Praise for *Bedside Manners*

"BEDSIDE MANNERS is extremely hard to put down....Phoebe Fox creates such a heartwarming cast of characters that you can't help but fall in love with them. Please, please, please Ms. Fox, keep on writing this series."

—Fresh Fiction

"A sequel that's even better than the first. Phoebe Fox takes the time to understand the human heart and mind."

—Dr. Duana Welch, author of Love, Factually

"A wonderful sequel to *The Breakup Doctor...* some very fine reading"

—A Simple Taste for Reading

"Amazing, belly laughing, full of honesty heart and truth... This series is not to be missed! 5 stars."

—Mrs. Mommy Booknerd

"There are very few times I have been able to say this, but I loved the second book MORE than the first. Great book – one of my favorites of the year!"

—Chick Lit Plus

"To me this series is perfect, I want to read more of Brook and her friends and I added it to my top 10 reads of the year. I'll be reading anything and everything Phoebe Fox writes with excitement!"

—Hello Chick Lit

"One of the great things about this series is the growth and change we see in each of the characters. The books are not just the same old, same old where the characters aren't learning from their mistakes. They actually move forward with their lives and relationships change."

—Susan the Book Bag

The Breakup Doctor Series

The Breakup Doctor (#1)
Bedside Manners (#2)
Heart Conditions (#3)
Out of Practice (#4)

Other Books by Phoebe Fox

A Little Bit of Grace
(coming August 2020 from Berkley Publishing)

Phoebe Fox

Author Phoebe Fox has been a contributor and regular columnist for a number of national, regional, and local publications, including the Huffington Post, Elite Daily, and She Knows. A former actor on stage and screen, Phoebe has been suspended from wires as a mall fairy; was accidentally concussed by a blank gun; and hosted a short-lived game show. She has been a relationship columnist; a movie, theater, and book reviewer; and a radio personality, and is a close observer of relationships in the wild. She currently lives in Austin, Texas, with her husband and two excellent dogs.

Bedside Manners

Phoebe Fox

For Joel, always and entirely.

Chapter One

Technically, lurking outside of an S and M bar to figure out whether I was going to have to go in wasn't part of my job description.

Mind you, as a therapist who specializes in helping people get through messy breakups, my usual menu of offerings was pretty broad. In the four months since my practice as the Breakup Doctor had taken off, it had included, but was not limited to:

- ✓ relationship dissection
- ✓ ego building
- ✓ organizational oversight (i.e., guiding my clients through removing the painful reminders of their ex from their everyday view until such a time as the memories don't confound their healing)
- ✓ personal shopping
- ✓ nutritional counseling (woman cannot live by Ben & Jerry's alone, no matter how big a jerk her ex is)
- ✓ deejaying (because endless, late-night loops of Fiona Apple and Joni Mitchell are just going to make you feel worse)
- ✓ image consultation, including hair and makeup referrals
- ✓ telephone/computer confiscation (some clients know they have no willpower and welcome the chance to remove temptation)

And that was in addition to the traditional therapy services I was actually trained, as a licensed mental health counselor, to provide. Intervention was strictly against my usual policy—I focused in counseling sessions on guiding people to move past the pain of rejection and abandonment and work toward making healthier choices in the future, but ultimately those choices were up to them.

But Cameron Fowler was way out of her depth. She'd moved here to my southwest Florida hometown just two months ago from hers, Fish Creek, Wisconsin—which made the fairly small town of Fort Myers seem like New York City by comparison. She was fleeing from the worst kind of breakup imaginable—being left at the altar by her longtime beau—and hoping for a fresh start.

Against all the odds in the dating wasteland that was southwest Florida, she immediately met "the perfect guy": Wayne Bukowski, owner of a local advertising agency that had made its reputation on two or three huge local accounts—a car dealer, a restaurant chain, and a mega gym. Wayne was older—in his late forties—but still handsome, with a perfect head of rich brown hair and a wide white smile, and he set about courting the young, fresh-faced Cameron with a ferocity and single-mindedness that drove her college sweetheart's betrayal right out of her mind.

Wayne and Cameron had been dating almost since her first day in town, when she'd met him in the grocery store as they were both checking out melons—Cameron the cantaloupe; Wayne, Cameron's. But lately, Cameron had told me on our first meeting, Wayne had begun to pull back—he was distant, distracted, and whereas he used to call her at all hours of the day and night, now she had to initiate most calls, and it would be hours before he returned her message when it slipped into voice mail more and more often.

Troubled, she'd finally sat him down to ask him what was the matter, and Wayne had forthrightly told her: He was worried she wasn't adventurous enough for him. Wayne Bukowski was a man of rapacious and varied appetites, and he was afraid that perhaps Cameron's delicate, sheltered upbringing meant they might not be right for each other after all.

Poor Cameron thought he meant things like bungee jumping and whitewater rafting. Wayne had to spell out for her that he was talking about their bedroom exploits.

Cameron Fowler had lost one man without ever having the chance to know what she did wrong so she could fix it. She wasn't going to let the same thing happen now. She'd said as much to me when she called me thirty minutes ago and told me what she was doing, with such ferocious, out-of-character adamancy that I'd walked out in the middle of a date and had been tailing her like a private dick ever since.

As I said, not part of my usual job description. But I was learning I couldn't always keep my personal concerns for clients strictly within the confines of our sessions together.

Now I was sitting in my car in the Southside Industrial Park late on a Saturday night, watching her loiter indecisively outside the tall, grim black doors of Sticks and Stones, and prepared any second now to break my policy of non-direct intervention.

She walked again past the matte-black doors, craning her neck to see inside when one cracked open for a moment and disgorged a laughing, stumbling couple in their mid-thirties, holding on to each other, the woman squealing in theatrical shock.

Drop-ins. They'd go home tonight and have "naughty" *Fifty Shades of Grey* sex with her restrained against the bedpost with some of his polyester ties, and feel dangerous and outrageous. Monday morning they'd casually mention at work that they'd hit Sticks and Stones over the weekend, and they'd enjoy the edgy street cred it gave them among their conservative coworkers.

Cameron made another pass by the doors and had to scurry out of the way, her gauzy skirt swinging, when a group of black-clad patrons seethed onto the front walkway from the parking lot on Work Drive. Now, this group weren't prurient tourists looking for a thrill. These guys seemed like regulars—leather clothes (chaps, I swore in one case, though it was hard to tell in the dim light from the single streetlight twenty yards away), the glint of metal, lots of piercings. One of them raked Cameron with an up-and-down investigation that made *me* blush sitting forty feet away in my car. She visibly contracted.

That's it, I thought. *This isn't your scene, Cam. Get back in your car and go home.*

Cameron pushed a strand of flyaway blond hair behind her ear with a hand I could see even from here was shaking, and finally turned to go back to her car. I hadn't thought she'd actually go through with it, but I'd had to show up just in case. Cameron was a sweet, naive Midwestern girl, and there was something about her I felt compelled to protect.

Just as I was turning my key in the ignition, Cameron lifted her shoulders, straightened her back, and reached for the door in a fast, firm motion. The club doors slammed shut, swallowing her.

Dammit. This was *not* one of the services I offered. I yanked the keys out, threw open my door, and scurried over to the entrance.

As soon as the imposing door sucked shut behind me with the muffled thunk of a vacuum seal, I was overwhelmed by sense stimuli. The unidentifiable house music was loud, a bass beat pounding so deeply it seemed to tremble the floor and threaten arrhythmia. Cool, slightly moist air rushed over my skin, as if I were standing in front of a window unit. The club smelled like perfume and incense, with the earthy undertone of sweat and something else I couldn't place, something slightly sharp and vaguely troubling.

My eyes adjusted to the twilight lighting and I realized the cavernous room was packed wall-to-wall. If I wanted to venture into the bowels I was going to have to forge a trail through the close-pressed bodies. Cameron couldn't have made much easier progress; she had to be nearby. In her flyaway floral dress she should be easy to find—everyone within my sightline wore either dark, shiny clothing of some nonporous fiber, or very little in general.

There was no sign of Cameron amid the crush, and I was surrounded on all sides by people with no seeming knowledge of the accepted personal space of Western culture. I tried to keep moving, but was stuck. I tapped the shoulder of the petite woman in front of me. She turned around to reveal herself as a very short man. He angled his body so I could make six inches of progress, and in that way I started working toward the rear of the club. People were tapping me for the same reason—or so I thought at first, until the tapping became touching, and the touching became groping, and by the time I was too deep inside to turn back, I had mystery hands copping a feel anywhere they could reach, their owners vanishing into the crowd as soon as I craned my neck to identify them.

I cursed Cameron Fowler, cursed the manipulative Wayne Bukowski, and again cursed my own overprotectiveness. The only thing that kept me moving forward instead of shoving a path back toward the exit was that if *I* was a little freaked out, sweet little Cameron Fowler had to be about to lose her mind. I wondered if she was regretting her ill-conceived plan to learn to be someone she absolutely wasn't, to try to please her boyfriend.

Motivated now like a mother lifting a car off her child, I blazed a path amid the revelers, grimly ignoring the expanse of my body I was leaving wide-open for free gropes. I hadn't had this many hands on me at once since offering myself up for the "light-as-a-feather-stiff-as-a-board" séance at a sleepover in fifth grade.

Once I was through the initial crush, the crowd thinned out ever so slightly—enough for me to at least move relatively unmolested. This part of the club was like a maze, the open floor plan narrowing into walkways divided by what looked to be office cubicle walls, only painted the same flat black as the front doors, instead of carpeted in the usual corporate beige. At intervals the makeshift walls parted to reveal small rooms behind them, each one filled with a tableau that was hard not to stare at as I determinedly kept moving, knowing if I looked too closely there would be too many things I would never be able to unsee: a man wearing only what looked to be a diaper, seated in a slightly reclining chair, each of his limbs secured at uncomfortable angles, two silver clamps attached to his nipples like tiny voracious piranha. A woman on her knees, blindfolded, a man standing in front of her holding a riding crop.

I passed a handful of rooms like that, each one filled with mise-en-scènes that made me feel like Doris Day in a Nicki Minaj video. Cameron was so far out of her depth. We both were.

So it was a shock to come to the next peep area in the wall and be faced with my client in her lightweight, flowery dress, her baby-fine blond hair slicked behind her ears, and a long, narrow wooden paddle held firmly in one hand.

In front of her was a mound of ass. That was really about all I could register at first: two globes of naked white flesh jutting up like the white peaks of Kilimanjaro above a pair of startlingly hairy legs. The rest of what I assumed (and hoped) was the man who belonged to them was apparently draped over a sawhorse contraption in a dirty downward-facing dog, and he was doing some kind of wiggly little dance on it that suggested he was awfully excited over what was to come. From all appearances, Cameron was about to administer some stern corporal punishment to the man's evidently quite anticipatory backside.

Holy cow. I really didn't think she had it in her. It wouldn't be the first time I'd been wrong about a client—but I was pretty sure it would be the most memorable. I started to push back out the way I'd fought a path in; it wasn't my job to judge my clients or decide what was best for them. If this was what Cameron wanted, then she was an adult and could make her own choices. I would just be there later in session to help with any fallout that resulted.

But right before I turned away, I saw it: Cameron's chin was shivering like an earthquake was happening underneath it. That was a woman fighting back hard sobs, or I had never seen anyone in distress before.

Only one way to test the theory.

"Cameron!" I called sharply.

Her head shot up and her eyes wildly raked the crowd at the doorway, a beaten dog seeking salvation. I saw the moment she registered my presence: She looked confused, then stunned, then delivered. The paddle dropped out of her hands, but she didn't seem to notice, and Cameron took a shaky step in my direction. I reached out a hand: *I'm right here.*

Then the crowd closed in, and she was forced to a stop. "Brook?"

"Come on, Cam. You're okay," I encouraged.

Again she made motions to leave, but her audience was having none of that. They were primed for a good show—sweet young thing turned dominatrix—and they didn't seem willing to sacrifice the expected spectacle. They swarmed her like angry bees, urging her with their mass and their not so gentle pushes back into the room. "Do it," I heard someone call out. And someone else: "Hit him!" The cries were picked up, the exhortations swelling through the crowd into a sibilant hiss of menace.

Things were careening quickly toward the unpleasant. This horde was stoked up. They wanted to see the girl next door turn into a BDSM mistress, and wouldn't be deprived of their payoff now. I wasn't getting Cameron out of here without some drastic action.

Well. Desperate times...

I shoved ungently at the shoulders nearest to me and forced a path to Cameron. As soon as I reached her I knew better than to hesitate or show any uncertainty. There was no time to communicate my plan or try to reassure her. Instead I grabbed her roughly by the arm, yanked her toward me, and bent her into a deep, possessive kiss.

...

Up until recently I would never have found myself in a situation like this, and certainly not for a client. I was a good therapist, but under the tutelage of my graduate mentor, Dr. Janet Evanston, I'd learned to keep a strict line between the personal and the professional. (Dr. Evanston had spectacularly broken that code herself when she tried to kill her husband with a carving knife while he slept, but I still followed the example she'd set for me up until she started serving her prison term.)

Since becoming the Breakup Doctor, though, I'd noticed an odd tendency in myself to be more personally engaged. More interactive. Even a little touchy-feely—sometimes a grieving, lonely person needed nothing so much as a comforting hug.

I wasn't completely comfortable yet with the new version of Therapist Me, but I was learning.

This, though, was pretty far outside my comfort zone.

I pulled back from my lip-lock with Cameron just enough to see her eyes wide on mine. "Just go along," I said, low, hoping she heard me over the din, hoping she understood. Then I straightened and swung her forcefully erect, using the momentum to shove her toward the exit from the room. Beside us the man bent over the sawhorse gave a tortured groan. I smacked his naked ass—hard enough to leave a vivid red handprint—and he groaned again, this time one of clear pleasure. I hoped my shudder didn't show.

"I don't share my toys," I snarled, loud enough to make sure the crowd overheard. Then I launched myself after Cameron, propelling her with a possessive hand on the back of her neck through the crowd at the opening to the hall—defused now, some of them laughing, idle applause from one or two—as smoothly as if the crush of bodies blocking the path had somehow become lubricated.

Which, come to think of it, they probably had.

We were almost to the front doors, pushing through the crowd like salmon swimming downstream, batting away free-ranging hands, when I felt fingers grabbing on and digging into my left cheek—and not the one on my face.

Fed up, furious, and ready to snap, I spun around, blazing.

And came face-to-face with Chip Santana.

He hadn't changed much. Same shaved head, same goatee, same slanted eyebrows over eyes whose unlikely teal color were presently concealed in pools of darkness in Sticks and Stones' dim, trespass-forgiving lighting.

Same overwhelming, animal jolt of...*something* that coursed through me the second I wheeled around and our gazes locked.

His expression morphed from sly amusement to disbelief to horror, until Chip looked as gobsmacked as I felt. We must have presented a monkey-see-monkey-do mirror reflection, both of us frozen, staring gape-mouthed at each other while the frenzy around us seemed to recede.

But the memory of his aggressive clutch on my nethermost regions stifled my knee-jerk chemical reaction like baking soda on a flame, replacing it with indignant rage.

"Hands *off!*" I growled, grabbing onto Cameron again with a grip I feared was harder than I intended, wheeling both of us around and pushing fiercely for the exit, my heart thunking into my ribs.

I kept my hand on the back of her neck even after the tall black doors disgorged us, a warning pressure telling her to keep quiet. A couple passed us on their way inside, the man sending me a nod of camaraderie as I noticed the collar around his partner's neck. *Just us two fellow doms out for a stroll with our pets...*

I didn't let go of Cameron until I opened the passenger door of my Honda and pushed her inside. Then I slammed it shut, went around fast to my side, started the engine, and squealed us out of the parking lot.

"I'll bring you back for your car tomorrow," I said.

Cameron's answer was to burst into sobs.

Pulling into a well-lighted gas station out on busy Cleveland Avenue, I put the car in park, then leaned across and took her into my arms.

"I'm sorry. I'm so sorry," she cried over and over.

"Shhh. Shhhh." I stroked her hair the way I would comfort a child, hoping she didn't realize it was the same hand I'd used on the naked guy's butt. "Nothing to be sorry for."

"I'm such an idiot. I thought I...But then when I..." Her breath was hitching. "And I don't know what to tell Wayne, but I can't. I just can't!"

What I knew but had never told Cameron was that Wayne Bukowski was a textbook Type Three—one of the several categories into which my best friend Sasha and I had slotted the available Florida males into throughout our lifetime's worth of experience in the local dating scene. A Type Three was an older man who courted only much younger women, dazzling them with his money and success, then moving on as soon as they aged out of his program. They dated their way through the pool of eligible, only-barely-legal hard-bodies, never intending to settle down or pursue anything more committed than tennis doubles.

Cameron, a newcomer to the area, and a charmingly ingenuous soul, wasn't familiar with our well-known local sharks. She was oblivious chum for someone like Wayne the moment she set one dainty, pink-painted toenail into the southwest Florida waters. But she was going to have to figure that out for herself. I didn't intercept her tonight to talk her out of Wayne. I came to talk her out of doing something that, knowing Cameron, I thought she might regret for the rest of her life. Now that she was out of that immediate danger, the rest was up to her.

"You can't do something that isn't right for you just to please someone else, Cam," I said, keeping my tone free of judgment. "You be true to you first—always. If someone genuinely loves you, that's all they'll want of you." I didn't spell out whether that someone was or wasn't Wayne Bukowski. I hoped that would become evident to Cameron as she thought about everything.

I kept stroking her hair, murmuring soothing sounds into her ear. Cameron said nothing; she just sniffled, but her sobs had dried up, and she was listening.

For now, that was enough.

Chapter Two

I took a shower as soon as I got home, hoping the steaming water would rinse away the feel of strange hands on parts of my body I usually kept private.

One invasive, inappropriate, outrageous hand in particular.

I hadn't seen Chip Santana in months. A bartender with anger-management issues, Chip was a former patient I'd been planning to terminate treatment with before my old mental health practice literally came crashing down under a wrecking ball, effectively ending our therapy work. He'd bordered on flirting with me back then in a way that was not only ethically questionable in the doctor-patient relationship, but personally unsettling: Chip Santana had a primal effect on me I could no more explain than control.

As evidenced by that animalistic jolt I'd felt tonight before rage had kicked in.

But rampant pheromones or not, I'd always kept personal and professional boundaries rigid and impermeable—up until the lowest point of my spectacular breakdown following my last breakup.

Miserable, lonely, and humiliated by breaking every one of my own breakup rules after Kendall Pulver dumped me, I ran into Chip at a party and we'd gotten a little too up close and personal...in a naked kind of way.

Luckily Chip and I had been interrupted from our middle-of-the-night clinch on the beach by the overzealous deputy who arrested us before we'd actually taken things to their logical conclusion—the only blessing of that ill-advised evening. The last time I'd seen Chip was nearly four months ago—the morning after we got hauled off to the poky for public indecency, when Sasha and I drove him home from the jailhouse and a silent, steaming Chip had stormed into his beach-basement apartment and slammed the door behind him.

He hadn't changed a bit. He was still breaking the rules and thinking he could get away with it, taking what he wanted—in this case, a handful of my ass—and disregarding anyone else. A pot-smoking bartender pushing forty who couldn't control his impulses. A man-child who'd never grow up. A mistake I'd made at the nadir of my life.

Until the worst of my behavior back then was staring me right in the face in the middle of an S and M club, I'd been trying to put that awful time behind me. And I had—with Ben Garrett, the man I'd been seeing for several months now. Ben, who'd started out as nothing more than a revenge date against my ex...and who had turned out in the last three months to be something so much more.

Ben and I had been midway through dinner at Angelino's when I got Cameron's distress call, and after dropping me off at my house for my car without a complaint, he'd asked me to let him know when I got home, so he didn't worry. It was late, but I wanted something good to end the evening. I poured a glass of wine and picked up the phone.

"Hey," Ben answered.

The sound of his voice made me smile. "Hey. I'm home."

"Was she okay?"

"She will be, I think. She's having a tough time, but we got her out of there before she did anything she'd regret." I'd told him a client was at Sticks and Stones, but that was all. "I'm really sorry about dinner."

"No big deal. Jake was pretty happy about your leftovers." I could picture Ben's enormous, shaggy Great Pyrenees—a dog I was pretty sure had ADHD—eagerly gobbling up the rest of my meatballs.

"Tell the big goofball I said, 'You're welcome.'" He chuckled and then fell silent. "I hate that we had our only date night interrupted, though," I added softly. Ben owned a construction company that was trying to create a niche as a green builder, and he'd recently landed a great project: designing and building a high-end green luxury home for a family in Cedar Key. Since it was four hours north, he'd been staying in a residence hotel there during the week.

"Me too," he said. "I miss you."

The simple words sent warmth spreading through my chest.

I miss you too, I wanted to tell him. *Come over.* But that wasn't something I could say.

Because Ben and I hadn't had sex yet.

Regardless of what men's magazines want you to believe, there's no unspoken five-date "rule." We'd had a lot more than that anyway—at least one night every weekend since we'd started seeing each other—and I knew Ben was attracted to me. I could tell by the way he took a quick breath in whenever he picked me up for dates before he complimented my appearance; by the way he let his hand rest in the small of my back when a host led us to our table at a restaurant; and I could totally tell by the way he kissed me good night at the end of the evening—never just a peck, and never an insistent, sloppy tongue job. Ben was a great kisser.

And it wasn't that I didn't want to sleep with him. Frankly there were some nights it was all I could do to pull away and say good night.

But during the worst of my breakup breakdown, I'd pretty much fallen apart for a while. And while I'd let go of judging myself for that—realizing that sometimes you have to get a little crazy to move past a broken heart—I wasn't eager to repeat it. No matter how great Ben was so far.

"Next weekend," I said instead. "And no clients that night—I promise."

"It's okay. I know it's hard for you to turn away from someone in pain."

I loved that he "got" me, but I wondered how long his patience would last. This wasn't the first time I'd had to change our plans for an emergency. "Who knew there were so many breakups going on in our sleepy little town?"

He chuckled. "Too bad you can't give seminars."

"Right?" I said. "TED talks for broken hearts."

We chatted for a few minutes longer before saying our good nights. "I'll see you next Saturday?" Ben asked.

"Absolutely," I said. "And this time no S and M bars."

"Oh, no. Now I have to come up with another idea for date night."

I was still smiling when I hung up the phone.

...

As late as it was, after the evening I'd had I couldn't sleep. I poured more wine and went outside on my lanai to listen to the still night, broken only by the sounds of occasional passing cars on Winkler.

What I'd told Ben was true—sometimes I couldn't believe how many people had their hearts broken in Fort Myers alone, and how many of them felt they had no one to talk to about it, or worried that they'd exhausted the patience of the people they did have to confide in. It could be hard to let go of heartache as quickly as well-meaning friends and family wanted you to.

I'd spent most of my life trying to figure out what my passion was, my calling, and I'd finally found it: I could help people. But there were only so many hours in a day—and I still had to leave time for a life of my own, or I'd have nothing to offer anyone else.

Too bad you can't give seminars, Ben had said.

It might be the answer I was looking for—a way to reach more people—to help them without burning myself out. But was that feasible? How could you group-counsel people who were going through something so private, and so particular to them?

As always when I had something to work out in my mind, there was only one person I wanted to talk it over with.

I called Sasha.

"What are you doing up?" she answered.

"What are *you* doing up?" I countered. She sounded too perky for me to think I'd wakened her.

And then I froze. *Ugh.*

"Oh, God. Did I call you in the middle of..." I couldn't even say it. "...with Stu...?"

"Sex, Brook. Sexual intercourse. I have it sometimes with your brother." I heard Stu's deeper laugh in the background.

After a lifetime where we'd all three practically grown up together, I was almost used to my best friend and my brother being a couple. I *was*. But no matter how close I was to Sasha, regardless of the excruciatingly intimate nature of the conversations we'd had over the years about every tiny nuance of our respective sex lives, with Stu involved I preferred to pretend that they had a close, loving, but platonic relationship.

At my awkward silence she finally let me off the hook. "But not at the moment. We got sucked into streaming *Game of Thrones* on Netflix and can't stop. Why'd you call if you thought I'd be sleeping?"

"I need to ask you something." I told her about Ben's casual suggestion, and how it was percolating in my mind. "So what do you think—can it work? Would anyone want to participate in something like that, or is it too weird to share that kind of suffering in a group?"

"Well..." Sasha mulled while I took a deep sip of my wine, letting the warmth spread down my throat and into my chest. "That's what alcoholics do."

I choked, the wine burning my esophagus. "What?"

But she went on as if she had not, in fact, made me begin to reevaluate my drinking habits. "Alcoholics are suffering from a pain that's really personal. And yet a lot of them find comfort in sharing their experiences with others who've had similar ones. Trust me on this one—I know."

She did. She'd attended a few meetings in her rabid dating days, because she thought it would be a good way to meet guys. For the bulk of Sasha's dating life prior to my brother, she'd been a little unstable where dating was concerned. And by "unstable," I mean borderline psychotic and occasionally criminal.

"But it's the same with any support group, right?" Sasha said.

"That's true," I said thoughtfully. "Grief, divorced parents, overeaters, parents of special-needs kids—there are groups for all of that. So maybe not seminars, per se. What if I could offer something like those support groups, but for people who've been dumped?"

Sasha made a loud explosion noise. "Mind? Blown," she said. "I love it. Cut and print."

I laughed. "Well, it's something to think about." I heard Stu murmur in the background and realized I'd been monopolizing Sasha. "I'll let you get back to your death orgy," I said reluctantly.

"*No spoilers,* Brook! Geez!"

"Sash, everyone knows everybody dies in that show. I've never even seen it and I know that."

"You suck. Hey, Stu, turn it off—they all die," Sasha said forlornly, and I giggled.

"Sorry."

"Whatever."

"I'll tell you about my night at an S and M bar, if that makes up for it."

"Well, of *course* it makes up for it," she said delightedly. "Girls only, or can Stuvie hear?"

This happened a lot lately—it was harder to have one-on-one girl talk with Sasha since she and Stu had gotten together. But I was the one who'd intruded on their night, after all—and I knew Stu would enjoy the story even more than Sasha would. "Put me on speaker," I said.

There ensued a good fifteen-minute conversation about my evening, with Sasha making the appropriate interjections of disbelief and incredulity and amusement, and Stu's contribution being frequent guffaws or snorts in the background. They had always been my best audience. I left out Chip—Stu didn't know about my winding up in jail with him, and I wanted to keep it that way—but by the end of my story I had them rolling with laughter over my smacking the prone Sticks and Stones patron's bald white ass.

"Oh, my God, Brookie!" Sasha sounded delighted. "Aren't you glad you got out of your boring old practice?"

If someone had told me six months ago, when I was contentedly ensconced in a nice, safe traditional counseling practice, that this would be the type of day I'd regularly have in my new career as the Breakup Doctor, I probably would have been horrified. But the truth was, I *was* glad. I loved it. What I was doing now was still helping people, but in a far more proactive, immediate-gratification, hands-on way. *Really* hands-on, in tonight's case.

"Thanks for talking," I told them. "I hope I didn't ruin y'all's evening."

"Are you kidding?" Stu called out. "My sister at an S and M bar is way better than medieval politicking."

I heard a smack. "She wasn't there for pleasure, freak. It was work."

"That sounds even better. That's what I'll tell people."

She giggled. "Stu! You can't say that."

"Maybe we should try some of that spanking therapy ourselves."

"In your dreams, buddy. Stu..." Sasha's tone was a warning. "Stu! No!" I heard a scuffle, a roar from Stu, a snort from Sasha, and then a long silence.

"All right, people, this feels a little voyeuristic." I sighed. "Conversation over."

No one answered me, so I hung up before I heard things a sister should never hear.

Chapter Three

A noise woke me early the next morning and I shot up in bed, still so woozy from my late night that I wasn't immediately sure where I was, or *who* I was. I blinked around the room, reorienting myself as my gaze finally fell on the phone lit up and vibrating on my nightstand.

I reached for it groggily, not recognizing the number. "H'lo?" I mumbled.

"Morning, Doc. Hope I didn't wake you up."

The low, gravelly, familiar voice crept across my skin like a porn star crawling across the covers. How had Chip Santana gotten my cell number?

Oh, right—I'd had our old office number forwarded.

"Chip," I said flatly, last night coming back in a rush. "It's"—I glanced at the clock—"seven thirty a.m. on a Sunday."

"Please don't hang up," he said quickly. "I want to explain."

"I think things were pretty self-explanatory."

"No! See...Geez, I knew you'd think that. Please—I just want to apologize."

I waited, but no apology was forthcoming. "Okay, Chip," I said finally. "Goodbye."

"Wait! Listen, Doc—Brook," he said. "I know what you're thinking, but it wasn't me who grabbed you."

I gritted my jaw. I'd thought we'd been doing some good work together when he was seeing me at my old practice. And when our building got razed for asbestos and my practice blew up along with it, I'd referred him to another therapist I knew had had great results with anger-management cases. But here he was, same old Chip, always blaming someone else.

"Chip, I *saw* you," I said wearily. "You were right behind me. At the *S and M bar*." It was probably slightly hypocritical of me to toss out that last with judgment dripping from my tone.

To my surprise, he laughed, a scrape of sound against his throat. "Yeah, I know how that must have looked. That's part of why I was so pissed off at my buddy for dragging me in there. And then when I saw him grope some lady, and you turned around and I realized it was you, I was so surprised I didn't know what to do. I just went deer-in-the-headlights. And then you ran out before I could explain."

I swung my legs over the side of the bed, staring at the wall while I considered his words. *Had* there been another guy next to him? Well, of course, I remembered—there'd been what seemed like hundreds of people crushing in around me and Cameron. Theoretically I suppose it could have been anyone who'd invaded my personal turf so egregiously.

Was he telling me the truth?

"I am so sorry, Doc," he said. "For what it's worth, I wanted to pound my buddy into the ground, but I kept thinking about you and how you helped me get hold of feelings like that, and I talked myself down." All the amusement had dropped out of his voice, and he sounded sincere.

I could at least give him the benefit of the doubt.

"Okay, Chip. Apology accepted. I appreciate your calling to straighten it out."

"I didn't want you to think...well, what I figured you were probably thinking." He paused. "I was pretty shocked to see you at a place like that."

"For the record," I added hastily, "I was there with a...a friend too. That's not somewhere I hang out either." It felt strange to be talking about this with Chip in bed, scantily clad, and I got up and pulled on a thick terry-cloth robe from my closet.

"No, no, of course—I figured."

"Okay, well, I'm glad we cleared that up. Thanks for—"

"Hey, I'm not at the bar anymore," he blurted.

For a second I thought he was still talking about Sticks and Stones, but then I realized what he was saying. "You mean you're not bartending at the Floppy Jellyfish?"

"I left the whole bar business, actually. It seemed like not the best fit for someone with my"—he chuckled—"triggers."

I remembered how many fights he'd gotten into at work—with customers, with coworkers, even with managers, until his boss told him he either went into anger-management therapy or he got fired. I felt a twinge of guilt. "You didn't lose that job because our therapy ended, did you?" I asked as I lumbered into the kitchen to start coffee.

"No. I took your referral and stayed in treatment. That's actually part of why I finally quit the bar—I started wanting to do better, you know? And being there...it wasn't helping my problems."

I stopped midway to reaching into the cabinet for coffee filters, leaning against the counter. Self-awareness and personal responsibility were new for Chip. "That's really great, Chip," I said sincerely. "I'm happy to hear that."

"I work at my dad's car dealership now—the Toyota one on Cleveland; you know it?"

"Of course. 'The vehicle you want at the price you need.'"

I heard a hitching blown-out breath and pictured Chip laughing through an exhale of smoke. "Yeah, that's it. Betcha can't see me selling cars."

"That's true, actually. Are you?"

"Nope. I'm helping out with paperwork after hours. Ask me why."

Despite my reservations, I was smiling now, enjoying playing along. "Why?"

"I'm glad you asked." He chuckled when I laughed, on cue. "I'm in school during the day. Finally finishing my chem degree."

This time he really had surprised me. "You are? That's wonderful! Congratulations." Part of me was jealous that I hadn't been the right therapist to help Chip as much as Jim Turner, the man I'd referred him to, clearly had. But mostly I was glad for him. This Chip was a far cry from the raging career bartender whom I'd worried would become a bitter, unhappy burnout.

"You really helped me, you know," he said softly. "I know you don't realize it, but you did a lot for me."

"Oh, come on," I said, pushing off the counter and turning to fill the coffeepot from the filtered pitcher in the fridge. "It was Dr. Turner who—"

"He was great too—don't get me wrong. But I've been able to tell him so. You I never thanked for it. So I want to now. Thank you, Doc. For believing in me and sticking with me, even when I know you must not have liked me all that much."

"Now, that's not true—" I said automatically.

"No, you know what I mean. I wasn't always the easiest guy to get along with."

"Well...thanks. It's really great for a therapist to hear they made a difference."

"You did. I've changed. A lot."

"It sounds like it."

"Yeah. And anyway, as part of that, there's something I...well, that I want to talk to you about." For the first time he seemed to be at a loss for words. I heard a clinking sound, like a spoon being stirred in a mug, and I wondered if Chip was doing the same thing I was: standing at his kitchen counter in pajamas, having coffee. The image was disconcertingly intimate. "The thing is, Brook...Man. It's harder to do this than I thought."

"Do what?"

He blew out a long sigh. "I have this thing I really need to talk to you about—you specifically, not my other doc. But not on the phone. Could we meet somewhere?"

The smell of coffee was starting to bloom into the kitchen as it brewed, echoing the renewed caution that blossomed in me at his words. "I really don't think it's a good idea to restart therapy after we—"

"No, no, I don't mean like an appointment. This is personal. I mean—that came out wrong. I can't really explain this over the phone, Doc. Could I just buy you a cup of coffee somewhere and we can talk? Just for a few minutes? Your opinion means a lot to me. I can meet pretty much any time you have open."

Theoretically I had a slot open to see Chip; I'd had a client cancel for tomorrow afternoon for an unexpected business trip. But was this a good idea?

I wasn't agreeing to take him back on as a client, though; he was asking for a onetime meeting. This was simply follow-up with a former patient. The exit session I had for closure with all my terminating patients that Chip and I had never had. I could meet him out somewhere—a neutral public place, rather than having him come to my home office, so it wouldn't suggest to him that we were resuming our professional relationship.

"Well...all right," I said finally. "Do you have class on Mondays?"

There was a long pause while I heard the scrape of a lighter and a deep inhale before he said, "How's sometime after, say, one o'clock?"

"Perfect, actually—I have three o'clock open if that works."

We settled on the Hot Pot, a coffee shop midway between the FGCU campus and my house, before saying goodbye.

Considering last evening, I felt surprisingly good about our conversation. The most rewarding part of being a therapist is seeing someone have that leap of understanding about the issues that brought them to therapy in the first place, the flash of insight that helps them make the changes they've been wanting or needing to make. I may not have been directly the cause of Chip's apparent breakthrough, but according to him I'd helped. And that felt fantastic.

He'd sounded so eager and proud to tell me of his achievements. *I've changed. A lot.* And despite the stumble of our inappropriate makeout session on Fort Myers Beach, it was endearing how nervous he was about asking to meet. *There's something I...well, that I want to talk to you about.*

As his words replayed through my head, I lowered the coffeepot I'd just finished pouring from, my heart thudding.

Oh, my god. Now that he was a "better man," had Chip come back to try to *date* me?

Chapter Four

Chip was waiting in front of the Hot Pot the next day when I arrived, a few minutes late, for our three o'clock meeting. I greeted him with a cautious smile, trying to get a read on his intentions from his expression, his body language, but all he did was call out, "Hey, Doc!" with a big, open grin, and fell into step with me as we approached the door. To my surprise he reached past me and held it.

Inside the place was bustling, as the locally owned coffee, tea, and doughnut shop always was—one reason I'd suggested it. A crowd seemed like a better idea around Chip than somewhere more intimate.

"Shall we order?" I asked, nodding toward the counter.

"How about you tell me what you want and let me get it?" he said instead. He *had* changed. The old Chip wasn't exactly chivalrous. "There's a table over by the window," he went on, "if you want to go hold it for us."

I asked for just a coffee and then sat where he'd indicated, checking my e-mails for a few minutes until he showed up at the table with a mug in one hand and a glass of iced tea in the other. He set them both down before taking the seat across from me.

"So…things are going really well for you, seems like," he said, leaning back. "I read your column. Hear you on the radio."

"Oh?" I didn't want to encourage social chitchat that might give him the wrong idea.

He smiled, sunlight revealing lines beside his eyes I hadn't noticed before, lighting up his teal irises like a crystal-clear lagoon. "It's really good to see you again, Doc."

"Thanks, Chip," I said warily. "You too." In the sense that I was always glad to see former patients. And, I had to admit, also in the sense that Chip Santana was purely good to look at: six-feet-plus of muscle and broad shoulders and edgy sex appeal. "You know I'm not actually a PhD, right?" I clarified. "I'm a licensed mental health counselor." Saying that used to make me feel inadequate, but not anymore.

"Yeah, I know. I just like it. Is it okay with you?"

"Whatever you like." Stirring sugar into my coffee, I gave him my neutral professional smile. "So what did you want to talk to me about?"

"Oh, boy," he said. "This is harder than I expected. Okay, here goes." He took a long breath and then let it out in a whoosh as I braced myself. "Look, Doc...I haven't always been the nicest guy in the world, and I've done some not-so-great things in the past. To some specific people. Female people," he said, shamefaced.

I was searching for the words to let him down without hurting his feelings, but he'd already plunged ahead.

"And the thing is...I need you."

Guilt flared up in me—along with an embarrasing secret thrill at his words I tried to ignore as I fixed a regretful expression onto my face. "Oh, Chip—" I said gently.

"This Breakup Doctor thing you do now...do you think you could help me make things right with some of them?"

I blinked. "What?"

He took a gulp of tea, an audible swallow. "I need to fix some things. Make amends. Whatever you want to call it. There are some women who...well, who probably hate me. And with reason. I can't really live with that anymore."

I leaned back in the upholstered chair, hoping to create some distance between his steady gaze and my heated face. "You...you want to *hire* me? To what, counsel your exes?"

"No, no. I just want to apologize for the things I did to them and, if they'll give it, ask for their forgiveness." He looked down at his glass. "That's not really something I'm so great at."

"But...I don't get it. What can I do?"

"I don't know. I guess help me do it. Especially the ones who'd rather see me dead than have a conversation with me."

"Wow."

He arched one of those slanting brows and a smile ghosted across his mouth. "Yeah, well, I did some pretty awful things to some of them."

I shook my head, recovering my bearings. "Chip, I don't know. I don't even think I'd know where to begin. This is something you have to find in yourself and—"

"I know! I will—I'm not asking you to do it for me. But..." He let out another sigh and played with the unused straw he'd never bothered unwrapping. He spoke without ever raising his eyes to mine, his long black lashes fanned over his cheeks. "You're the easiest person I ever talked to, Doc. You never made me feel like an asshole or an idiot—even when I was one. This kind of thing...it's not easy for me. I'm afraid I'm going to screw it up. Get frustrated and turn back into who I used to be. 'Sometimes people act hostile when they're really afraid of being vulnerable.' You remember saying that to me?" His eyes shot briefly up to mine before dropping to the table again, and I felt my heart soften at the naked uncertainty I'd seen there. "I really heard that. And I hated you for it then—but I get it now. I don't want to do that again, Doc. I don't want to be that guy again." He dragged in a breath and made a visible effort to look directly at me.

This truly was a changed Chip. It was impressive how far he'd come—and what he wanted to do was so healthy—righting past wrongs to move forward. Despite my lingering embarrassment, I couldn't suppress a little twinge of pride that I'd played a part in his transformation.

"This is admirable, Chip," I said genuinely. "Of course I'll help."

He smiled fully for the first time since we'd sat down, and my breath caught at the way his face lit up with it. "Thank you!" he blurted out. "Thanks, Doc! That's awesome!" He reached a hand across the table for a handshake, and accidentally knocked his tea over. I pushed back quickly to save my dress.

"Oh, crap—sorry," he said, reaching for his napkin and dabbing ineffectually at the table. "That didn't get all over you, did it?"

I had to laugh at his sudden little-boy demeanor as I reached over with my own napkin to help. "It's fine—no worries." We had insufficient napkin for the spill, and I started to stand to get more when he caught my hand with his and kept me from leaving.

"Hey," he said. "No bullshit—thanks. This means more than you know. You're helping me be the man I want to be."

A little shiver crested my shoulders—at the touch or the sentiment I wasn't sure.

Chapter Five

Here's something they don't tell you in grad school as a psych major: When awaiting your very first group therapy session ever outside of the mockups you did in class, your feet will sweat, your armpits will prickle, and your heart will beat fast enough to convince you that you are having a panic attack.

Jumping right into the idea had seemed fabulously proactive. But now that I was here, in a meeting room at the Fort Myers Yacht Club that Sasha had procured for me through an ex, waiting for the first attendees of the first Breakup Doctor group session to show up, I wondered what the hell I'd been thinking.

I'd mentioned the sessions on each of my radio appearances over the last two weeks, and Lisa Albrecht, my editor at the *Tropic Times* newspaper, had graciously posted a sidebar on it in the paper (graciousness from acerbic Lisa still freaked me out). Still, I'd been half-surprised when I began getting queries about it. Twenty-two people had inquired; nine of those had signed up, but now, at nine fifty, with the session scheduled to start at ten, I was pretty sure no one was going to show.

I was just about to pack up and flee when the first people began trickling in. Three women filed through the doorway, one after the next, but clearly not together as they found seats at a scattered distance from one another in the circle of chairs I'd created. I got a shy smile from one, a quick glance from another, and a third who avoided eye contact altogether.

"Hi, how are you?" I said. My relief made my greeting sound slightly manic, and I forced myself to sit back and simply offer what I hoped was a confident, welcoming expression as people continued to file in.

We had two men—Antonio Moretti, a tall, good-looking dark-haired man, the first to sign up for the group—and an older gentleman with thinning salt-and-pepper hair and kind brown eyes that drooped at the outside corners, giving him a slightly sad look. Sherman Schmidt, I remembered from the signup list. Every other attendee was female—but not a bad ratio, I thought. In total we had nine; we'd had a dropout at the last minute—"We got back together," the woman had explained sheepishly.

At exactly ten o'clock, I took a deep breath. "Ladies," I began, then cleared my throat to remove the quaver in my voice and smiled at Antonio and Sherman. "Gentlemen." A couple of people tittered. "Good morning," I tried again, and this time the group gradually quieted down. "I'm Brook Ogden—um, the Breakup Doctor. Well…let's go around the room and introduce ourselves. And you might say a little something about why you're here. Would you like to start?"

I looked at the woman to my left, a mousy brunette with her head tipped down toward her lap. In the silence that fell, broken only by the shifting of chairs and bodies, she glanced over at me and shook her head.

She was obviously either terribly shy or not comfortable enough yet to share, so all I said was, "Okay. How about you?" nodding encouragingly to the dark-haired woman beside her.

"Well, I'm Elisa. And I'm here because of a breakup."

Yes, clearly. The beginning was bound to be awkward, but things would get better once we got the ball rolling. I took a deep breath and tried again. "Okay, Elisa, thanks." I indicated the woman beside her, who gave her name as Carolyn and appended, "Breakup." The next woman and the older man followed suit. The rustlings in the room got louder.

"How about you?" I asked the petite woman who was next in the circle, hearing an edge of desperation in my voice. *Please let her say more than three words.*

She let out a noisy sigh and rolled her eyes to the ceiling. "I'm Dina. And big surprise! I'm here because of a breakup!" She said it in a singsong, like you'd speak to a stupid child.

I forced a chuckle. "I guess we can assume we're all here because of a breakup, huh?"

"You think?" She heaved herself backward in her chair and crossed her arms over her chest.

I was losing the group already, and we weren't ten minutes into it.

"Well, I'm Betty Mitchell," the woman directly to my right spoke up. She was older, perhaps in her late fifties, and had a kind face. "And I haven't had a breakup, so that shakes things up a little." She laughed uncomfortably. "My husband and I are still living together, trying to work it out, but he's told me he's not sure he ever loved me, so…Well, that's not the most fun thing in the world." She gave a smile that trembled around the edges, and before I could check myself I laid a hand on her knee.

"It gets better, Betty," I said quietly. "I promise."

I heard a snort across from me, and looked up to meet Dina's scornful expression. "Awesome," she muttered.

I looked directly at her and made myself offer a pleasant expression. "Dina, let's go back to you. Would you like to talk more about your situation, what brings you here?"

"I thought you were the expert."

"I am trained as a therapist, yes," I said neutrally. "But we work together in counseling. This is a partnership. So if you can tell us a little about your situation, we can talk about it a bit."

"I don't think so."

I didn't even know what to say to that. I glanced around the circle. Most of the attendees looked confused or uncertain. Skepticism was creeping across the faces of a couple of them.

Why did this woman even come here?

"Well," I said, clearing my throat. "Would anyone else like to share a bit more to get us started?"

No. Apparently no one at all would like to do that.

"Okay," I said into the heavy silence. I reached into my bag and brought out the prop I'd thought of last night: a hand-held garden cultivator, its three pristine bent prongs glinting with reflected light betraying the fact that I'd never actually used it.

"This is a cultivator, for those of you who don't garden. Like me," I said with a smile. "I had to actually look up the name of it last night." A couple of the women giggled. "This sucker's kind of intimidating-looking, to me," I went on, turning it so the sharp ends of the prongs bristled at the group. "It can hurt you accidentally if you aren't careful with it. It can be used as a weapon." I batted it in the air as if bludgeoning a head. "But it can also be used to ready the ground for planting something new and fruitful." I turned it prongs-down and made a raking motion with it. "And so it reminded me of relationships. And of what we're hoping to do in here."

"Ha!" Betty cackled, and Elisa and Antonio shot me a grin.

"Nice one, Brook," Antonio said.

"You gonna use that on us if we piss you off?" came a voice, and I didn't have to look to know who it was.

"Of course not, Dina."

"Hey, JK," she said. "Don't get your bra in a bunch."

This was when psychology was hard. When the human response—to bite Dina Jones's head off, to say something scathing to put her in her place, or to poke her in the eyes, the way my basic nature was strongly suggesting was a great strategy—directly conflicted with the clinical one that would yield positive, constructive results. Which in this case, I decided, was to ignore her provocations the way I would a tantruming child—pretty much what she was.

"We need some way to honor the person sharing and remind ourselves that we won't interrupt," I went on. "Even in support. It's hard to talk about some of this, and sometimes we need the space of silence to formulate our thoughts as we do. So who wants the claw first?" I held it up, prongs toward me, and panned it around the circle.

A derisive noise emanated from the Dina portion of the circle.

"Dina, you seem to have some thoughts about this process," I said calmly. "Would you like to talk about those with the group?"

"I thought that was your job?" she snapped. "You're the Breakup Doctor, right? I thought we were paying you to tell us what to do, not make us do all the work. I thought you were going to make it *better.*"

Even in the face of her rage, a wash of sympathy came over me—because in a flash I thought I understood where it came from. Dina was young and pretty, with a mass of perfectly highlighted curls and the face of an adorable pixie. I suspected she was the kind of girl who'd made me entirely insecure in school—the popular girl who led a charmed life.

And someone had broken her heart. If I was right about Dina, it might be the first time that had happened. And it probably shook everything she thought she knew about her life and herself. Dina didn't know how to handle what most of us had learned to deal with, at least on some level, from a young age: rejection. Like a hurt dog, she was snapping at anyone who approached her to help.

"You're in some pain right now, aren't you, Dina," I said gently.

"No. I'm not in *pain,*" she sneered. "I'm pissed. At my asshole ex. And right now at you, because you want us to strip it all down and give it to you right in the feels. But why should we trust *you*? What makes you so much better than us?"

Once upon a time I prided myself on my therapeutic demeanor—and not just in the office. Like my old professor Janet Evanston, who'd never let on that she was brimming with homicidal rage until she snapped and tried to stab her husband, I thought that what made a therapist good was her ability to stay neutral, collected, always a calm, confident authority figure.

But I'd learned after having my own breakup breakdown that that was a lie. It might have been good clinical therapy, but the kind of work I was doing now was all about human connection. Being real. So it was time to take down my own guard if I wanted anyone in this group to feel safe enough to let down theirs.

I turned to look directly at Dina. "I'm not better than you, Dina—any of you." I stood up and took a deep breath as all eyes glued onto me. Then I slowly unbuttoned my blouse, turned around, and slid one sleeve down my arm to reveal my own badge of shame—the one I'd never shown nor confessed to anyone but Sasha: my donkey tattoo. I was one treatment into the removal process, but I knew it was still clearly visible against my pale skin, huge and colorful—with a huge equine hard-on behind a vivid red void sign, over the caption, "No More Jackasses!"

I listened to the group take a collective gasp, and then I heard a few hesitant laughs, and then the entire room burst out in guffaws. I felt my face heat up, but I calmly rebuttoned my shirt and then turned to face everyone head-on, waiting out their amusement.

"I'm Brook, and I lost my mind after my last breakup, because I felt powerless and unwanted and small. I stalked my ex, almost had the world's worst rebound sex," I added wryly when the laughter finally subsided, thinking of Chip, "and wound up getting a drunken tattoo one night. Knowing what to do—and not to do—doesn't always mean you do it. That is, if I'd even been sober enough to make that judgment call," I said sheepishly, and the class laughed again—with me this time, not at me.

"I've fought some of the same battles a lot of you are facing," I went on, now to everyone. "And I still am, and I'll probably fight more in the future. But this last time through the wringer I learned that you can't keep it all bottled up—you have to let it out. And you can't do it alone—you have to be brave enough to share it with people who care about you. You have to let yourself be vulnerable enough to accept help. I hope that's part of what we're able to offer one another as we work through our situations in here."

At first I wasn't sure what the slapping sound was, or where it started. But then I realized that the woman whose husband didn't love her anymore—Betty—was clapping. A second later someone joined her—Carolyn, an older woman in a twinset and pearls. And then the woman beside her, and Antonio and the other man, Sherman, and in just a few seconds the whole circle had erupted in applause, the participants smiling, laughing, shooting me thumbs-up and "okay" signs.

Dina Jones was *not* clapping— slumped back in her chair, arms still crossed over her body. But I hoped that as the weeks went on, even Dina might find some relief here.

"My husband left me for a younger woman," the carefully groomed Carolyn blurted out as the clapping died down. "I've been stewing in that for more than a year. I feel ugly and undesirable and old."

I turned to look at her. "Carolyn, thanks for telling us that. It takes courage to talk about the vulnerable parts."

"My girlfriend dumped me because she got a psychic reading that told her she was going to meet the love of her life." This was Elisa, the dark-haired woman two seats to my left. There was laughter and a few snickers. "I know!" she said. "I feel like an idiot for being with this woman. And extra stupid because I..." Her voice broke, but she went on: "I actually loved the moron. What does that say about me?"

"It says you're human, and you invested in someone you cared about, Elisa," I said. "You're not responsible for her decision-making process."

She nodded, shrugged, and then gave a weak smile.

"I'm Antonio," the dark-haired man said into the commotion of voices that had started to fill the room, and everyone quieted at his loud tone. "I'm here 'cause my wife wants to leave me...because I've been cheating on her a little bit." He had the grace to look embarrassed. "I'm hoping you guys can help me turn this thing around."

"Admitting it's the first step, honey!" Betty called out. "It's great that the spirit is willing, but you gotta keep that flesh in your pants!"

The group laughed.

One by one each spontaneously shared their stories—and how their broken relationship made them feel—everyone but Dina, that was, and the mousy-haired girl who sat watching everyone else share like a scared rabbit. But they were listening, and they hadn't left.

And I was beginning to think that this crazy idea might actually work.

Chapter Six

Ben picked me up that evening at six, as he often did on Saturday nights, and drove us downtown. When we pulled into the parking lot of the Plantation, I slanted him a look.

"Pretty fancy," I said, my eyebrows lifted.

One side of his mouth rose. "We have to celebrate."

The 1902 manor had been refurbished and operating as a restaurant since I was a kid, but I'd been there only a few times—once with a prom date when I was a junior, and with Mom and Dad for my graduation from both high school and college. It was designed for special occasions—a wood-lined bar that looked painstakingly hand-carved, chandeliers over each linen-covered table, and a brick fireplace in the center of the main dining room.

The host seated us at a table by the staircase in a corner, in a cheery yellow room I suspected was once the formal parlor, and Ben ordered a bottle of red wine for us. When the sommelier arrived with it he flourished the bottle toward me and then Ben, opening it with great flair and making rolling hand motions over the neck, presumably to waft the aroma toward us. Then he tilted the bottle over one of the balloon glasses to pour off a taste, finishing the pour with a stylish twist of the bottle to avoid spilling a drop.

"Monsieur," he said with a slight bow, proffering the glass as if it were frankincense and myrrh.

Ben tried to hide his grin, but I saw it playing around his lips when he noticed mine plastered across my face. "*Merci,*" he said, schooling his expression and taking a sip. "Excellent, thank you." He gestured toward me. "Please pour for the lady."

"Just so, sir." As the man spilled the dark red cabernet into my glass, he added, "If I may be so bold, might I recommend the veal this evening? It's supremely satiny and tender. Fed entirely on a diet of vegetables and squash." He brought his bunched fingers to his lips and kissed the air an inch in front of them. "Exquisite."

By this point I had my face buried in the bowl of my wineglass.

"Thank you, my good man. We will certainly give that our deepest consideration," Ben said seriously.

As soon as the sommelier was out of the room and well away from earshot, I giggled. "Oh, my god. I love him."

"Vegetables *and* squash. That must be why the veal is so satiny."

"'My good man'?" I teased. "Have you been taken over by a Jane Austen novel?"

"I couldn't help it. He was contagious."

I reached across the table spontaneously and clasped his fingers in mine. "You didn't have to do this, Ben. But it was very sweet. Thank you."

"To the Breakup Doctor's new venture," he said, holding his glass aloft. I lifted mine to meet it.

"I should be taking *you* out—it was your idea for me to do these in the first place."

"Tell me how it went."

And I did—through the appetizers we ordered (crab cakes and oysters Rockefeller), and into the entrée, a fancy chateaubriand we shared that required half an hour to prepare. I didn't mean to hog the conversation, but Ben asked question after question, so interested in the session and me and my work that my tongue tripped along of its own accord. He always really listened, and had such an easygoing good nature. Those shouldn't be such unusual qualities—they seemed like just basic human decency—but I'd dated enough to know a man like Ben was rare.

Finally we moved on to other topics, like the house he was building for a quirky millionaire in Cedar Key, who wanted the design to include a sensory deprivation room—black floor, walls, and ceiling, with no windows, where he could go and "commune with his inner oneness."

We talked and laughed through the entire meal and dessert—a crème brulee so silky it was almost imperceptible on our tongues except for the explosion of sweetness and the crunch of the sugar topping. When the bill came I tried to split it with Ben, but he refused.

"I wanted to do this, Brook. I want tonight to be special," he said, and the sincere expression he wore kindled a little glow inside me.

And suddenly I wanted the night to be special too. I'd been holding Ben at arm's length for so long, telling myself I was making sure we weren't a rebound relationship, that I wasn't jumping in too fast, that I was being careful. When the truth was that I was being cowardly. So afraid of making the wrong decision again that I made no decision at all.

I made one at that second. I'd found an extraordinarily good man, and—for better or for worse—I was ready to move things forward and see what happened.

"Ben," I said, my voice sounding breathless in my own ears. "Can we go back to my house?"

...

I'd realized on the charged drive home what my invitation had sounded like, but once inside I guided us to my sofa in the living room, and I turned on two lamps instead of the candles I usually preferred in the evenings.

I wanted to come clean, and I wanted to be well lit to do it.

"There are some things I need to tell you," I said. Ben just looked at me with a calm, patient expression I wished I could take a picture of. It was exactly how I always thought of him: steady and open.

It was time I was open with him.

"This is about me, not you," I began. "And not *us*."

He smiled slightly, but I could see a hint of unease behind it. "Is this how the Breakup Doctor starts a breakup? Because if it is, you can just be honest with me."

"What!? No! Oh, my god, I'm sorry, I'm just not sure how to..." I blew out an impatient breath and stood. "Okay, let's just dive right in." I reached to unzip the side of my dress.

Ben's eyebrows lifted.

"Oh! Not *that*. I mean, yes, I want to do *that*, but not...Oh, good lord. Just...here." I turned slightly so he could see my shoulder as I revealed my giant tumescent jackass in all its hideous glory.

Ben's eyes widened. "That's quite a statement," he said.

I didn't know if he meant the tattoo itself or the actual statement inked underneath it.

"Inadvertent," I said. "I was drunk and made a really stupid decision."

"That doesn't sound like you."

Bless him. "That's what I want to talk to you about. It *wasn't* like me—at all." I pulled my sleeves back up over my arms and zipped the dress, sitting back down on the sofa next to Ben. "Can I tell you how it happened?"

"Of course you can."

"Okay." I took one more fortifying breath, and then plunged in. "A little over a year ago I was engaged."

His eyebrows crept up his forehead, but he didn't interrupt.

"A month before the wedding my fiancé got cold feet—I didn't know why then, and I still don't. But instead of trying to find out, or talk to him, or even work through it on my own, I acted like it was fine. Ate all the deposits, got my things, and bought the first house I found that I could afford, just to prove that it didn't impact my life at all."

Ben nodded, some understanding lighting my murky past. "That's why this was such a fixer-upper when I met you."

"Right. Mortgage in haste, repent at leisure. Although I love it now." I looked around at my still-in-progress living room—Ben had drywalled for me after Sasha and I stripped the wallpaper, although I hadn't figured out what color to paint, and I hadn't hung curtains or accessorized yet—but I felt a fierce rush of pride. "I love that it's *mine.*

That I did this—but that it also represents pieces of all the people I care about who've helped, like my dad, and Sasha, and Stu—and you. Thank you for that, Ben."

"You're welcome," he said simply.

This man deserved every last bit of honesty I could offer him. I reached over and took his hand, and he wrapped his fingers around mine. "I was pretty devastated by my fiancé's...by Michael's decision." Despite how long I'd refused to say his name—to let anyone else say it—speaking it aloud to Ben seemed to rob it of the power it used to hold over me. "But I didn't know it at the time. Or I didn't let myself feel it, anyway. Instead I jumped right into another relationship—Kendall."

"The guy you were dating when I met you in the hospital?"

Ugh. I'd landed in the ER for a tetanus shot after a fight I'd had with my ex, when I'd tromped down on a carpet tack strip while venting my anger on home repairs, instead of to Kendall, where it belonged. For a therapist I'd made every mistake in the book. When I'd met Ben—in the hospital with a broken arm from a job site—and he'd been kind to me, I'd blurted out that I had a boyfriend. Which I had, at that point—until he broke up with me by text message the next day.

I nodded. "Yes. It ended right after that. Badly. And I kind of lost it. Hence"—I pointed a thumb over my shoulder—"the tattoo. It wasn't about Kendall," I added. "Or it kind of was. And it kind of was about Michael too—I'd never really dealt with my feelings about our breakup." I looked down at where our fingers were still entwined. Where Ben hadn't let go, despite my revelations, and I wondered why I hadn't told him sooner.

"I didn't used to deal with a lot of things. I thought it made me strong if I didn't let anything affect me—so I shut everything down and didn't show anyone anything but the 'good stuff.' But I'm trying not to be that way anymore. I like you, Ben." I squeezed his hand, and he squeezed back. "I mean I *really* like you."

"Brook," he said, his voice barely a vibration of the air. "I really like you too." He lifted my hand to his lips and pressed a soft kiss to my fingers, and inexplicable tears pricked my eyes.

"I don't want to shut down with you," I whispered. "But I'm trying to take baby steps, or I'll freak myself out. And that's why...Well, that's why we haven't...um..."

"Brook, I'm really only in this for the sex."

I froze. "What?"

"I'm kidding." Ben grinned at me, and my heart started beating again. "Look, I love your company. I have a great time with you. You're fast becoming my favorite person to talk to. This is a good thing—a really good thing. Things will happen when they happen. So just don't worry, okay? I'm happy."

My chest felt so full I figured I'd grown a cup size. "I'm happy too," I said. And the truth of that felt like a flower opening up all around me.

He reached over and stroked his fingers down my arm, and I shivered. "For the record, that's not to say that I don't *want* to do those...other things," he said in a voice so low and sexy it vibrated my Fallopian tubes.

I let out a shaky breath. "Me too, actually. Some nights it's all I can do to stop."

He was still grinning. "Good."

And now that we'd talked—now that Ben knew everything, and the sky hadn't fallen and a nuclear bomb hadn't detonated and I wasn't left in a helpless puddle of patheticness on the ground—it seemed ridiculous to wait any longer. I liked Ben. I trusted him. And, god, I wanted him.

But he was already standing, holding out a hand to pull me to my feet. "I'd better get home," he said, bringing me close. "Jake and I are working on the Fiat first thing tomorrow morning with my buddy Malik." I'd met Malik—he and Ben had been rebuilding an old Spider convertible together for the last year and a half.

I let my arms wrap around Ben as if they belonged there. "Jake's helping, huh?"

"Are you kidding? If that dog had thumbs he'd have his own auto body shop."

He leaned in and kissed the smile off my face.

Chapter Seven

"So, what's happening with the sex?"

Sasha was lying on my outdoor sofa on my lanai, her body sprawled across the seat and her legs angled up over the back. Periodically she reached for the daiquiri I'd planted in front of her and held it down below the sofa, where she could sip from the bendy straw by just turning her head, rather than going to all the trouble of lifting it.

I was cradling my drink in my fingertips to avoid melting it too quickly with the heat of my palms, balancing the glass in my lap in the overstuffed patio chair cattycorner to her, my feet propped up on the wrought-iron cocktail table. Frozen drinks seemed a little like overkill for a Sunday afternoon, but it felt like ages since I'd gotten to sit like this with Sasha—just Sasha—and lazily talk over our lives, and it felt like an occasion.

"Nothing," I said. "Nothing is happening with the sex yet. I told you that. We're—"

"'—taking it slow.' Bleh. Bo-ring." She slurped her drink. "I'm assuming that when it happens I'll know about it?"

"Almost before he does," I assured her. A smile crept across my face. "We talked about it, though."

Swinging around to sit up, Sasha folded her legs underneath her and regarded me rapaciously. "Phone sex? Hot. Tell."

"Not phone sex, pervy. I mean we talked about doing it, what it means...why we're waiting. You know."

"Oh." She sounded like she'd opened a gift and found a vacuum cleaner, slumping back in the sofa. "Still boring."

"Smart," I corrected her. "I like him, Sasha. I mean, a lot—more and more, actually. And I don't want to ruin it, or move too fast, or do anything before I'm more certain. You have to admit I've had a bad run lately."

"True dat," she admitted. "And you are the responsible one of us. Look at me—I've leaped all the way in with your brother."

"Well, in your defense, you *have* known him for nearly twenty years."

An expression took over her face that I could only call *dreamy*. "Yeah. It's crazy. But it feels so...normal."

It tickled me to death to see her like this. For once, Sasha seemed secure. Content.

"And you know the best part?" she asked softly.

I smiled back at her. "What?"

"We have *so much sex*. Everywhere. All the time."

"Agh! Stop it! Why do you always do that?" I said, jumping up and snatching her nearly empty glass away.

Sasha was practically doubled over with giggles. "Oh, god," she said, trying to catch her breath. "Because it is *hilarious*. It never gets old."

I was a mental health professional. I knew that if I stropped reacting, she'd stop provoking. And yet she got me with it—every single time. "You're disgusting," I said. "I'm getting more drinks. Subject change when I get back."

By the time I'd blended another pitcherful, Sasha came in to scavenge for food, and we took a ragtag assortment of cheese and crackers, candy bars, beef jerky, and grapes outside with us. I knew Sasha would probably only eat the grapes.

"So," I said as I ripped into a piece of jerky. "I tone hin aba Maca."

She lifted a brow. "Beg pardon?"

I finished chewing and swallowed. "I told him about Michael."

"Stop it! You just said his name!"

"Yup. And I said it to Ben."

"No. No way. What did you say? What did *he* say?"

I recapped our conversation to her—adding the bits about Kendall too, and I even told her about showing him my tattoo.

"Who are you?" she asked, shaking her head in wonder. "I can't believe you said all that. Out loud. To a *boy*. It's like...Oh, my gosh, Brook, it's amazing." Her eyes grew wide and solemn. "It's like you're becoming *human*."

I threw the last bite of beef jerky at her.

I'd missed talking things over with her like this. I loved that she and Stu seemed so happy together, but sometimes it felt like I'd lost a bit of each of them—like I was on the outer valence of their atom of two. And Sasha must have sensed my feeling of neglect—she'd suggested this aimless afternoon on my lanai before we headed over to my parents' for Sunday dinner.

"Hey," I said, readjusting myself sideways in the chair and swinging my legs over the arm to face her. "You remember that guy from Faryn and Jan's party last March?" I asked. "The bartender?"

Raising her eyebrows, Sasha drawled, "Uh, the one I bailed out of jail, along with you, after you two sneaked out of the party in the middle of the night and nearly humpback-whaled on the sand? Your former patient? Chip Santana? *That* bartender? No, not really."

"Shut up. I'm seeing him again."

"*What!?*"

"No, no—not like that! He just asked for my help."

"Brook, is that a good idea?"

"I think it's okay." I told her about Chip's mission to make amends to his exes. "I'm not taking him on as a client. I'll just be sort of...well, an adviser now and then. I think it's healthy."

"For him, maybe. But is it healthy for you?"

"What do you mean?"

"Um, naked horizontal beach volleyball? The fact that the guy flips your switch? *Ben?*"

To get out from under her laser stare, I reached for my drink. "I thought about all that. It's strictly professional, Sash. He asked for my help. And he's changed."

"People don't change."

"Of course they do!" I yelped. "Otherwise you just invalidated my entire profession!"

But Sasha shook her head adamantly. "Not like that. Not guys like him."

I sighed. "Sash, I appreciate your concern. And I get it—normally I might agree with you. But you have to trust that I'm a professional. I know when a change like this is genuine, and believe me—Chip Santana is a different man. He wants to be a better person. How can I turn down someone who comes to me with a request like that? That's the whole reason I got into this line of work in the first place."

"Well, if you're sure." But she still looked doubtful. "Be careful, though, okay? There's something about that guy...I just don't trust him."

I wondered where these cautious instincts had been when she was dating every bad boy within a hundred-mile radius, but the only reason I opened my mouth was to put my straw into it and take a long sip of my daiquiri.

"Don't worry," I said after I swallowed. "I'm always very cautious."

Sudden pain knifed through my brain as my entire cerebellum cramped, and I groaned and grabbed my head.

"Brain freeze?" Sasha asked conversationally.

"Aggghhh," I moaned, managing only a nod.

"Reassuring. Way to be cautious."

She leaned forward and plucked my drink from my limp hand.

...

Chip and I met at a diner on Estero Boulevard late Monday afternoon.

"I want to start with Katie," he said, stirring a cup of coffee.

I took a sip of my own coffee. "Okay. Tell me about Katie."

Katie was the Big One—the one who'd broken Chip's heart the worst. They'd met at his bar and fallen "wildly in love," he said. He moved into her place within the week, and it was the most intense, best relationship he'd ever had.

And the worst.

"We fought. Like, not all the time, but a lot."

I nodded. "What did you fight about?"

"Stupid shi— stuff. I didn't answer all of her calls. I didn't seem interested enough in her stories. I was hanging out too much with the guys."

"Sounds like she wanted more of your attention than she was getting?" I asked.

"Yeah, I guess. It seemed like she was always on my case about it, though, you know?"

"Is that why you broke up?"

He made an odd little gesture—a twitch of his shoulder that was meant to be a shrug, I thought, but just looked like a tic. "Yeah. No. Kinda."

"What do you mean?"

The server came back to our table to refill our mugs, and Chip raised one slanted eyebrow at me. "Hey, you want to order some chow? They've got great grits here."

"No, that's okay. You go ahead if you want to, though."

He shot that incandescent smile of his at the tired-looking woman in a worn apron. "Ma'am, do you mind bringing us a plate of your cheese grits? And two forks?"

She perked right up, lifting one spotty, lined hand to smooth the ashy blond hair at her temples. "Sure thing, honey. What else can I do for you?"

"You're already doing just right. Thank you." He kept the grin on her till she turned away, and I saw a pink flush creeping into her cheeks.

Amused, I looked back at Chip, who was adding creamer to his coffee. The woman had to be pushing sixty, and he'd just effortlessly reduced her to a blushing schoolgirl. At least I wasn't the only one susceptible to his charms.

Chip was telling me something about this restaurant, and how he used to come in here for breakfast after his closing shift at the bar nearly every night. I focused back on him and waited until he took a breath.

"We were talking about Katie," I reminded him. This was an odd circumstance—not quite therapist/client, not quite friends—and I wanted to keep things out of the social realm. "And why you broke up."

He looked down at his cup. "Oh. Right. Look, Doc, I don't want you to think badly of me."

"Chip, I'm not here to judge you or your actions. You asked for my help. I can't really offer it unless you give me the full story."

He leaned onto the table on folded arms and blew out a long breath that smelled of coffee and cigarettes and faintly of cinnamon, but strangely it wasn't unpleasant. "Okay. Crap. Maybe I should have started with Amelia. She dumped me cold and I didn't do anything wrong to her."

"We can start with Amelia, if you prefer."

"No. No. Okay." Another sigh, and he scrubbed his cheeks with his hands, making a rasping sound against the stubble. "I messed around on Katie."

Well, that was about what I'd expected. It was funny that Chip—who'd once had a penchant for punching people in the face—was this embarrassed about cheating on someone.

I kept a neutral expression. "Okay. Is *that* why you broke up?"

He nodded. "Yeah. Eventually."

"You mean she didn't find out right away?"

He pushed back from the table and slouched in the red booth. "Oh, no. She found out. I was late coming home and she drove to the bar and caught us in the beer cooler."

"Ah."

"I screwed up—I knew it. I didn't even like the girl. She was just there, and Katie'd been mad at me for some stupid thing, and...you know how it goes."

Once upon a time I'd have said I didn't. But considering that, when I was having relationship woes of my own, I'd almost done something almost identical with the very man telling me this story, I no longer rode my old high horse. I nodded. "I do know how it is to do something out of anger or hurt that you later wish you hadn't done."

Chip looked up from mutilating an empty packet of sugar. "Thanks, Doc. It helps that you understand."

There it was again—that genuineness I never saw in Chip until recently. This new version of him could be disarmingly sincere.

The server showed back up tableside at that moment, setting the grits in front of Chip with a smile curving her newly lipsticked mouth. "Here you go—cheese grits." She turned her head as if to address me as she set a roll of silverware in front of each of us, but her eyes stayed on Chip. "Extra fork."

Chip sat up straight. "All right! These are worth getting out of bed for."

"What else can I get for you, honey?"

"This is perfect, just like the service. Thank you." He winked at the woman, and she visibly preened.

"It's my pleasure." She gave a wink back before turning and walking back toward the kitchen with a spring in her step that hadn't been there before. I felt a strange tenderness ooze into me like smoke. I'd thought flirting for Chip was an autonomic response, like breathing, but here he was trying to make a worn-down woman with a thankless job feel good.

He unrolled his silverware and dug a fork in. "Get on in here, Doc—you won't be sorry."

I smiled at him, making no move toward my utensils. "You just made her day, you know."

Chip looked up at me, chewing his first mouthful, a question in his ocean-colored eyes.

"The server," I explained. "You made her feel really good."

He swallowed and flashed that same luminous smile at me, and something jolted alarmingly inside. "Oh, I don't know about that. Come on, Doc—try these."

As I reached over with a fork and scraped the barest taste from one edge of the grits, I warned myself to never let my guard down with Chip Santana.

Chapter Eight

After Chip polished off the plate of grits, I got the rest of the Katie story.

He'd been candycoating.

Katie was more than pissed. When Chip got home, everything he owned was lying on her front lawn—not in suitcases, but spread out like mulch—and Katie was waiting in the kitchen.

With a gun.

Which she shot at him.

I was glad at that point that I hadn't laid into the cheese grits, because it wouldn't have been a pretty picture with my mouth hanging nearly down to the tabletop. "Are you shitting me?" I cleared my throat, mentally hunting down Wise Therapist, who was nowhere to be found. "Sorry."

Chip waved a hand and lifted one side of his mouth in a sardonic grin. "Nah. Nice to see the armor get dropped."

I didn't have time to chew on that, though, because Chip was going on with the story: "I tried to grab the gun away from her, but I slipped in the blood, and—"

"The *blood*?!"

He raised an eyebrow. "Well, yeah, Doc—she shot me."

I had no answer to that—no words at all, actually.

"In the calf—I mean, she wasn't totally nuts—and believe me, if she'd wanted to hit an artery, she'd have done it, even from across the house. Katie could shoot." He actually looked fond for a moment. "Anyway, I guess she thought I was lunging for her when I slipped, and she reared back and belted me in the side of the head with the barrel, and that's when I got pissed—sorry, mad."

"*That's* when you got pissed?"

He went on as if I hadn't interrupted. "I didn't mean...well, I guess I didn't really know what I was doing, and I just grabbed her by the ankles and yanked her down—the floor was pretty slippery at that point—"

I cringed.

"—and then I...Aw, shit." He didn't even correct his language this time—just pushed the empty plate away from him and propped his elbows on the table, dropping his head into his upraised hands.

We sat like that for a moment or two. I caught from the corner of my eye our server sending me a hot glare, as if I were responsible for Chip's upset. I averted my gaze from her and broke the silence, afraid he'd just sit like that forever if I didn't.

"And then what happened? Chip?" He looked up, his eyes bloodshot, and suddenly I was afraid of the answer.

He wanted me to help him make amends to her, I reminded myself. At least I knew he hadn't killed her.

Probably.

"What happened next?" I asked quietly.

"I'm sorry," he whispered.

Oh, shit.

"I...I tried to strangle her." His voice was choked, as if he himself were strangling, and my stomach dropped to the floor. "And then...and then we were...having sex"—a whisper—"both of us going at each other like crazy right there, on the kitchen floor. And then afterward I just..."

I felt ill.

"I just left her there. I never saw her again."

...

The whole story was so much worse than I'd first imagined...but on the other hand, not as bad as I'd begun to fear.

Glass half-full, I suppose.

I didn't even know what to say after Chip's last verbal bomb. In my old practice I'd dealt with depression and narcissism and even mild schizophrenia, but this was so far out of my depth I couldn't even come up with something as textbook as, "So how did that make you feel?"

Besides, it was pretty obvious how Chip felt. The guy who usually had one emotional setting—rage—was sitting across from me looking destroyed.

I let out air I hadn't realized I was holding in, and the breath quavered. "Chip." I shook my head. "That's awful."

The words were out before I could censor them, and I knew they were all wrong—you didn't judge; you didn't make someone in pain feel worse.

But he nodded eagerly as if I'd offered at least some slim solace. "I know."

"Why did you do that?"

"'Cause I was pissed. I was shot. I loved her." His voice was ragged. "I don't know. It was so...*bad*, like you said. I gotta start there, right? If I can't make this right, then there's no point to any of it, is there?" His eyes were searching mine almost desperately, and he was pulling at his goatee with his fingers so hard I worried he'd rip it off.

I reached across and grasped the hand yanking at himself, pulled it down to the tabletop and kept mine resting firmly over it. "Don't do that, Chip."

He turned his hand over and clutched my fingers so tightly I nearly cried out. But I just squeezed back instead, and we sat in silence for a moment.

"I can't fix this, can I. It's too bad." He looked beaten.

"Well..." I thought for a moment. "What do you mean by 'fix'? What do you want to come of this?"

"I want her to forgive me," he said without hesitation. "The only way I can live with this forever is if she says it's okay."

I tried to soften my words: "I don't know if that's possible, Chip. That's up to Katie, not you."

A thwacking sound on the table made us both jump, and I didn't realize until I saw our server standing there like a Valkyrie that our fingers were still linked across the table. I jerked my hand back guiltily, pulling toward me the plastic check tray she'd slapped down.

"You pay at the front," she snapped, and then stalked away.

I focused back on Chip, who was slumped in the booth, staring at his lap. "Then there's no point to any of this," he said so quietly I almost didn't hear him.

"There *is*." I leaned forward. "This isn't about her forgiving you, Chip. It's about you asking for it. Taking responsibility for what you did, and showing your true remorse over it."

He looked up at me as if I were crazy. "What does that accomplish? It doesn't erase anything."

"Erase it? You can't do that anyway. Even if she forgives you. It happened, Chip. You did it. You have to own up to that."

"I did! I just told it to you!"

"Yes. And that's a good start. But you told me you want to make amends, didn't you?" He nodded, more a jerk of his head. "Okay. Then you have to do it with her—with Katie," I said. "Without any expectation in return. She may accept it—she may forgive you. But she may not. All you can do is try."

He looked forlorn. "She's never going to take my call."

"Then go see her."

"She won't see me, either."

"Then write her."

His satyr's brows came together for a moment, and then his forehead cleared. "Yeah! Okay! I like that. Like a text—'I'm sorry'?"

I didn't know whether to laugh or shake him. "I don't think a two-word text is going to do it, Chip." I spent a little time explaining how to formulate an apology letter, keeping it strictly to general guidelines: I wanted Chip to come up with the actual words.

"Okay, I'll give it a shot," he said doubtfully as we rose and moved toward the register. "But will you take a look at it before I send it?"

"I'd be glad to," I said. Reaching into my purse for my wallet, I felt a warm hand on my elbow.

"Let me get this, Doc."

"That's okay, I asked you to meet here. It's a business expense."

He frowned. "Oh, well...okay. Thanks. Um, I guess...what do I owe you for the consultation?"

I shook my head, having prepared for this conversation. "This is a bit odd, I know, but I don't think resuming our counseling relationship is a good idea, considering...well, we stepped over some boundaries in the past," I finished lightly, my face on fire.

Chip didn't say anything, his eyes glued on me.

"But that's behind us, and I do want to help you," I went on. "I'm happy to meet now and then if you need further help with this, just as...well, not a friend, exactly." I smiled to soften the words. "More like a mentor, of sorts, if you need a little extra help with this. Sound good?"

He was still fixing me with that intense stare, but slowly his expression cleared. "Okay, Doc. Whatever you say. I'm grateful for whatever help you can offer—really. If I need to pay you just let me know, okay?" He gave that slow boyish grin that always did disturbing things inside me. But this time all that struck me now was how straight and white his teeth were.

A knot I hadn't even known was in my stomach loosened. This might be a good idea for me too. Maybe meeting Chip in this safe middle ground between professional and personal was a way to remove that inexplicable draw I'd always felt to him. If he had a lot more stories like the one he'd just told me, I suspected it wouldn't take any time at all before I was finally completely immune to Chip Santana.

Chapter Nine

Mary Lynn Moretti had given her husband an ultimatum: He either cleaned up his act and quit cheating, or he had to pack his bags and get out, and he could kiss goodbye any hope of winning custody of their three children.

Antonio Moretti, unsurprisingly, was the first one to share in the group meeting that Saturday.

Antonio couldn't imagine life without his kids—or Mary Lynn, whom he loved "more than life itself," he told us. So he agreed, and swore that his womanizing was behind him.

That very same night he'd wound up in a bathroom stall at the Drink Tank in North Fort Myers with a woman whose face he couldn't remember even as he drilled her from behind.

Antonio wasn't usually the type of client I worked with. I was more likely to be consulted by the wife in a situation like this one, or one of the many girlfriends, wondering why "her" man couldn't commit to her, or why she kept going back knowing that he never would. It was a new experience for me to be on this end of things: counseling the person I'd usually be counseling his partners to run far away from.

But when he called the show asking for my help, it had been hard to turn Antonio away. In person I could see he was as sincere as he'd sounded—his eyes were dark and haunted, despite his easy smile and outgoing personality, and I heard self-loathing in every word that I doubted even he knew was there. He'd started today by asking all of us to help him figure out why he had such trouble with fidelity, and how to do something about it.

So far I was wondering what we'd taken on. In the past three weeks alone, he told us, he'd been with four different women, and the lengths he went to so he could conceal his transgressions from his wife boggled my mind. One was at a gas station on his lunch hour, when he went in after a fill-up to get a beef jerky and instead got jerked off in the restroom by the attendant who was in there cleaning it. One was a woman who worked in his building on a different floor—they went up to the smoking area on the roof midmorning and she gave him a blowie behind a shrubbery. The other two were similar stories—women he met entirely casually who almost immediately offered him sexual favors in inappropriate places at the unlikeliest of times.

Why would a man who clearly loved his wife so much betray her?

I tried to imagine my dad in the same position and couldn't. Even though I knew—from his own lips—that he'd once cheated on my mom, the woman around whom his entire being revolved.

There are those who claim that monogamy is unnatural, goes against biology and every instinct we have as animals. Maybe so, but what makes us human is our free will. We're not slaves to our base impulses—we choose. *Why* we make those choices isn't always apparent to us—that's the raison d'etre for my entire profession. But we have to accept that these decisions are under our control.

Our impulses may be instinctive, but our actions are up to us.

Sherman Schmidt watched Antonio talk with wide eyes. A couple of the women—Carolyn, whose husband left her for a younger woman, and Rebecca, whose boyfriend was cheating on her with her boss—sat back in their chairs, arms crossed and matching accusatory glares on their faces. Sheila stared at her lap—all she ever did, I'd already learned. Dina seemed equal parts fascinated and repelled by him. The others simply listened as if sitting around a campfire hearing ghost stories—I had to admit that Antonio's tales were pretty wild, and he was a talented storyteller.

I couldn't understand the appeal he apparently held to so many females—and males, as he confessed to having accepted the occasional hand job from unusually persistent homosexuals, although he hastened to assure everyone that he was the farthest thing from gay. Antonio was good-looking, sure—dark hair and olive skin, eyes so big and brown he looked like Black Beauty, and a tall, fit body that he held with an appealing confidence. He was an attractive man by any standard, but I didn't feel any compulsion to rip off my panties and throw myself at him.

"It's not like I even liked the girl." Antonio was telling us of his most recent transgression, sitting at an angle in the ladder-back chair at the yacht club with one leg bent up on the rung of the chair beside him and the other on the floor. I didn't think he was conscious of the pose; it was just his instinct to put his junk on display.

"You've said that a couple of times," I observed. "Why is it that you want to point that out?"

Antonio looked over at me and slowly sat up. "That's funny. I thought you were gonna ask me why I did it if I didn't like her."

"That's what we're hoping to get at eventually, isn't it?"

He sighed like a released balloon. "Yeah, I guess."

"So why is it you want us to know you didn't even like the person you were sexual with, Antonio?"

He gave a half grin. "Geez. You don't let things go, do you?" I shrugged. "Well. I don't know. I guess...Am I, um, am I trying to shock you guys or something?"

"Are you?"

He glanced around the circle of people, then shook his head. "Nah. If you haven't been shocked yet, then I got nothin'." He stared at me, eyebrows pulled together, but I didn't think he was glaring at me so much as thinking hard. "Maybe I'm trying to convince myself? Or...I dunno, maybe I think it makes it less bad if I don't like these women? Maybe that makes it less awful for Mary Lynn?"

Suddenly he blinked. "Shit. Oh, wow." He shoved a hand to his face, index finger and thumb wiping at his eyes. "Shit. How about that. That's it, huh? I think that makes it better for her somehow, if I don't even care?"

I softened my gaze. "Is that how it feels? Like it's less hurtful to your wife if you're removed from these women?"

"I guess, yeah. That's what I think," he whispered. "Like that's not really cheating."

I wanted to talk his realization out—why he felt that way, what drew him to other women, whether he consciously picked women he knew he wouldn't care about. It was "circling the drain," as I liked to call it: working our way slowly toward the crux of the issue—why Antonio felt a compulsion to cheat—without shoving the client where I thought he needed to go. Realizations had to come from my patient, not me, to have any lasting impact.

But group therapy didn't work quite the same way as one-on-one sessions.

"I think you're a sex addict," Dina Jones piped up.

Antonio's gaze shot to her face. "What? Nah. No way. Look at me." He spread his arms so we could take in his fit body so clearly outlined by his tight black T-shirt that we could see every muscle of his six-pack. "I take care of my body and my health. No way I'm any kind of addict."

I thought the jury was still out, but it wasn't productive to push Antonio in a direction he wasn't willing to go in at this point.

"Maybe you have mother issues?" This was Betty Mitchell, whose husband told her he'd never loved her. "That Oedipus thing?"

"Oh—yeah—or were you not loved enough as a child?" Sherman, who hadn't yet shared about himself. "I read an article about that once."

"Nah, are you kidding?" Antonio grinned, spreading his arms out again. He liked to take up space. "Look at this. What mother couldn't love this? But not in a weird way," he hastened to add, looking at Betty.

"Okay, let's not get off-track here," I tried. "Let's let Antonio—"

"Oh, I know!" Elisa jumped in. "You have to be in control. You cheat to feel powerful. Like my asshole ex-girlfriend."

"Or is your wife frigid?" Dina asked bluntly. "If you're not getting it at home then I can see why—"

"Okay, hang on a second, everyone." I stood up to get their attention—the group was fast spiraling into chaos as everyone put in their pop psychology theories. The Internet had made everybody an expert in everything—but this kind of "pick a card, any card" snap diagnosis wasn't going to help Antonio see and evaluate his own behavior.

"Maybe he's overcompensating for something," Dina plowed on deliberately, looking at me.

"Dina, let's let Antonio talk without—"

She moved her gaze to Antonio. "Is that it? Do you have a tiny penis?"

"Dina, Antonio has the claw." It was all I could do not to shout it at her. "We need to not interrupt when someone is sharing. And it's not helpful to try to diagnose. We're here to talk about our own situations and hopefully reach some useful conclusions for ourselves."

"Then what do we need *you* for," Dina muttered.

I pretended not to have heard her. "Go on, Antonio."

He sat back. "Nah, that's it—I'm done. I'd rather everyone just tell me what's wrong with me, anyway—sounds a lot easier!"

"Told you." Dina smirked.

Ignoring her wasn't working—she'd just work harder and harder to get my attention.

So if that was what she wanted, that's what I'd give her.

"Dina, it's great that you take an interest in other people's stories," I began, standing to take the claw from Antonio. Plus I wanted the height advantage. "But there's a reason I brought the claw in, and that we try to honor each person when they're sharing. It's hard to do sometimes—to talk about these vulnerabilities, our pain. It's important that we respect one another's time to talk. Can you try to hold on to your feedback until someone has finished sharing?"

She leaned back in her chair, staring up at me with her chin tipped down and her eyes angling up in an insolent stare. "What? You heard him—he was finished."

I forced a smile onto my face. "Okay. I'll tell you what, Dina. Since you have a lot to say right now, we'd love to hear your story. You haven't shared with the group yet." I advanced on her, making sure to hold the claw nonthreateningly, prongs-in, though every primal instinct I had screamed to flip them around to bristle at her. "You've got the claw."

Her elbows were propped negligently on the chair back behind her, and she lazily lifted one hand to wave me off. "Nah, I'm not ready yet."

Next to her, Carolyn Hendry was staring back and forth between the two of us as if watching a Mexican standoff. I felt every other eye fixed on our face-off too, but the room stayed deadly silent.

"I think it's a good idea for you to share your story with us," I said implacably, holding the claw just above her inert hands in her lap.

Dina smirked at me, and I wanted to scrape the expression off with the cultivator. "I don't think so, thanks. You said we didn't have to share until we were ready. I'm just not ready."

"I can certainly understand that." I held my smile firmly in place. "We want this to be a safe place where we all feel comfortable and secure talking about these intimate things. Where we can take the time we need to gather our thoughts and know that we can reveal some uncomfortable things if we need to, because we're all in this together. So I'd like you take the lead here, if you would, and let us in on *your* situation."

Dina was starting to look uncomfortable. This confrontation had clearly gone on longer than she expected, and I wasn't backing down. So neither was she—she was holding her awkward position so stiffly I knew her neck and arms must be aching. But I suspected she had no intention of "losing," and she proved me right when she shook her head. "No, I'm going to skip it for now, Brook, but thanks," she added sarcastically.

But Dina didn't realize I was holding the trump card.

"If you can't share with the group, Dina, I'm afraid I'm going to have to ask you to leave."

No one moved. There wasn't even a rustle in the room.

Dina shot up in her chair, eyes narrowing at me. "That's not fair! I don't have to share until I'm ready—that was *your* rule!"

I said nothing, just stood in front of her with the claw like the original immovable object.

"That girl hasn't shared!" Dina blurted, pointing across the circle at Sheila, who—as usual—dipped her head so her long bangs covered her eyes. "And you're not kicking *her* out!"

"That girl's name is Sheila, and you're illustrating my point," I said calmly. "If you don't take the trouble to learn anyone's name, why would they feel safe sharing their vulnerabilities in front of you?"

Dina shrugged nonchalantly, but I could see color flood her face. "Whatever. Sheila. You still don't make her share."

"Sheila will share when she's ready, I'm sure." I turned slightly to offer the other girl a reassuring smile, but Sheila was curled in on herself, head down, as if trying to be absorbed into the chair. I hoped Dina's turning the spotlight on the poor girl didn't scare her out of the group. I looked back at Dina. "But she isn't jumping in on everyone else's time either. You are. So what'll it be, Dina? Are you going to give everyone the same opportunity to hear your story? Or would you prefer not to be part of the group?" I held out the claw like an ultimatum.

Dina glared at me so hard, I began to reconsider whether offering her a weapon was really a good idea.

Or whether this whole confrontation was. I'd introduced a combative energy into the group that might make *me* to blame for removing the sense of safety I hoped everyone would feel in here. If Dina kept at it, or even if she left, too stupidly prideful to come around, then it might alter the energy of the group irrevocably. And that would be my fault for forcing this issue. I'd given her no way to save face— and I realized belatedly that she wouldn't so much as bend without that.

And then Betty Mitchell rode to my rescue.

She was staring directly at Dina from her position immediately beside her. "I've been sitting here too chickenshit to talk," she broke the room's tense silence in her hale, blunt manner. "Watching you and thinking, 'Now, *that* girl's got a set of nuts'—excuse the French." A few others tittered with nervous laughter. "You ain't afraid to talk, and I've been sitting here trying to screw up as much chutzpah as you have. Share your story with us, Dina," she said, patting Dina's leg. "If *you* don't get the ball rolling, there's pretty much no chance I'm gonna find my own backbone."

Dina had turned her truculent expression toward Betty as she addressed her. Was it softening? I couldn't tell. She just stared at the other woman for a long, awkward beat.

And then after a moment Dina smiled. A real smile. And damned if that girl wasn't gorgeous when she wasn't wearing the butt face she usually sported in here.

"You're Barbara, right?" she said to her.

The other woman grinned. "Betty. Close enough."

"Sorry. Heck, yeah, Betty, I've got a story for you guys." She turned her face but not her eyes in my direction and snatched the claw from my hand. "I've got the claw, folks! Buckle up. Wait'll you hear this."

I could practically feel the group relax as the heavy tension was defused. I shot Betty a grateful glance, and her grin broadened.

And then I turned around and went back to my seat, ready with everyone else to listen to Dina's story.

...

Dina's tale actually filled me with compassion I wasn't sure I could feel for her. It was painfully similar to my own: a month before her wedding, her groom abruptly—and with no explanation—called it off.

In that way, I could empathize with her. The pain of a broken engagement was bad enough, but it increased exponentially the closer you were to the wedding, in my experience. When Michael got cold feet weeks before ours, it had been a blow that took me to my knees.

If I were honest, I still wasn't sure I was over it. Michael yes—I thought so. But the pain of someone you loved, someone you planned to spend the rest of your life with, telling you at the eleventh hour that they'd changed their mind...that was a wound that took a long time to close.

I could almost understand why Dina was so disagreeable.

I hadn't been too off the mark in my original assessment of her. Dina and Luke met in college in Gainesville, at a Greek mixer for their respective houses. He wasn't quite the quarterback—he was a defensive end—and she wasn't exactly a cheerleader—she'd headed the sorority—but I was close. They were the golden couple all through school—Dina's words—and had their future mapped out: They'd marry, move near her family in Captiva, and she'd stay home so they could start their family while he went to work.

"The thing is," she said, addressing the group as a whole, "I could understand it if he met someone—if he was fooling around on me. I mean, he'd be an idiot, but guys think with the little head, right?" She lifted her eyebrows in Antonio's direction, and I could see it took all he had not to pipe up. Instead he nodded furiously. Dina went on. "But he didn't. And trust me—I would have found out. No one keeps secrets from me." She trailed off, spinning the claw in her lap, not sure where to go, I thought, without verbal validation from the group.

After a moment or two of silence, I said, "Anything else you want to add, Dina, before we open it up?"

She shot a glance over at me—fleeting, but minus the raging hostility I was used to. Telling her story seemed to have lowered her defenses just a little.

"Yeah, that's it for now, I guess. It sucked. But he blew it. I'll never take him back. I hope he's miserable forever."

I stood and walked to her, holding out a hand for the claw, which she proffered—handle-first, surprisingly. I stayed facing her directly for another moment. "Thanks for sharing," I said. "I'm sorry you had to go through something like that. It must have been horribly painful, and embarrassing. And it's much worse when you don't know why."

Dina nearly did a double take. "Yeah," she said in a surprised tone. "It is."

"It passes," I said quietly. "Eventually." I leaned over to touch her briefly on the shoulder, then turned to walk back to my chair, not sure I wanted to see her reaction. "Okay...guys?" I said, panning my gaze around the group. "Anyone have thoughts for Dina?"

Antonio's hand was in the air before I'd finished speaking, and I nodded toward him.

"Okay, first off, I gotta say that guy's a moron. You're hot as Satan's ball sac, honey."

It wasn't entirely appropriate, but the room bubbled into laughter, and Dina gave a real smile. I wondered if she knew how much of her prettiness she sacrificed with her habitual smirk.

"Thanks, Anthony. You're not so bad yourself," she said.

"Antonio—but you can call me whatever you want, sweetheart."

"Okay," I said into the fresh wave of laughter, holding up my hand with a smile. "Let's try to keep it more constructive."

"Sorry—*Antonio*. I sort of suck at names," Dina said. "But I'll work on it," she added, sending an apologetic glance to Betty.

That was as positive a sign as I'd seen for Dina's growth, and for the first time I thought she might get something out of being in here.

"Okay, hang on, I had a real therapy thought too, though," Antonio went on. "This guy—we'll call him Shithead"—more laughter, but I let it go. Antonio was great for group morale—"he bailed on you because he's a jerk. *He's* the one with problems, not you."

"Exactly!" Dina said, nodding.

"Hang on." Holding a hand up again, I looked around the room. "Yes, people's behavior is because of their own issues, that's true. But it's not healthy, or productive, to assign blanket blame to one party in a breakup." I was thinking of Michael again, and my role in the rift that developed between us without my realizing.

Dina's hot glare was back, fixed on me. "Are you saying it's my fault? That *I* made him walk out on me right before our wedding?" Her tone was razor-edged.

"Not at all. What he did was cowardly. Unconscionable. Cruel." Dina's face softened just slightly. Encouraged, I went on. "But *he* thought he had a reason for it—however misguided his actions might have been. Sometimes it's more useful to examine both sides of the coin in trying to figure out what went wrong. Not to assign blame—on either party. But because, for all their painful after-effects, breakups are one of the greatest learning opportunities life offers us. They teach us what we want—and what we don't want. And let us learn what we might do differently in our next relationship."

"Not pick a douche bag, for starters," Dina muttered.

"See?" I said. "Already you've learned one excellent strategy for next time."

For a moment she looked at me, eyes narrowed, before she realized I'd made a joke.

"Right," she said, her stiff posture relaxing a bit. "First check box: No douche bags."

"But don't feel you have to have that tattooed on to remember it," I said dryly, tapping my own shoulder to remind them of my "No more jackasses" tattoo.

Laughter filled the room again, and the smallest of smiles graced Dina's lips. "Yeah, okay, Brook—I think I can remember without that."

I smiled back at her, and then addressed the group again. "Okay, who else has something to offer Dina?"

Betty raised a hand. "I know we need to be balanced and positive and constructive and all," she began when I indicated she had the floor. "But first she can bash him a little, can't she?"

"It can help healing to lance the poison first, sure," I agreed. "But only if that's helpful to the person going through it."

Betty looked at Dina. "How 'bout it, honey?" she asked.

Dina sat forward in her chair, now fully engaged. "Oh, hell, yes, Betty. Let's bash that bastard for a while."

I sat back, content to watch as the group started verbally lynching a man they'd never met, and Dina's smile grew dazzling.

...

My own smile stretched my face as I walked out to my car afterward, and it broadened when my phone rang and I saw that it was Ben. He'd had to stay in Cedar Key last night for an early meeting today with his client, and I was looking forward to his return for our date tonight.

"Hi!" I chirped. "Perfect timing—the session just let out, and it was so good, Ben! One of the participants had a breakthrough—well, not a breakthrough so much as sort of a melting of her polar ice caps—and the whole group kicked in to support her, and...it was just everything I hoped for when I started these. It was fantastic!"

"That's great. Congrats, Brook. I know you must be so proud."

"Thanks—I am. I feel *awesome.*" I heard traffic sounds in the background. "You're already on the road? Your meeting must have let out early."

"No," he said. "I had to leave in the middle of it."

"Uh-oh." I laughed. "That couldn't have made the temperamental millionaire happy."

But Ben didn't laugh. His tone was flat and tight when he said, "My mom's in the hospital."

Chapter Ten

I broke land-speed records sailing up McGregor and across Gladiolus to the condominiums where Ben said his mom lived.

He hadn't told me much—she'd fallen and hit her head on her tile floor. Jake started barking nonstop until an irate neighbor finally came over, looked through the front sidelight, and saw his mom's legs in the hallway. He called an ambulance and the police; the latter broke into the house so the former could help her.

Now Ben was flying down I-75 and straight to the hospital as fast as he could—"Please be careful," I'd pleaded uselessly—and I was headed to get Jake.

"I'm sorry to ask," Ben said. "I know you have clients who—"

"Ben, please," I'd interrupted. "Of course I'll go get him."

On the way I rescheduled for tomorrow the two appointments I'd had on the slate this afternoon, though I usually tried to keep at least Sundays free. I wished I could cancel them altogether—I didn't know whether Ben might need me—but when someone was dealing with acute heartbreak, you couldn't leave them hanging.

Ben's mom lived in an over-fifty-five community of tile-roofed stucco town homes tucked away behind the upscale Bell Tower shopping mall. He'd started to give me intricate directions to her unit, but I knew he had other things on his mind. "Just give me the number—I'll find it."

I should have listened. After fifteen minutes, I understood why they called it a "complex." Every time I thought I was headed to where the map showed me, I wound up at the community pool—each time via a different street. It occurred to me that when you're planning a community for an aging population, it's not a great idea to create a maze.

Finally—through sheer luck more than planning—I saw her building number, 826, on the side of a building as I cruised past, and I whipped into a visitors' spot. Ben's mom's unit was around back, along a sidewalk that wound through head-high hibiscus and oleander bushes.

Ben had told me where to find the spare key—tucked under a garden gnome in a bed outside her front window—but there was no need, I saw as I rounded the corner: The police had kicked the door in, and there was a half-inch gap where it no longer latched.

It was dead silent inside, and my heart pounded—had Jake gotten loose in all the confusion?

But when I pushed the door open, there he was: sitting facing me as if he'd known I was coming—or was guarding the door, I realized uneasily, as I saw that his hackles were up. I slowly crouched just inside the entry. "Come here, buddy. It's okay. It's me. Brook," I added inanely, as if that would help him recognize me.

Jake let out a bark so loud I swear my heart stopped beating, followed by a terrifying growl, and for a moment I was certain Ben would come hours from now to find out why I hadn't picked up his dog, and find my gutted body on the floor. But then I heard a soft whine from his throat, and the big white dog lowered himself to the ground and laid his head between his paws, his big brown eyes looking weary and sad.

I stood up slowly, and Jake's brushy tail began to gently wag. Either this was a clever con to get me within eating distance, or the poor dog was simply confused, scared, and perhaps grieving.

I decided to bank on the latter.

Walking to him with my hand extended, I said in a soothing voice, "Okay, Jakie. It's okay, buddy. Remember me? Daddy's...um, friend?" He didn't move from his prone position, but his liquid eyes stayed glued on me, and—I made sure to notice—his tail still swayed gently.

I stopped two feet away, took a deep breath for courage, then gradually lowered myself into a crouch again, and then to a full sit on the floor. I was either laying myself out as an entrée or making myself unthreatening. I'd find out which one in about two sec—

A hundred pounds of Great Pyrenees lurched onto me with the force of a cannonball, and I went over backward, hands flying up to protect my face.

From his tongue. His really slimy tongue. Ew. "Okay, Jake," I said, futilely pushing him away. "Okay, pal, that's enough."

He was straddling me on all fours, but as my hands grasped his huge head he *flump*ed down, sprawled out on top of me with his head resting on my chest.

I was completely pinned, and frankly I felt Jake was taking liberties with my body we hadn't really discussed yet. But as he let out an enormous sigh that spoke of nothing so much as relief from his troubles, I couldn't help bringing my hands around his big torso and petting his soft fur. "That's a good boy, Jakie. It's okay, buddy. I've got you," I murmured softly.

After a few minutes of this sort of thing I stirred, and Jake reluctantly lifted himself off me. I stood and made a quick circuit through the house to make sure no one had taken advantage of the broken door. Jake literally dogged my every move, staying pressed close to my side and nudging his head under my hand as we walked through the condo.

I didn't know how Ben's mom usually kept house, but unless she'd been broken into by a meticulous maid service, I realized no one had been inside. The only sign of what had happened was the broken lock and an overturned sofa table near where she must have collapsed. No blood, thank goodness, and I hoped that meant she hadn't been badly injured. I righted the table, along with the lamp that had fallen with it, unbroken on the tile floor but for the shattered bulb.

I pulled my phone from my pocket and dialed Ben as I peered into closets looking for a broom.

"Hey, Brook. Did you find Jake?" he answered.

"I've got him—he's fine," I said quickly, hoping to assuage some of the tightness in his voice. "Any word on your mom?"

"I've been calling the hospital—they say she's okay, but I haven't been able to talk to her. Thanks for doing this. With all this, worrying about Jake was..." He trailed off.

"I'm glad I'm here. And I think Jake is too," I said, twisting my fingers through the long fur on Jake's head, pressed into my thigh.

"Do you mind taking him home with you for now? I promise I'll come get him later—I just don't know what time I—"

"Don't worry about it. He can stay with me as long as you need. He's a good dog," I said, as Jake looked up at me as if agreeing with my assessment. "But listen, the police had to break in, and your mom's door doesn't lock anymore. I hate to leave the place open like this. Want me to have someone come fix it?"

"Would you?" he asked, his voice heavy with relief.

"It's done. We'll hang out here till we get someone out—Sasha used to date a locksmith who I'm guessing owes her a favor." Because he nailed one of her coworkers in a bathroom on a night Sasha took him to a newspaper party, I didn't feel the need to add.

"Thanks. Really, Brook—thanks a lot. I'll call you later."

After we hung up I called Sasha, who called her ex-beau and I presume guilted him into dropping everything to come fix the door, since she texted right back and said he'd be there within the hour.

While I waited I found a broom—hanging neatly on a rack just outside the door to the garage, of course—and cleaned up the glass shards, trying to keep Jake at a safe distance. He wasn't much on personal space, though, so after I finished I sat on the floor with him, carefully running my fingers over the pads of his paws to check for glass. Jake lay on his back while I did it, his tongue lolling out as if I were giving him a foot massage, so I presumed he was uninjured.

I found his leash on a hook inside the kitchen pantry—everything had a place in Ben's mom's house—and put it near my purse, Jake taking that as a cue to leap around the room like a giant white bunny. Assuming that to mean, "I have to pee," I walked him in the small yard outside the condo unit until the locksmith arrived, and while he worked I wandered with Jake through the house, looking at the pictures on every wall and flat surface: A black-and-white wedding photo of a handsome couple I assumed was Ben's parents. He had a crew cut and a square face, with crescents for eyes when he smiled. His mom was striking: long dark hair that looked insanely thick, huge dark eyes, and full lips. I couldn't see Ben in any one feature on either of them, although there was a clear family resemblance.

In the living room I saw the same man in a military uniform, and a police uniform, and later a suit. The two of them holding a baby that had to be Ben, chubby and smiling. Toddler Ben standing at the shore of a lake, covered in mud. Naked Ben, three or four years old, in the middle of a street in the rain, a bar of soap in his hand and a delighted grin on his face. Ben graduating elementary school; Ben graduating high school; Ben graduating college. What seemed like annual family photos lined the wall leading back to the master bedroom, and I walked along it like a time line, watching the man I was dating grow from a baby to an adolescent. His smile struck me in every picture—he seemed like such a happy, easy kid. It reminded me of Ben now: He had a way of looking at everything as if he found it wonderfully engaging—including me.

The photos stopped when he looked to be in his late twenties or so, and I noticed that there weren't many pictures of any of the family after that. His dad died, Ben had told me the first day I met him. It was as if his mom had stopped commemorating their lives after he was gone. As if there were nothing worth remembering.

The thought made me sad. Was her life empty since her husband passed away? Had she given up since then?

If something happened to her, then Ben, an only child, would be alone in the world.

I still had a knot in my stomach about that when the locksmith finished and I paid him, then leashed Jake back up. For all the vaunted empathy of dogs, Jake seemed to have no sense of my state of mind, crammed into the front seat of my Honda Accord with his head out the window and his lips flapping into a giant grin in the breeze as we drove back to my house.

...

Three hours later my doorbell rang, and apparently it heralded the coming apocalypse, because Jake started up a ferocious chest-deep barking that sent a tsunami of adrenaline rushing through me. A burglar would have to be *really* stupid to break into any house where Jake lived.

I opened the door to Ben, and Jake did the bunny-bounce thing again before flopping onto his back and wiggling like a hookworm. Crouching down, Ben scratched his belly, rubbed his ears, and finished up with a few pats to the dog's side before standing back up to greet me.

"How is she?" I blurted. I'd spent most of the afternoon gnawing over the fears that had sprung up at his mother's house.

"She's got a nasty bump on her head, but she's awake, she's talking, she's lucid, nothing broken."

He looked exhausted—worn out from the emotion of it, I guessed—but I could hear the lightness in his tone, compared to earlier, and a weight lifted from my chest. I hugged him. "I'm so glad. How are *you*?"

"Better now. She had me worried there for a while." Jake was still bounding between us, and Ben leaned over to stroke his head, which seemed to calm the dog down. "Sorry you got stuck with the Kraken here," he said.

I waved a hand. "He was fine. He's really sweet."

"He is, but I know he's a handful. We're working on the crazy, but Pyrs are a little willful."

I'd rather noticed that, as I'd spent much of the last few hours alternating petting the enormous head pressed firmly into my lap with saying, "Okay, go lie down now," only to have the cycle repeat about twenty times. But it was hard to say no to those big brown eyes. We get enough uncertainty and inconstancy from the people in our lives. It was nice to have a creature seemingly woven up of unabashed affection and need.

"He's really a good dog," I said.

Ben's expression clouded. "Well, you haven't seen the full-on Jake, then. It's my fault. I'm not here often enough to give him consistent training. And Mom can't—" His voice grew rough, and he shook his head. "It's my fault."

I heard what I thought Ben was really saying: This wasn't about Jake, who truly, except for a little too much enthusiasm, seemed to be a fine dog. No, I thought Ben was blaming himself for what happened to his mother, for not being here. His guilt-stricken face broke my heart. "Come on into the kitchen," I said, putting an arm around his waist and giving a tiny squeeze. "You need a beer."

He followed me, but protested, "I can't—I need to go and sit with her. I just wanted to take Jake off your hands and get him fed before I go back to the hospital."

I was already in the refrigerator and had a bottle uncapped. Setting it in front of him, I walked past him to the pantry closet and opened the door, gesturing to the floor, where three small bags of dog food resided. "We stopped at PetSmart on the way home. I didn't know what Jake likes, so I let him pick. So relax and have a beer—I can keep Jake."

Ben was looking at the food with an odd expression—like it was either a van Gogh or roadkill; I couldn't tell which. "That's...Brook..." He stood up and pulled me against his solid body, his tight hug telling me everything he didn't say.

Chapter Eleven

That first night was an adjustment for both of us. Jake prowled the parameters of my room as I as I brushed my teeth, sniffing every inch of the floor, my bed, the nightstand, and my person.

When I got in bed the entire mattress dipped as he put his front paws on it and reared over me like a ghostly white specter. "Get down, Jake," I mumbled wearily. For about an hour after that he kept pulling me back from the brink of sleep with intermittent barks. Finally, sometime in the middle of the night, he started regular, pathetic groaning noises, as if he were having an existential crisis.

I rolled over to look down at him, and saw him flat on his side as if he'd been deflated, facing me, his eyes glinting in the spill of light from the streetlight outside seeping between my curtains. "You okay, buddy?"

Jake moaned.

Reaching an arm to the floor, I rubbed his ears, and he nuzzled his nose into my palm.

...

The first of my two rescheduled clients from yesterday was due to my home office in twenty minutes when Ben called to say his mom would be released around one, and he'd be over once he got her settled. He sounded worn-out.

"Everything okay?" I asked before we hung up.

"She'll be fine. I'll tell you the rest when I see you."

By the time he showed up later that afternoon, I'd worked myself back into a dull knot of worry for him. He looked drawn, his face absent its usual color and the skin under his eyes dark.

"What's wrong?" I asked before he'd even made it over my doorjamb.

Ben shook his head, but his reply was waylaid by a joyful Jake greeting his father as if he were the second coming of Christ.

Ben knelt down to pet the dog. "Hey, Jakie. Hey, buddy. How's my boy?"

Jake was quite well, he let his father know with a toothy doggy grin, some really intensive sniffing of Ben's entire person, and a tail that wagged so hard his whole butt swayed back and forth. His antics at least brought a small smile to Ben's weary face.

"Thanks for looking after him," he said, glancing up at me. "I know it's not easy."

"It's my pleasure. How's your mom?"

He stood and I led us into the living room. "She's okay, the doctors said, as far as her head—no concussion," he said as we sat side by side on the sofa. "But the problem was her knee, apparently. I didn't know how bad it was; she's got pretty much no cartilage left in there, and she's been in constant pain."

"That's why she fell?"

"She says it just went out on her. Turns out she needs a replacement."

"That's good, right? They can fix the problem."

"Yeah. We scheduled it for end of August, as soon as I finish the build in Cedar Key, so I can help take care of her."

I frowned. "Will she be okay till then?"

The tight expression returned to his face. "The doctor has her on a pain management regimen for now. Not much else we can do at the moment." He reached over to rub the top of Jake's nose, which was resting on his thigh. "Meanwhile she can't keep Jake with a bum knee—he's way too intense for that."

We both looked down at the dog as he stood gazing adoringly at Ben, head still pressed to his lap. "Well, why don't I just keep him till you get back?" I said.

I was as startled to hear the words coming out of my mouth as Ben looked at hearing them. Jake, apparently, did not find this offer to be a surprise at all. At the sound of his name he bulled his way past Ben's legs and shoved his nose under my arm. I scratched his ears, and his eyes narrowed into slits as he started a contented panting. "There you go. See? He approves."

"That's incredibly nice of you, Brook, but I can't ask you to do that. Jake's probably functionally insane."

He was a handful; that was true. And I certainly was no expert on taking care of a dog—or any living thing, actually. The dead aloe vera on the sill behind Ben's head testified to that. Seriously, it takes work to kill an aloe vera. In *Florida.*

But I wanted to do it, I realized. Not too long ago I was actually reluctant to even meet Jake, afraid the dog would get attached to me and make things with Ben and me feel way too serious. But I was kind of falling in love with him already.

The dog, that is.

"Let me do this," I said. "It's just for a little while. And I like him. He likes me." Jake surged forward and buried his head between my legs. "Maybe a little too much," I joked as I pushed the dog away.

I could tell Ben was considering it. Taking Jake to his residence hotel and leaving the poor guy alone all day couldn't be what he wanted.

I gave the boulder one last shove over the edge: "Seriously, it's no big deal. I have a fenced yard, and I work at home. It'll be like doggy summer camp."

I knew the moment a smile crept over Ben's face that the battle was won. "If you're sure...that would be awesome. Thanks, Brook— really."

Jake scooted closer, sitting at my feet and looking up adoringly at me. Already he was calming down. I petted the dog's smooth head and returned his smile. "It won't be any trouble at all."

...

We went to get Jake's doggy gear and took another big leap forward in our relationship: I met Ben's mom. He'd thought it would be easier to transfer the extra set of bowls, dog bed, and a few toys from her condo, so that when he came home on weekends he still had supplies at his own house.

I'd heard about Adelaide the first time I'd met Ben, when he realized who I was—his mother had been a fan of my newspaper column from the beginning. As we came through the door of her condo she was lying on the sofa with a leg propped up and capped with an ice pack, and her face lit up when she saw me.

"Brook Ogden!" she said. "You look just like your picture in the paper. How delightful to finally meet you. I'm sorry I can't get up at the moment."

"Please don't," I said, coming across the room and offering a hand to shake.

She laughed and lifted her arms. "I'm afraid it has to be a hug. I feel like I know you already, between my son and the column. And you were such a dear to have my door fixed."

I leaned in for her quick firm hug; she smelled like rosemary and clean linen. Stepping back, I watched mother and son together while she and Ben chatted about her knee and she absently stroked Jake's soft white head. In person there was a stronger family resemblance—I could see now that the laugh lines around Ben's eyes were Adelaide's, and the fullness of his lower lip, the slight overlap of his two front teeth.

Ben had told his mom on the phone that we were coming, and that Jake would be staying with me for a while. While he went into the kitchen to gather the dog's supplies, I held the leash and sat at a chair where Adelaide could talk to me without craning her neck. Jake stretched the leash to get to her, and she reached out a hand.

"Despite what my son seems to think, I'm not made of glass," she said. "You can let him go." He went immediately to Adelaide, sitting beside her and gently bumping her shoulder with his nose until she petted him. "I'm going to miss this boy. He's good company."

Guilt pricked me. "I'm sorry—I think Ben's just worried that—"

She waved a hand, which Jake followed with his nose like a bouncing ball until she dropped it back onto his head. "It's for the best, I know. Jake doesn't seem to know his own size."

I smiled. "He is kind of a giant lapdog."

She moved her gaze to me. "It's nice of you to take him for a little bit. I'm so glad Ben has someone he can count on."

Her words gave me a strange little lurch in my belly.

"I presume Ben told you how much I love your column?" she went on. "And your radio appearances."

"Thank you."

"I expect you help a lot of people. You give such kind, positive, practical advice."

I was trying to resist basking in her compliments like a lizard on a rock. Generally I could control my childhood insecurities, but Adelaide was offering the kind of unvarnished approval I wished I could hear from my own mom, and rarely did.

"Thank you," I murmured again, rather than throwing myself belly-up on the ground like Jake and lapping up her praise.

Ben came back in with a brimming grocery bag in one hand and a plush dog toy in the other. "I left the treats, Mom, in case I bring Jake over for visits when I'm home on weekends."

"Oh, please do. The house is going to feel a little empty without him." A shadow crossed her face, and—like a patellar reflex—I wanted to fix it.

"I can bring him over now and then to see you," I blurted.

She and Ben looked at me.

"Really?" his mom said. "Well, I'd love a visit, if you have time. From both of you."

"Done." I pulled out my phone and we exchanged numbers.

...

"That was nice of you to offer to visit my mom," Ben said once we were outside at our cars. I'd followed him over, since he had to leave directly for Cedar Key. "And unnecessary. I know how busy you are."

"I don't mind. I liked your mom." I grinned. "And she likes my column. Maybe I'm just being self-absorbed."

He moved closer, pressing me against the warm metal of my Honda behind me, and pulled me to him with the hand not holding Jake's leash. "I don't think so," he said in a low tone I felt shiver through my body. "I think you're pretty great, actually."

I wrapped both arms around him, liking the feel of his hand at the small of my back. "You do, huh?"

He nodded, a tiny grin flirting with the corner of his lips just before he lowered them to mine.

Heat flared up inside me, and I pushed away from the car and angled into him, sorry as hell that he was about to get in his car and head out, and I had to get in mine and head home without making the kind of intimate connection Ben's kiss was making me crave.

I yelped as something jabbed me right between the butt cheeks, and spun around to see Jake grinning up at me, wagging his tail.

That wasn't exactly the kind of intimate connection I'd had in mind.

Chapter Twelve

"What the hell is that? A polar bear? A yeti?" Sasha took a step back on my front walk, eyeballing Jake, who'd scrambled past me the moment the door cracked open. She and Stu had come to pick me up for Sunday dinner at Mom and Dad's. Not attending was not an option, short of being unavoidably out of town, hospitalized, or—in the case of my mother for a few difficult weeks I wished I could forget— suddenly separated from your husband of thirty-three years.

"It's Jake—Ben's dog," I said. "I'm watching him."

"Oh, my god!" Stu exclaimed, stepping inside as Sasha followed and I closed the door to keep Jake from bolting. He dropped to his knees in front of the dog—he'd wanted one ever since our German shepherd, Mugsy, had died when we were teenagers. But my mom disallowed another pet "when you kids are going to be going off to college soon and leaving me and your father to take care of it," and running his own business since then meant he wasn't home enough to be a good dog owner.

"Look at him! Who's a big, beautiful boy?" Stu asked Jake, working the dog's ears and head like a human car wash. "Who's the best doggy? Who is it? Who is it?" He sounded like a crazy person, but I couldn't help grinning. My brother was just a big kid. He and Jake might have been meant for each other—Jake's tail was wagging so hard I was grateful my living room was bare of knickknacks, and his long pink tongue was lapping all over Stu's face and into his laughing mouth. I grinned at Sasha's revolted expression.

"FYI, it may be days before I come near you now that I've seen that, Stuvie," she said. "There's not enough mouthwash in the world."

"It's just doggy slobber," he said, still in his crazy-baby voice. "There's nothing dirty about that, is there, Jakie? No, there isn't! No, there's not!"

Riled up to new heights of ecstasy at having found his soul mate, Jake plowed right into Stu as he knelt, knocking my brother over so hard we heard his head crack against the bare concrete floor. I cringed, but Stu only laughed, letting Jake plop down on top of him and wrapping his arms around the dog's huge furry body.

"That is one big bastard," Sasha said.

Jake seemed to notice her for the first time as she spoke, and he scrambled up off of my brother—I worried he might puncture a lung with all his weight on the long nails on his giant Grinch paws—and beelined toward Sasha.

He lunged and shoved a nose between her legs and I scrambled for his collar, buried amid all that fur.

Sasha took a quick step backward and pointed a finger at Jake. "That is *not* how you greet people. Sit."

Jake's butt dropped to the ground in front of her as if it were magnetized, and he sat staring patiently up at Sasha.

My mouth fell open. "How did you do that?"

"He's a dog, Brook. You're a human. You have to know who's in charge."

"I do know," I muttered. "It's Jake."

"Aw, don't be mean to him," Stu said, sitting up. "He's just a big bear. Aren't you, you big bear?"

Jake trotted back to Stu, tongue lolling happily at his playmate, until Sasha made a sharp, staccato noise in her throat—a loud "eh-eh!" sound that startled me and Stu as much as it did Jake, who froze in his tracks. "Sit!" she commanded again, and Jake did.

"Seriously, Sash, this is amazing," I said, stunned. "I had no idea you were so good with dogs." Her parents had never let her have a pet. They could barely be bothered with Sasha; the last thing they could have wanted was another creature demanding their attention.

"It has nothing to do with being good with animals. It's just setting parameters. Get up, Stu—you can't encourage him to have no manners like that."

"Yeah, okay, you have a point," he conceded, pushing Jake back so he could stand, and again I was shocked—Sasha handled my brother as well as she did Jake.

"Stay," she commanded, and neither Stu nor Jake budged, both looking at her, waiting for her next decree. She winked at Stu. "Okay, goofball. Now that he knows he's not in charge, you can play with the doggie."

She might as well have fired a starting gun—Stu dropped down again and buried his face in Jake's ruff, rubbing him all over and making muffled exclamations into his fur about Jake's goodness and handsomeness and general state of perfection as Jake's eyes practically rolled back in his head in delight.

I sat watching them. "Isn't he the cutest?"

Sasha raised an eyebrow, but she was smiling too. "So's the dog," she said with a wink.

But as right as she was—both of them were adorable, lost in their mutual love fest—it wasn't what I was thinking. Seeing my brother and my best friend with Ben's dog gave me a glimpse of what they might be like as parents—Stu the perfect playmate and hands-on daddy, Sasha the one who kept order—and I couldn't keep the smile off my face.

...

I left Jake behind at my house—there was no way my mom was going to tolerate slobber and dog hair and nails scratching her hardwood floors. After corralling him in my bedroom, I secured every single thing on the floor that I thought he might use as a chew toy— shoes, laundry, even electrical wires—and put actual chew toys on the floor as a distraction. Maybe I was getting the hang of this caretaking thing.

Mom was bustling over the stove when we arrived at six, the smells of roast chicken and rosemary and sautéing onions wafting through the house. I still wasn't used to seeing the kitchen so thoroughly changed from the one of my childhood. My dad had been working on renovations for my mom for months during which she'd had to operate in a gutted kitchen, with cookware stashed in closets and drawers all over the house and a two-by-four counter set up on sawhorses. For a long time I wondered if that had been part of the reason for her abrupt decampment from our family.

Now the kitchen looked like an ad in *Martha Stewart Living*: sleek granite countertops set off by tiles of smooth glass in rich spice colors that inexplicably made me want to lick them, new stainless appliances, all framed by the glowing wood cabinets my dad had made himself over painstaking, careful months in his garage workshop while my mom grew bored and restless and finally left, like a Hollywood-movie cliché, to get back to her long-delayed "career" in theater.

I set the salad I'd made on the granite counter and leaned in to kiss her cheek as she stirred a brown gravy on the stove.

"Hi, Ma. Smells good."

"I overcooked the chicken. It'll be dry."

At least she wasn't any easier on herself than she was on me.

"I'm sure it'll be delicious." I poked into the sauce a finger that my mom summarily swatted away.

"Your brother's late. Can you set the table?"

There was no mention of Sasha's tardiness—all our lives, she could do no wrong. "We rode together. He and Sash stopped in the garage to say hi to Daddy." I went to the silverware drawer and pulled out what we'd need, then fished cloth napkins from the pantry. Paper ones were *not* okay for Sundays.

"So how are rehearsals coming along?" I asked as I butterflied the edges of the first napkin.

"Oh! Slowly. *Virginia Woolf* is chockablock with dialogue, and you can't paraphrase Albee. Our George is terribly uncertain with his lines, and he'll skip whole pages when he flounders. I'm having to learn his part too so I know how to get us back on track."

For all her disparaging report, her face glowed—the way it did every time she spoke about anything to do with theater.

"You've got pretty big chunks of your own dialogue to learn too, though, don't you?"

"I do." Mom nodded, then looked up directly at me. "How did you know that?"

I shrugged. "I rented the movie with Liz Taylor when you got cast."

She turned back to her gravy, but not before I saw the expression of pleased surprise creep over her face. I was trying. We both were.

I finished laying out the place settings just as Stu and Sasha came in from the garage and Mom called out the three-minute warning—everyone's cue to wash hands and report to the table. Sasha and Stu headed to the guest bath, so I wandered into Mom and Dad's bedroom to use theirs.

Mom's suitcase was neatly tucked into a corner, mute testimony to their strange new relationship. From Tuesday to Saturday, she lived in Naples in the tiny studio apartment she'd rented after her first foray back into theater last year—when she'd garnered fantastic reviews and grudging admiration from me for her real gifts onstage in *The Lion in Winter*. As soon as her rehearsals let out on Saturday afternoon, she came back and lived the other half of the week with my dad. He seemed okay with it, and I had to admit my mom was happier lately than I'd ever seen her.

Dad had come in from his workshop by the time I came out of the bathroom.

"Doll!" He threw his arms open wide and I stepped into them for one of his all-encompassing bear hugs. Dad always made you feel that seeing you was the best part of his whole day.

"Hi, Daddy."

He'd changed too in the last months, in some ways for the better— like my mom, he seemed happier most of the time, the heaviness that had overtaken him during her absence lifted. But now and then it seemed to me he was trying too hard with her, his smile a little too broad, his laughter a little forced. Sometimes I wondered if he was working extra hard to make sure she loved him.

I knew what that felt like.

But I couldn't Breakup Doctor my mom and dad. They didn't ask me to, and I wouldn't have known where to start if they had. They had to work their marriage out for themselves, Stu and Sasha and I had decided. Meanwhile, we carried on as best we could as if everything were normal, I think all of us hoping that by doing so, we would make it true.

"What's new in your business, Stu?" my mom asked as we started passing around dishes and serving ourselves. "Did you get the Windward Apartments account?"

My brother nodded as he plunked a precariously heaping spoonful of herbed rice onto his plate. My mother cleared her throat and Stu's second scoop was more moderate. "Yup. Twice-a-month landscape care half the year, and monthly after that, with regular seasonal plantings at the entrances to the parking areas and buildings."

"Attaboy! Knew you'd win that account," my dad put in.

"Contract?" my mom asked.

"Two years."

"Signed?"

"All over the dotted line. Nice and legal, Ma."

After a few more parental probes at Stu it was my turn. Yay.

"I had my first Breakup Doctor group therapy yesterday," I floated tentatively.

My dad's reply was instantaneous: "That's wonderful, sweetheart."

"That's ridiculous. Why would anyone share their personal business like that in a group?" my mom said, and I swear I *heard* the sound of my balloon popping.

"I don't know, Mom," I said, sitting up straighter and looking back at her. "Maybe because I can *help* them?" My tone was terse. Mom knew how to push my buttons, and I reacted with knee-jerk defensiveness every time.

"I think it's a genius idea," Sasha gushed. "People need something like this."

I gave her a grateful nod. "Thanks, Sash."

Mom tightened her lips and said nothing.

Sasha stared at my mom as if she could hypnotize her with her gaze, nodding like a bobblehead. "Don't you think so, Mrs. Ogden? That it's so cool that Brook can help people through their tough times? Don't you think it's really great of Brook to want to reach out to more people?"

I knew she was only trying to help, but Sasha was laying it on really thick. Mom would see through it in a second, and it would crush Sasha to be on the receiving end of my mother's disapproval. I kicked her to get her attention.

"Ow!" Stu said, glaring at me.

"Bedford-Stuyvesant Ogden! We do not shout at the dinner table."

"She kicked me, Ma!"

"Brook Lyn!"

"Sorry." I shoved my fork into the rice. "My foot slipped."

"You shouldn't be fidgeting at the table."

"Sorry, Mom."

"You kids settle down," my dad admonished mildly. "Your mother worked hard on this meal."

At least it was a new record—this time it had taken almost half an hour at my parents' house for us all to be reduced to adolescence.

...

Dinner wrapped up a little earlier than usual—a fact I was grateful for. I didn't want to leave Jake alone too long. Sasha and Stu dropped me off in the driveway before zipping off together.

I was looking forward to having a living creature waiting for me when I came home for a change, but as soon as I opened my bedroom door my stomach sank.

Big mounds of snowdrifts covered every inch of my room.

Because while I'd carefully dogproofed everything on the floor Jake could possibly get into mischief with, I had neglected to consider that he was *six feet tall* on his hind legs. And Jake had helped himself to my comforter, all my pillows, and the curtains, shredding everything with his sharp piranha teeth into piles and piles of fluff. It looked like werewolves had had a throwdown in my bedroom.

He looked up with a big proud grin as I entered, raising his head from the pillow cadaver he held between his huge paws, tufts of foam spilling from his mouth.

"No!" I screamed, advancing on him. "Bad dog! *Bad* Jake!"

He cowered and slinked backward, toward the bed.

"Why?! Why did you do this? I left you a monkey!" I shouted, picking up the stuffed animal and brandishing it at him like a weapon. "I left you a big squeaky banana!"

I'd backed him against the corner where the bed and the wall met, and he couldn't retreat from me any further, so Jake ducked his head, shooting quick, repentant looks at me with liquid brown eyes.

Guilt pinched me, but I couldn't get hold of my anger. Every single textile in the room was ruined. I reached down and grabbed his collar, and he flinched.

"Outside!" I barked. "Now!" I walked him directly to my back door and nearly shoved him out.

I cleaned up the mess as best as I could, scooping the piles into Hefty bags with a dustpan and vacuuming up the rest. Jake had pulled the curtain rod off one bracket, and they hung askew—what was left of them, which was about three feet that ended in a wet, ragged hem. I pulled them off the rod.

Now I had no bedding and no window covering. I guessed I'd be sleeping in my office tonight.

I brought Jake inside and fed him in silence. I'd calmed down enough to be gentler with him, but I was still seething. What was I going to do about the dog for the next however many weeks until Ben came back? It was too late to back out—I was the one who'd talked him into letting me take care of Jake.

He could have warned me, I thought with a flare of resentment. And for that matter, so could his mom. Maybe Adelaide's show of reluctance to lose the dog was for Ben's benefit. Maybe the crazy animal had been tearing up her house for weeks already.

"Come on, Jake," I said wearily when he'd finished his dinner. "Let's go to bed."

I changed my mind about the office when I carried an armful of blankets in there and saw my nice sofa. At least in my bedroom, hopefully the damn dog had done all the damage he could do. He trailed me back across the house, and I folded up one blanket for a pillow, then lay down on my bare mattress and drew the other one over me.

"Try not to eat these off me as I sleep," I grumbled as he collapsed down beside me with a weary *hrrrmmfff*.

"What's the matter?" I muttered. "Did you wear yourself out destroying my house?"

Jake lifted his head and nudged my arm with his nose. When I ignored him, he nuzzled me more insistently, and finally I grudgingly gave him a few strokes.

"I'm going to take that as canine for 'I'm sorry.' But you're on probation, dog." I scratched his ear and he leaned into my hand. "Now go to sleep."

Like a magic trick, he did—curling up contentedly on the floor beside me and almost immediately starting a low but steady snoring. Between that, the uncomfortable blanket under my head, and the light from a street lamp streaming in through the bare windows, I, on the other hand, was up most of the night.

Jake was definitely getting the better end of this roommate deal. And he didn't have a radio show to do at six a.m.

Chapter Thirteen

Even though getting up at four thirty a.m. was among the worst parts of my week, I'd pushed hard for my odd on-air schedule on KXAR, the station where I hosted an hour-long relationship advice show first thing Monday mornings and on the rush-hour drive home Friday afternoons. I figured that the time when people most needed to talk to someone was either right before the weekend, when they might be tempted to do something ill-advised, or right after, when they already had.

By six o'clock the next morning I was sitting on my stool on the opposite side of a bank of electronic equipment from Jim Veneer, real name Norm McGayhay, host of the A.M. Drive Time Morning Show, with headphones clamped to my ears. Before Jim had even introduced us both we usually had a lineup of callers, and today was no exception.

He pressed one of the lighted buttons. "Okay, caller, you're on the air."

"Um, hi. Dr. Ogden?"

"Morning, caller. Would you like to give me a name?" I asked into my mike.

"Sure. Um." He faltered. "Ri...er...ban."

I went with whatever a caller offered me—people calling in about their most naked feelings or embarrassing behavior didn't always want to lose their anonymity. "Okay, Rierban. What's on your mind?"

"Uh, my...my wife. She's...I think she's, uh...you know. Probably having an affair."

Oh, boy. First thing on a Monday morning, that was deep territory to mine. "What makes you think that?"

He was silent for a second, and I glanced up at Jim. When I'd first started coming onto the show he got nervous when callers faltered for their thoughts—dead air was apparently the cardinal sin of radio. But over the last few months he'd gotten a little more familiar with the rhythms of rejection—he wasn't even looking at me, just sipping his coffee and glancing over some notes.

"Okay." My caller cleared his throat. "Well, she joined a gym. She lost weight. She's, uh...can I say this on radio? She got waxed. You know. Down there."

That caught Jim's attention. He looked up at me, grinning.

"I take it this is all fairly out-of-character behavior for her?"

"Oh, my gosh, sure it is. She's never done anything like *that* in the last forty years, I can tell you. We don't do that sort of thing. We're *Christians.*"

Now Jim was having a hard time keeping in his laughter. I felt a giggle welling up too, but I tamped it down. My caller's pain was real.

"Well, Rierban, I can see that when someone we think we know inside and out starts behaving differently, it can be disconcerting. Is there anything else that leads you to think she might be looking outside your marriage?"

"Well..." Whatever he was trying to say, I could tell my caller was having a hard time coming out with it. "She's, uh...Oh, boy. She's *forward* with me now. Like, she always wants...*it.*" The last word was almost whispered.

Jim's face had turned red and his lips were pressed so hard together to keep back a laugh I worried he wasn't breathing. I had to look away.

"So she's getting fit, taking care of herself, fixing herself up, and she takes more romantic initiative with you than she used to?"

"Yes! Exactly!" The relief in his tone was immediately colored with despair: "What do I do?"

"Well, for starters, Rierban, enjoy the *hell* out of that."

Jim couldn't take it anymore—he guffawed. Luckily his mike was off, but I hoped my caller wouldn't hear it in the background and think he was being laughed at.

"Then make sure your wife knows you're noticing the changes in her," I went on.

"What?"

"Does she seem distracted when she's with you? Does she disappear and you don't know where she is? Does she not take your calls when you phone her, act evasive or distant with you?"

"Uh, kind of the opposite right now. She's..." He hesitated and then blurted, "She's all over me! That's why I think she's found someone—it's got her all, you know...sexed up."

Jim completely lost it, snorting with laughter; then he was up and moving, letting himself out the studio door with a wave at me behind his head to indicate I was on my own. Good—I had an unharried minute to talk to this caller.

"Rierban, I can't say whether your wife is or isn't having an affair. But it sounds to me like she wants to—with you."

"Huh?"

"What you've described to me sounds like a woman who desperately wants her husband—and wants him to notice her, to pay attention to her as a woman, a sexual creature, not just a wife or a partner or the mother of your kids."

"But...but I respect her."

"Good! That's the best basis there is for a healthy relationship. Now show her how much by taking her sexuality seriously. She's clearly changing—whether it's her time of life or some kind of awakening she had or just her wanting to shake things up. Find out what it is—meet her there. Are you attracted to her?"

"Of course I am! She's so beautiful."

I couldn't help smiling at his fervent answer. "Okay. Let her seduce you. Respond to her advances. And in between enjoying what I think most callers would agree makes you a very lucky man, *talk* to her. Find out what's going on—what she's thinking, how she's feeling, what's changing for her. *See* your wife—really see her as a separate, growing person. Be a part of her growth. It sounds to me like she's asking you to be—not as though she's looking elsewhere for that."

"Okeydoke," said my caller. "I'll give it a go. But, uh..."

The door opened and Jim came back into the studio, having managed to compose himself.

"...but what if the old Johnson's not as reliable as it used to be?" the man finished sheepishly.

The door wasn't even fully shut behind Jim before he wheeled around and went right back out, his face red. I wrapped it up with the caller, telling him that there were treatments that could help him, and to talk to his doctor. "But most important," I stressed again, "talk to your wife."

He thanked me and hung up just as Jim came back in, holding a tiny Styrofoam cup of the bitter station coffee and hustling over to his mike.

"That's our own Breakup Doctor, working it hard so you can too," he said on air, winking at me. "Next caller, you're on the air!"

"Morning, Doc," an instantly familiar gravelly voice drawled, and my heart slammed into my ribs. What the hell was Chip Santana doing calling in?

"Morning, caller," I said cautiously. "What's on your mind?"

I heard a heavy sigh, as if he were exhaling smoke. "Well, I've been seeing someone."

I blinked. "You...What?"

"I mean a therapist. And I'm trying to make amends to some women I've, well, maybe not been great to in breakups."

"Oh?" I kept my tone neutral.

"So my therapist has me writing a letter to one lady I dated, and I'm kind of stuck. I don't know what to say. And I can't show up for my next session with my therapist without the letter. She's a whip cracker."

I smothered a smile. "Sometimes we need to be held accountable, caller."

"Oh, I know it, Doc. I need her to stay on top of me."

Heat poured into my face at the sudden image his words conjured. "E-excuse me?"

I heard his raspy chuckle. "I just mean I'm a dude, Doc. This feely stuff she wants me to write isn't my forte. You got any ideas?"

Glancing up from where I held my finger poised over the mute button, I saw that Jim was looking at what must be my bright red face with his eyebrows up at his hairline. I needed to get my mind out of the gutter. "Well," I said, my tone crisp, "I think your therapist might tell you to start with a thumbnail outline of what you want to say to this woman. Just off the top of your head, but from your heart. And then write it out—don't judge it. Just say what you'd say if you weren't worried about her reaction, or that you're being too revealing. You can go back and tweak it later if you need to. The important thing is to be honest about what you're sorry for, and apologize— if you're genuinely sorry, if you've truly changed."

"I am. And I have, Doc. I've changed a lot. I promise."

He sounded so sincere, so eager, I wanted to believe him. "Okay, Ch— caller. Get busy on that letter. You don't want to disappoint your therapist."

"No, ma'am," he said. "I definitely do not want to do that. Thanks, Doc. See you soon."

Jim disconnected the call, shooting a quizzical look at me at Chip's parting words. I just shrugged, nodding at him to put the next caller on the air.

...

Ben called about ten minutes after the show ended, as I was getting into my car in the station parking lot. I could hear the rumble of equipment in the background.

"Morning," he said. "Good show today."

"You were listening?"

"Had it on my computer in the construction office. I think our office manager is hooked on it."

I pulled the phone away as a loud regular beeping sounded on Ben's end. "How can you hear it over all that?"

"That just started. It's pretty quiet around here before seven thirty. How are you doing with Jake so far? Everything okay?"

Except for the fact that your crazy dog ate my house? Sure, everything's aces. But all I said was, "He's all right."

"I'd totally understand if you changed your mind about keeping him, Brook. The last thing I want to do is make your life harder. You've already got your hands full."

The worry in his voice—and his consideration—made a snap decision for me. "Everything's fine," I lied. "Jake's...very sweet." That part was true, at least.

"Good." Even in that one syllable I heard Ben's relief. "I wasn't sure how he'd do on his first night somewhere unfamiliar. Sometimes he gets a little scared."

I remembered Jake's fearful eyes when I'd backed him into a corner. It hadn't even occurred to me that the oversize dog might be feeling disoriented, taken from his two familiar people and places by someone he didn't know that well, and then left behind all alone somewhere new.

"Poor Jakie," I said, imagining him cowering in my bedroom right now, thinking he'd been abandoned again. "I'm just...I forgot how to take care of a dog," I said guiltily. "But I'll learn."

"My mom's amazing with him—she's like the Dog Whisperer. It makes me forget what a pain he can be."

I pressed down on the accelerator and edged up past the speed limit down Highway 41, anxious to get home. "I'll take good care of him, Ben," I promised. "I want to."

"I know you will, Brook. I never doubt you."

I vowed to earn his faith.

"If he gets to be too much, promise you'll tell me," Ben went on. "I'll figure something else out."

"We'll be fine," I said firmly.

And we would be. Whatever I had to do.

...

"Chip, it's probably not a great idea for you to call into the show while we're working together," I said as we sat across from each other in my home office later that afternoon. I wouldn't make a habit of it with Chip, but until Jake felt more comfortable I didn't want to leave him alone. Presently the dog lay sprawled beside me, finally having calmed down after Chip's arrival.

Jake had been fine when I got home that morning, sitting in my bedroom waiting for me like a perfect gentleman, as if the night before had never happened. Only the shambles around him gave his previous destruction away. Maybe he was settling in.

Visitors were a fresh excitement each time, I'd learned with my first client of the day, when Jake heralded his arrival with a crazy spasm of barking that sounded like Cujo. I'd been a little nervous about how he'd react to so many strangers, but as soon as someone came inside they became his new best friend, and after a good sniffing (which I fruitlessly tried to curtail and then profusely apologized for) and my verifying each visitor was okay with dogs, Jake would settle quietly next to me for the duration of the session. In a couple of cases, he'd actually seemed to relax my clients.

Chip looked up at my firm admonition, instantly contrite. "Oh, I'm sorry. I thought you said we weren't really working professionally together?"

"That's true," I conceded. "But..." It was hard to argue with my own words. "But I think it's best if we keep it off the air, okay?"

"Sure, of course—sorry if I put you in a weird position. I just was a little stuck and hoped you could help point me in the right direction." That smile. "Which you did."

"So what do you have to show me?"

Chip leaned forward and reached into a back pocket, coming up with a square of paper. "I went old-school," he said, unfolding it and handing it over. He sipped his iced tea as I started to read.

Dear Katie,

I wish things hadn't ended so badly with us. I know you probably didn't mean to shoot me. I never loved anyone more than you, which was probably why I choked you, but I shouldn't have done it. I hope you're happy now, and I just wanted to say that I'm sorry, and I wish I could have told you that then. If you're willing to talk to me, I'd like to tell you in person, and I want to pay for all the stuff that got broken that night.

Take care,

Chip

It was short, but better than I expected, actually. Chip hit all the right elements of making amends—he took responsibility for specific actions, expressed remorse, and offered to make it right. But there was one key element missing.

"You didn't mention your cheating on her," I said.

Chip gave an impish grin. "Yeah, I know. She can get kind of nuts. I was afraid to set her off."

"But that *was* what set her off to begin with, wasn't it? It was what brought on all the other stuff you're apologizing for. You haven't apologized for doing the thing that hurt her so much in the first place."

His dark eyebrows drew together. "But I didn't think that was half as bad as the choking."

"I'd suggest that, to Katie, it was probably the worst thing of all."

"Really?" Chip looked bewildered.

I leaned forward. "Of course! If your relationship was everything you told me it was, there was something real between you. Katie loved you. And you..." I searched for a nonpejorative way to put it. "You shared yourself with someone else, which must have felt to her as if your love for her was a lie, or didn't mean as much to you as it did to her. Imagine how that would feel."

He slumped over, elbows on his knees and face furrowed. "Well...I guess I can see that."

"Look at it this way: How would you have felt if she cheated on you?"

He looked up sharply, and his furious expression stood every hair on my body on end. "I'd have *killed* her."

I reared back at his explosive response. Jake stiffened and gave a little growl, and I reached down to scratch his head.

Chip's face cleared like a passing cloud. "Sorry, buddy," he said to Jake with a chuckle.

I didn't move, keeping a wary stare on him. "That's a disturbing sentiment."

He winked. "Oh, come on, Doc. I didn't mean it."

"Really? This is a woman you choked. You've had impulse-control issues in the past. To be honest, Chip, this is a little concerning."

"It was a joke."

"It was a bad joke."

His teasing expression sobered. "I apologize. I know that was in bad taste and offended you, and I wish I could take it back." A grin lit up his face. "There—see? I've got this amends thing down pat."

I frowned. "This isn't really something to take lightly. Are you sure you're ready to do this?" I asked him. Chip might not have quite as firm a handle on his temper as he wanted me to think.

"What? Yeah, of course I am! That's why I came to you."

"You still seem to have some residual anger toward Katie. I'm not sure that's the best time to try to make amends. You might want to do some more work with your anger therapist before we—"

"No, Doc, listen—I'm so sorry." His face softened into repentance. "You know, sometimes I feel like I know you so well, I can be really relaxed with you. And I tease hard like that with my best friends. I just...I forgot we aren't friends, not really. You always feel like one to me, rather than just some therapist."

I chewed my lip. Maybe he was right—god knew I'd overreacted to a perfectly innocent comment he'd made on the radio this morning. I was a little hypervigilant with Chip, and perhaps I needed to ease the reins, give him the benefit of the doubt. "That's a nice thing to say," I offered finally.

"I'm not just saying it. I've got a handle on my anger now. I really want to do this. Please, Doc. You know I need your help." Chip's eyes were on me, and they were earnest.

"Okay," I said slowly. "But, Chip, if you get to talk to Katie, and you truly want to make this right and show her you've changed, you can't make jokes like that. They're disturbing."

"Right, right, my bad." He held up his hands, palms out. "I'll remember, Doc. I was just teasing with you, and I shouldn't have. And I won't with her. I promise."

I nodded and gave him my careful professional smile. "Okay. Let's talk about what you want to say if she gets back to you about the letter."

Chapter Fourteen

By Thursday, it was plain that I was going to have to kill Jake.

He'd stopped chewing things up in the house—but possibly only because I almost never left him unattended. He stayed at my side from the time I woke up and throughout my client appointments during the day.

At night I remained glued to the house, unwilling to trust him alone with my textiles. I'd replaced my bedspread with a cheapie from HomeGoods (because I didn't want to drop a wad on something that might end up in Jake's intestinal tract), and bought him a blankie of his own for beside my bed, hoping that if his fabric-eating pica struck in the night, he'd at least focus on the bedding nearest to hand (or paw).

But that wasn't what Jake did at night. No. At night Jake apparently lay vigilant, alert to any moment I slipped into REM sleep. At which point he set up a deep, full-chested barking that yanked me, terrified, from slumber. He would keep it up long enough for me to say, "Jake, stop it! Jake, be quiet!" over and over until I was good and truly awake; and only then—once he was assured that I'd be up for at least an hour trying to fall back to sleep—did he deem it right to flop over and start his instant snoring.

As if taunting me.

For the first time I understood what it might be like to be a new mother. Jake's regular clarion calls kept me up every couple of hours, and by the time I finally drifted back into sleep he'd start the cycle up again.

I tried everything I could think of: extra chew toys, treats, a bowl of food, and taking him outside (I'm sure the neighbors loved me for that, as he continued barking at the apparently dangerous air). Then I attacked the problem from the other end, with earplugs and sleeping pills for me, neither of which was a match for the Death Bark.

After a few days of this I was at my wit's end. And I couldn't ask Ben what to do about it when he called, because he was already so worried and apologetic about Jake being any kind of imposition, I didn't want to add to his concerns.

But today I had a battle strategy.

Lying exhaustedly awake last night during the dog's small-hours alerts, I'd had plenty of time to ruminate about my problem. And then I remembered Ben's words about his mom: *She's kind of like a Dog Whisperer.*

Adelaide had asked whether I might bring the dog over for visits. And she seemed not to have had any of the troubles I was having with him. Maybe, under the guise of a visitation with her granddog, I could pick her brain for what the hell to do.

She'd sounded delighted when I called, and we'd agreed to meet tonight at seven. I was more nervous than I expected as I rang her doorbell. I hardly knew the woman, and here we were having an evening together, just the two of us.

Well, three, I amended as Jake leaned his entire body against my legs.

But Adelaide didn't answer the door. I rang the doorbell again, and when there was still no response, pressed my ear to the door.

Which was of course when Ben's mom threw it open, and down I went at her feet like a carnival duck. Which Jake thought was a great game, and he hurled all hundred pounds of himself on top of me, wagging his tail and grinning up at Adelaide as if to proudly show that he'd pinned her some prey.

"Oh, my goodness!" she said, herding Jake up and off me. "Are you all right?"

"Fine, yes—I'm fine," I babbled. Jake sat at attention beside her, looking at me as though for the life of him he couldn't fathom what I was doing on the floor.

I pushed myself to my feet. "Never let it be said I don't know how to make an entrance," I joked weakly.

"Are you sure you're okay? That looked like quite a tumble."

Waving off her concern, I leaned over to take the leash from Jake's neck. "It was my own fault. I was a little worried when you didn't answer, and I was listening at the door like an old spy film. It was stupid, really."

"Not at all. Sweet of you to be concerned. I'm just not moving as fast as I'm used to at the moment." She indicated her knee, swollen to twice the size of the other one, but I could see the frustration behind her smile.

"Does it hurt?"

"It does, actually. But it won't forever." She gestured me inside, and as I watched her limp in front of me toward the kitchen, I marveled at her easy acceptance of the pain. It was the opposite of my family: Our way of dealing with pain was to deny its existence. I'd learned the hard way that that was only a temporary solution.

Jake trotted obediently after her like a damn show dog. Either he was the greatest con artist on earth, or he was actually a pretty good dog, and it was only me who couldn't control him.

"I made supper—hope that's okay," Adelaide was saying from the oven as I entered the kitchen. "Just an enchilada casserole. I hope you like Tex-Mex?"

"Love it. I eat anything. Literally."

Pulling out a casserole dish, she hobbled toward me to set it on a hot pad on the counter. Cheese bubbled on top of something that smelled spicy and delicious. "Isn't that refreshing! I love food. I can't fathom all these young girls starving themselves."

I thought of Sasha, who was as gorgeous a hardbody as I'd ever seen, but lived on sprouts and tofu. I shuddered. "Me either. Pass the cupcakes."

Adelaide laughed. "I knew you'd be funny from your columns. I just love them. Wish you'd been around in my dating days."

These could be her dating days, I wanted to say. But Ben had told me his mom had no interest in dating.

It was too bad—in her mid-sixties, she still seemed young, in both appearance and attitude. If she wanted to get back out there, Adelaide would be a catch—especially in Florida, where she was a hot little spring chicken in the snowbird demographic.

"What can I do?" I asked, standing uselessly at the edge of the kitchen.

"It's all done. I'm sitting around enough with this knee that I'm actually glad to be up and around. You can have a seat there at the breakfast bar and keep me company. Any chance you also enjoy an occasional cocktail?"

A grin spread across my face. "One might say so, yes."

"Fabulous! I made margaritas. Jim and I lived in Texas for a bit and got spoiled for them made from scratch, with lime juice—now that's the only way I can drink them." She pulled a glass pitcher from the fridge and poured into two martini glasses on the counter. "Oh—hope they're okay straight up? Another Texas carryover."

"Sounds great. So Ben grew up in Texas?" It was funny that I didn't know that.

"Not that he'd remember. We moved all over. Jim and I liked to see other places, and we'd always get a seven-year itch—with where we were living, not each other," she said. She raised her glass to me. I tinked the edge with mine and we sipped.

"Wow!" I said. "That's the best margarita I've ever had."

Adelaide nodded. "Once you've had them from scratch, you can never drink sweet-and-sour again. I'm sorry—I've ruined them for you now."

"That's quite all right. I'd love the recipe."

"Done. Now I *will* trouble you to carry the enchiladas into the dining room, if you would, and we can eat and then I'll visit with Jake so you're not stuck here all night long. I know you didn't come here to chat with your boyfriend's mother."

I wanted to protest that I was happy to be here, that she was good company, but I was so tripped up on *boyfriend* that I was tongue-tied.

Ben and I hadn't used the word yet. We hadn't defined what we were at all—which I liked. But had he told his mom we were something more?

And if he had...did I mind?

"How are you doing with our Great White Terror?" Adelaide interrupted my thoughts as I stepped over the dog and put the dish on the trivet between the two place settings.

"Oh, he's a good dog. We're doing fine." I scooted Jake out of the doorway with a foot so he wouldn't trip Adelaide. She followed me into the dining area with our drinks and we sat.

"Brook, I'm a pretty straightforward person, so you don't have to sugarcoat things for me." Adelaide extended a hand for my plate and I passed it over. "I love Jake dearly, but he's a Pyrenees."

My brows furrowed as I watched her cut and serve me a square of the casserole. "What?"

She looked up. "You don't know?"

"No, I know he's a Pyrenees, but...what does that mean?"

"Oh, my." A rueful smile curved her lips as she cut a piece of the casserole for herself. "They're willful. Stubborn. Independent-minded to the point that obedience is an uphill battle—they're bred to think for themselves, as herd dogs. Oh, and that also means they'll herd you—by leaning, pushing, pawing, and generally having no regard for your personal space. And they're bred to guard, so they have extraordinary hearing and they bark to alert—at everything, and fairly nonstop."

I gaped at her. "You just described Jake exactly. You mean they're *all* like that?"

"Pretty much. We had one when Ben was little, and he adored her—and vice versa. Pyrs are wonderful with children, and she was big enough to stand up to an energetic little boy. I'm sure Alexandra was why he got Jake."

I grinned. "Alexandra? That's a lot of name for a doggie. Did Ben name her?"

"Yes. Alexandra the Great...Pyrenees."

I laughed. "Clever little boy."

"He was that," she said with a fond smile. "And still is. I've been very lucky to have Ben."

So am I, I almost said, but didn't.

As we ate she asked me about my Breakup Doctor practice, and how I'd gotten into it. She listened attentively, laughing in all the right places as I related how my old practice got demolished and told her about my initial efforts. The evening felt easy and fun—as if I were with a friend, rather than someone's mom. It was certainly more comfortable than it would have been with my own mother, when I'd have been on the defensive all night against whatever advice she wanted to hammer at me, and mentally editing my every word to avoid saying something that would yield her pointing out whatever I could and should be doing better.

The thought gave me a pang of guilt. I loved my mom, and I was trying to work on a relationship with her. It was just so hard when we'd spent a lifetime picking at the same scabs.

After dinner Adelaide reluctantly acquiesced when I insisted she let me do the dishes, but she perched on a stool at the breakfast bar and we continued chatting as she iced her knee. Afterward we sat side by side on her sofa while Adelaide pulled up articles on Pyrenees on her iPad to show me what she'd told me before—that most of Jake's crazy behaviors I'd come to her to learn how to control were actually bred into him for hundreds of years.

"But he never seems to do any of that with you," I said as I scrolled through one of the articles. "Ben says you're a dog savant."

She waved off the compliment. "Oh, anyone can learn how to handle a dog properly—you just have to know how they think. They want structure and leadership, and a good dog owner—or temporary one," she added with a nod at me, "makes sure to provide it."

That was exactly what Sasha had said.

"But if these behaviors are innate, that's just who Jake is, right?" I asked. "Trust me, I'd love to get a full night's sleep, but how can I change what's bred into him?"

"You don't. You can't change a creature's nature. You just have to let them be who they are, and figure out how to find a way you can both live with it. And not everyone can—there are plenty of people who don't like a Pyrenees."

I looked down to where Jake had his head resting in my lap, looking up at me with adoring brown eyes as I stroked his giant head. "How can anyone not like them? Look at him—he's so affectionate and loyal and protective."

Adelaide smiled. "That's true to the breed too. But they're not for everyone."

"He can be a pain," I admitted with a laugh, and then heard what I'd said. "I mean, he's great, and no trouble—" I added quickly.

Adelaide interrupted. "It's okay, Brook. It's still nice of you watch him for Ben."

"No, really—he's sweet and I do like him. I'm happy to have him. I just..." I caught her eye. "He's been a little hard for me to control, but I didn't want to worry Ben. I saw how good you are with Jake; I thought you might be able to give me some tips."

"Well, that I can do." She pushed herself to her feet. I reached out a hand to steady her, but she caught her balance on the arm and I dropped my arm before she saw, instead holding Jake back from surging toward her.

"Jake, come."

He scooted instantly to her and planted his butt.

"Lie down."

He gazed at her, his tongue lolling in a happy grin, and pawed at her with one long limb.

Adelaide looked over at me. "Now we're in a battle of wills," she said. "Exactly where you don't want to be with a dog—especially a Pyrenees. They will outstubborn you every time." She sidestepped his paw and moved two steps away, not looking at him, and he hastened over to sit in front of her again, pawing her leg. "You have to give him something he wants more than he wants to follow his own mind. And Jake—bless his sweet heart—wants my attention. But he has to earn it."

Still ignoring him, she moved back to her original position and Jake followed. This time he sat still, not touching her, and after a moment Adelaide met his eye and stroked his head. "Good," she said calmly. "Now lie down, Jake."

He threw himself to the floor, and I laughed at his fervor.

Adelaide winked at me, but again said only, "Good," in a light, approving tone, and bent to rub his ears for a moment. "Stay." She straightened and looked at me as Jake remained planted to the floor as if glued there. "It won't always work with a Pyr, but remember that consistency is the most important thing. And don't overpraise him— he's not curing cancer; he's just obeying a command. If a dog gets too much attention for doing things that— Ahhhh!"

Jake had shot to a sitting position and pawed at her leg again before either of us could react—this time directly on her bad knee. Adelaide's yelp was followed by her crumpling to the floor, and Jake surged over her, delighted.

"Jake!" I cried, already on my feet and lunging for him. I grabbed his collar and tugged him off her, then sank down beside her.

"Adelaide! Are you okay?"

A groan seeped past tight lips, but Adelaide was already pushing herself up to sit. "Just a moment." She was holding her knee gingerly, her face pale and her eyes shut.

After a few moments she opened her eyes, reaching with a hand for my arm and squeezing. "That felt fairly awful. Help me up, would you, Brook?" Gingerly I did, and walked her carefully to lie on the sofa, Adelaide putting as little weight on the leg as she could manage by leaning on me. I ran to the kitchen for ice, and when I came back she was reclined against one arm with her leg propped on the couch, Jake face-first in her armpit.

"Jake! Stop that!" I barked, but Adelaide only patted his back.

"It's okay. He didn't know he'd hurt me."

I held the ice pack to her over Jake's long body, and Adelaide laid it over her swollen knee, letting out a held breath. "That's a help. Thank you, honey."

She didn't seem to realize the endearment had slipped out, but it spread over me like warm syrup. Perching on the club chair cattycorner to her, I leaned forward. "Jake was the reason you fell last weekend, wasn't he?" I said quietly.

Adelaide lowered her eyes to the dog with a soft smile, stroking his fur. "You didn't tell Ben you were having trouble with Jake because you didn't want to worry him or make him feel bad when there was nothing he could do about it," she said. Her gaze shot abruptly to mine and she held it. "It's very lovely that you were able to take care of his dog so he could give his full focus to this project that's so important to him."

She spoke slowly and carefully, and I heard what she was really saying.

"I won't tell him," I promised.

Chapter Fifteen

Another middle-of-the-night klaxon call tore through my consciousness and plucked me out of a sound sleep.

"Gooboy. Thas gooboy, Jakie," I mumbled reflexively. "Go sleep now."

Closing my eyes, I was just drifting back off when another growling bark yanked me awake again. "Okay, Jake," I muttered, trying to sound authoritative while half-conscious. "I'm safe. That's enough."

I rolled over and squeezed my eyes shut, but I knew it was no use now—I was fully alert. Dammit. I sighed and twisted onto my back, dropping a hand to pat Jake, hoping it would keep him quiet and soothe us both to sleep.

When the next bark came, though, I realized it had followed another sound—the bleep of my phone.

My heart gave a thud. Middle-of-the-night calls never meant anything good. I pushed myself up and leaned over to the nightstand, grabbing it off the charger. Three texts.

Hey, Doc.

Doc, you awake?

Brook?

What the hell was Chip Santana doing texting me at—I peered at the time stamp on the last message—three fifty in the morning? Way out of bounds. I let the phone drop to the nightstand and flopped back onto the bed. Sleep was off the table for a while, but I pressed my eyes closed anyway, hoping it might sneak up on me.

My phone beeped again. Jake let out another bark.

Annoyed, I sat up and grabbed for the phone.

Really need to talk, the message read.

Chip, it's 4 in the morning. We can talk tomorrow. I hit send.

I sat there in the darkness holding the phone for a few moments, but it stayed blank, and after a moment I set it back down and lay back against the pillows.

Beep.

"Rrrruuuffff!"

Was he kidding? I shot up, yanking the phone to me to tell him this was inappropriate and unacceptable.

Sorry. I know its late. Just really in bad shape and u always help. Talk 2mrw. Night, Doc.

I held the phone in my hand, staring at the lit screen.

No. This was a bad precedent to set. Whatever was troubling Chip would wait till morning. And he needed to learn to self-soothe. I set it down and lay back, willing myself to go to sleep, but monkey mind took over.

U always help.

Up until recently I would have said Chip Santana would never have admitted he needed help, let alone asked for it. This was another milestone in the journey he was working so hard to make.

I sat up yet again. I'd just make sure he knew this couldn't become a habit, I decided as I reached for the phone.

What's the matter?

His reply came back almost immediately: *Talked to Katie.*

Oh, boy. *Are you okay?* I texted. Although considering their history, "Is *she* okay?" might have been the better question.

The phone stayed silent in my hand for so long I wondered if my text had gone through. Just as I was about to resend, his reply came.

Shattered.

I frowned. *What happened?*

She called & agreed to talk. Met here—work. Got ugly.

She came to your dad's dealership? Why would she agree to meet Chip in such an isolated place after all that had happened between them?

There was another long pause, and then: *Wanted to talk face2face.*

So the two of them met in the all-but-deserted car dealership after hours to talk about...what? And what did he mean by "Got ugly?" And where was Katie now? There was a stubbornly paranoid part of me that kept reverting to fear for her safety. If Chip's anger had gotten the better of him and he got violent, would he tell me?

It was ludicrous to try to have this conversation via text, and my instinct was just to dial his number. But that felt like another boundary I didn't want to cross—middle-of-the-night texts were bad enough without adding middle-of-the-night consultations. And I guessed there was a reason Chip hadn't called in the first place. It might be easier for him to talk about what had happened in the more impersonal milieu of texting.

So what happened? I prompted when no elaboration seemed forthcoming.

After a lengthy pause I got three texts in a row: *She spent an hour telling me all the ways I was a bad byfrnd. Knew all that. Said I wanted to make it right. She said no way. Tried to say sorry and she said she wldnt accept it. We argued a lot. Ill nvr be able to make this right. She hit me—just whaled on me.*

Did you hit her back? I texted quickly, my heart pounding.

No answer.

Chip—did you hit her back?!

No, Doc, come on! I wldnt do that. Pls believe me.

Guilt pricked at me, but not too long ago that question wouldn't have been so out-of-the-box with Chip. A certain shooting/strangling incident came to mind.

And then I remembered how that incident had ended.

Did you have sex? I texted.

A few seconds ticked by. *Would you be mad if I said yes?*

My lungs deflated. What was the point of working so hard—with Chip, with anyone—if people just engaged in the same behaviors over and over, and then kept coming to me wondering why their life didn't look the way they wanted it to? What good did it do to push myself so hard if I wasn't really helping anyone?

These are your decisions, I texted wearily. *It's not up to me to be mad.*

His answer came quickly. *I was just joking, Doc. Bad taste again. Sorry. No, didnt sleep with her. Promise.*

*Chip...*My fingers hovered over the keypad. What? Was I going to go into his inappropriate sense of humor now, at—I glanced at the phone—four fifteen in the morning? Why bother? If I just ended this pointless communication and tried again for sleep, maybe I could get a couple more hours and at least salvage something of this night.

Another text came in as I sat there, undecided.

U make me nrvs, Doc, and I say stupid things. Pls 4give me.

I sighed, rereading his message several times.

It's ok, I finally wrote. *You don't have to be nervous with me, Chip. I'm on your side, and I won't judge you.*

I waited a few moments, but when no reply came I finally put the phone back on the charger and flopped exhaustedly onto my back. Chip and I had arranged to meet again on Monday, four days from now—well, three, since it was technically already Friday. We could finish discussing this then.

It took a long time, but finally my mind quieted in the silence and I felt the edges of consciousness begin to blur.

My phone beeped again—I'd forgotten to silence it. Jake barked. Sighing, I groped for the phone and brought it to my face.

U r everything I wish I deserved.

...

I had a hard time concentrating with my clients the next day, and had to work to stay focused in my radio appearance on the Kelly Garrett show that afternoon.

Chip's last text had thrown me. What did he mean by it? Was he just feeling bad about himself? Did he mean he didn't think he was up for working together to make amends to his exes after all?

Was it some kind of declaration?

I was still parsing out the single sentence by the time Ben swung by on his way into town that night to pick up Jake—I actually felt a little sad to see the dog go, though I'd get him right back Sunday. We had a date scheduled for tomorrow—Friday he planned to spend with his mom, running her around to take care of errands she couldn't handle on her own, and then taking her out to dinner.

After he left I called Sasha.

"Hey," I said without preamble. "What are you doing tonight?"

"Dinner, movie, then a ton of sex. You want to join us? Not for the sex part."

"Ugh—Sash, please!"

Part of me did want to join them. But what I really wanted was an evening with my best friend—to talk about Ben and figure out together our relationship. About Jakie, and my efforts to yield some kind of obedience from the willful dog. About Adelaide, and my guilt because I'd spent the kind of evening with Ben's mom that I'd never had with my own.

About Chip, and what the hell his cryptic last text message meant.

We couldn't do any of that in front of Stu. I loved my brother, and we were closer than a lot of siblings. But he was still a man, still my brother—still Stu, for that matter, with whom trying to discuss emotional nuances was like describing a rainbow to a meatball.

"I'll catch up with you guys on Sunday at my parents'," I said. "Go have couple time."

She made an attempt to change my mind, but it didn't take much to convince her I'd be better off staying home and getting some much-needed respite from my overfull schedule.

I loved that she craved solo time with Stu, but sometimes, like tonight, I couldn't help a twinge of jealousy.

...

Antonio Moretti was full of remorse.

"It was a total accident, you guys. I swear," he said as soon as the session started that Saturday morning, practically lunging for the claw.

I barely held in an exasperated sigh as I saw a few of the women roll their eyes. We were seeing a familiar pattern in his sharing, but Antonio never seemed to be progressing—just repeatedly *trans*gressing. "What happened?" I asked reluctantly.

He regaled us with the story of his latest conquest: While he was taking Mary Lynn's car for an oil change, the woman in the waiting area next to him started chatting.

"I tried to ignore her. I had a magazine and I just buried my face in it—figured she'd get the message, right?"

"And did she?" I said automatically, already knowing the answer.

"Nah, she starts in on her divorce, and how it was just finalized, and her husband used to take her car in for her too, like I was doing for my wife—what a good husband I was. And then she started to cry, you guys, and tell me how lonely she was, and...I swear to God, I didn't mean to do it." He shrugged and put the claw back in the center of the circle, then sat again.

"But you did do it." My tone was flat.

"Well, yeah, of course. But it wasn't my fault—I really tried not to."

"Oh, for god's sake, Antonio, if your dick came out of your pants who else's fault is it?"

In the silence that greeted my outburst, Antonio and everyone else in the group stared at me with a shocked expression I was pretty sure mirrored my own. That was not how I talked to clients. Ever.

I shot to my feet, hands clenched at my sides. Muttering, "Excuse me for a moment, please," I beelined out of the room, hearing a buzz of curious chatter fire up among the group as I stalked down the hall of the yacht club and into the ladies' room. I slammed the door shut behind me and locked it from the inside, then leaned back against it. My hands shook.

Where had that come from? Yes, I was frustrated with Antonio. I thought we'd been making some good progress last week when he'd finally realized how much his behavior hurt Mary Lynn, no matter how he tried to justify it. No wonder I was irritated with him—here he was again, abnegating responsibility for controlling his impulses, as if we'd never even had that session.

And here *I* was, I realized, abnegating responsibility for not controlling my own.

Classic: The therapist mirroring the patient's behavior.

I don't think I'm better than any of you, I'd told the group at our first session. But that was a lie, wasn't it? I'd been sitting in judgment of Antonio for doing the exact same thing I'd just done—letting my base impulses take over my better judgment.

I rubbed my eyes, scratchy with lack of sleep. I'd thought last night I'd sleep like the dead with a respite from Jake, but I'd found I missed his breathing, the sound of him moving around beside me.

That and I'd lain awake gnawing on Chip's message again like Jake gnawed on my textiles.

I was tired, I realized—exhausted. Too much work and not enough sleep was lowering my usual resistance to the knee-jerk responses a good therapist learned to control. It was normal to feel the things I was feeling lately with my patients—annoyance, frustration, futility, anger. But it was not okay to express them—not if I considered myself a good therapist. And whatever else I doubted myself on—and there was plenty—that was the one thing I knew for sure.

Okay. I took a deep breath, and then another. I just needed to relax, accept what I felt instead of denying it, and then let it go. I told my patients that all the time.

And sleep. God, I needed to get some sleep. Once I caught up, everything would be fine, and I wouldn't be so tired all the time that my normal filters vanished.

Taking one more breath, I let it out slowly, counting to ten, and then unlocked the door and twisted the knob.

Antonio was up when I came back in, pacing the room. The rest of the group was still in their seats, but they talked among themselves in little subsets—Carolyn and Betty; Sherman, Rebecca, and Elisa. Dina sat slumped down in the chair, arms crossed, looking bored, and Sheila was in her usual position: huddled over her own lap, staring at the floor, her hair curtaining her face.

As soon as they saw me all conversation stopped and Antonio froze in his tracks. Eight pairs of eyes fixed on me, staring in silence.

"I apologize for my comment, Antonio," I said levelly. "I apologize to all of you. That was out of line."

His arms hung by his sides like dead pythons, his shoulders hunched and eyebrows drawn, but he made no reply.

I pushed on determinedly. "If I've made you feel you're no longer comfortable with the group, or"—I swallowed hard—"with me as a therapist, I can offer some refer—"

"Are you dumping me?" he asked, his tone sharp.

"What?"

"Are you dropping me from the group? Because I banged that girl?"

"Antonio..." I came fully into the room, headed to my chair, but he put himself directly in my path. I stopped in front of him. "No, I'm not dropping you. I'm...I wanted to give you the chance to take some time to regroup and decide whether I'm the right therapist for you, in light of my inappropriate reaction to your confession."

From the corner of my eye I saw Dina watching us with a rapacious expression.

"Inappropriate reaction to...Can we just talk normal again? You're pissed at me, right? Because of that girl? No, no, no—wait—I know. Not because I banged her. You're mad because I said it wasn't my fault, right? I'm right, aren't I?" His expression was pregnant with all the expectant pride of a remedial student who's finally sure he has the right answer.

"Yes," I admitted. "That was what made me angry. But it's not my place to judge you or to react that way, and I'm sorry. That's not good therapy. That's why I thought you might prefer to—"

"Fuck good therapy, Brook." A few people stirred behind him at his outburst. "You called me on my bullshit."

I shook my head. "That's not really how the therapeutic relationship—"

"You're right—it was my fault. I'm the one that banged that girl. I wanted to bang her—she was hot, and she was practically begging for it. I always want to bang these women. I want to bang you right now."

I took a step backward.

Antonio held up a hand. "Just making a point. I like banging." He turned and stepped beside me, so that we were both facing everyone else, and addressed the group. "That's on me. I gotta know that, right? I gotta cop to that or else I'm not going to be able to figure out how to stop. Right?" He turned toward me again. "Isn't that what you've been trying to get at all this time?"

I opened my mouth, but no proper therapeutic platitude came out of it.

Antonio filled the gap. "But I love Mary Lynn. Honest to god, I do. And my kids. God, my kids..." Tears filled his eyes. "So I gotta accept that I love sex—with a lot of women—but that doesn't fit with keeping my family together. So I have to choose, right? I mean, really, that's what it comes down to—I gotta decide which one I want more?"

He was staring at me with a nakedly pleading expression, and I felt the tension in my face soften. "Well...yes, Antonio. I guess that's pretty much what it comes down to." I wanted to say more—felt I should. Antonio was at a really powerful transition point, and my job was to help ease him over it. But I could no more ask him some clinical question about how he felt about that than I could take off my clothes and lie down to let him "bang" me. So we just stood there for a long time, face-to-face, looking at each other as though we were alone in the room.

"So what do you want to do now, Antonio?" I asked gently.

"Do you think I'm a sex addict?" He directed the question to the group, and suddenly sixteen eyes looked anywhere but at him. Antonio turned back to me. "Do *you*?" he asked me point-blank.

I knew the "proper" answer: *Do* you *think so?* But that wasn't the one I gave.

"Yes. I do," I said quietly.

"*Shit.*" He looked away, toward the floor, then after a few moments met my eyes again. "Will you help me?" He looked around the room. "Alla you guys? Will you help me figure out what to do with that?"

Faces softened, heads nodded, and I heard a few soft "yeses" and "yeahs."

Antonio looked at me. "Brook? You too? You'll help me?"

I reached out and laid a hand on his shoulder—under the circumstances I thought a hug might send the wrong message—and squeezed. "Yes, Antonio. I will."

...

As I threw my bag into my car and climbed in, I thought about the session.

I'd been a good student in school—I made the honor roll every semester, worked hard in my classes, built relationships with my professors to make sure I was doing everything exactly right. When I began practice I carried that philosophy in with me—I'd help my patients by being the perfect therapist, doing everything by the book.

Despite my mom's view that I'd chosen the second-tier road to becoming a therapist, I'd decided deliberately to pursue an LMHT license. It allowed me to start working with patients sooner than slogging through a PhD, and I had no interest in treating people with pharmaceuticals. I wanted to help them talk through their troubles, to get into the trenches with them, let them feel there was someone on their side, and use the tried-and-true techniques to help them.

But being the Breakup Doctor didn't seem to lend itself to standard clinical practices. Every broken heart was different, and every person needed something unique to figure out how to heal it.

Although...it was the same with any other psychological issues, wasn't it? Maybe it wasn't that my patients and my practice had changed. Maybe I had.

My outburst with Antonio had thrown me. Yes, I'd realized a long time ago—with Lisa Albrecht, my editor at the paper and my first client—that sometimes it was more effective to be direct with my clients, to call them on behaviors that in my old practice I'd have spent weeks or months slowly getting them to see for themselves.

But I'd never flat-out yelled at a client before. I'd never attacked his behavior so directly.

Half of me was waiting for the avalanche to drop: the recrimination, guilt, self-doubt that had been my loyal companions for so long.

But I felt...good. There was no denying that Antonio had had a breakthrough today—a meaningful one. Was it less powerful because he got pushed there, instead of gently shepherded along to the finish line?

And the way everyone else had jumped in to help him be honest with himself, to support him...

When Sasha and I had ever had our hearts broken—or even just our egos bruised—we'd always taken solace in each other. We were a community of two, creating an environment where we could talk it out—often ad nauseam—where we could work through what had happened for as long as it took, cheering each other on the whole way. So often the worst part of a breakup was the feeling of being alone in your emotional pain—Sasha and I had never had to do that.

By the time everyone in the group started to weigh in with Antonio, to offer encouragement and support, it felt just like that to me.

I hadn't known exactly what the Breakup Doctor support groups would entail, what they would look like. When we first started them I wasn't even sure they were a good idea—heartbreak was so personal.

But it was also universal. And being able to share your deepest wounds with people you trusted, who understood your pain because they were feeling something similar—that was the key to getting past it.

I wasn't a good Breakup Doctor because of years of study, or my insight into psychological practices and my expert application of the theories in the field. It was simply because I'd had my heart broken—stomped on—and I knew what it felt like.

Just like everyone else in that room.

The thought should have made me feel inadequate.

But instead, I drove down McGregor with a nonstop grin on my face.

...

Ben came over at six to pick me up for our date, Jake bursting through the door ahead of him to greet me with his big goofy grin and a paw to my groin.

I sidestepped. "Ah-ah, boy. Sit."

Jake whined, wagging his tail, but I didn't look at him, meeting Ben's eyes with a wink. When Jake still didn't calm down, I let myself greet Ben instead with a hug and a kiss, which sent Jake into a fresh frenzy of left-outness, thrusting his nose between our bodies and then pulling back to bark at us.

Finally I turned back to the dog. "If you want some love, then sit."

Down went his butt.

"Jakie!" I exclaimed in shock. What the hell—it actually *worked.* I leaned over and started agitating his floppy ears, Jake groaning in pleasure. "Good boy! Good boy, you smart, smart dog!" I gushed.

At my excited tone Jake got charged up again, doing the bunny hop around me and Ben and giving out gleeful little yips.

Oops. Adelaide said not to overpraise him, I remembered too late.

I was too happy to see them both, though, and too thrilled to see any kind of progress with Jake's obedience.

"Okay, crazy, torque it back," Ben said, laughing at the dog's antics. He looked back at me with the smile still on his face. "Well, you seem to be handling him awfully well."

I shrugged. "No big deal."

"Pretty impressive, actually. I know Jake."

A sheepish grin crept over my lips. "I have to confess I got a coaching session from your mom."

"You did? She didn't say."

I'd promised not to reveal Jake's knocking her down. "Because I asked her not to tell you how grossly incompetent I was with him at first. But you're right—she's a dog genius. How is she?"

"She's in pretty good spirits, actually, just a little stir-crazy."

An impulse struck me, and I grabbed it: "Let's go get her."

He shot a quizzical look at me. "For date night?"

"Well, we don't have to. It just must be hard for her to be cooped up. She seemed like a pretty active woman."

"She usually is," he admitted.

"Hang on." I darted into the den, Jake right behind me, then grabbed yesterday's newspaper and brought it back to Ben in the living room, Jake still bounding happily after me as if we were in the world's best game of chase. Next to my most recent column—"Letting Go of the Grenade," about getting out of a volatile relationship before you got badly hurt—was an ad for the summer movie series downtown in Centennial Park.

"Look—I saw this this afternoon. We can even take Jake."

Which was how we found ourselves sitting on the grassy banks of the Caloosahatchee River with several hundred other Fort Myers residents at sunset—well after eight o'clock in summertime—Adelaide, Ben, and me on blankets, Jake pinballing between us, too excited to sit, bags of sandwiches and a bottle of wine in a cooler, waiting for the outdoor movie to start.

I unpacked the sandwiches on the blanket we'd brought, while Ben got his mom settled in a chair we'd carried out and tried to contain Jake, who was greatly overstimulated to be out with all of us: surrounded by other people, a plethora of kids charging around the grass between the many blankets and chairs spread out on the lawn. The family next to us was enchanted with the dog, and Jake agreeably sprawled himself across their blanket as their three kids—ranging from age seven down to around three—climbed all over him like baby goats.

We ate as the sun began to sink into the river, conversation relaxed and easy. I'd forgotten matches for the candle Ben had tossed in with our things, and the couple on the other side of us offered a lighter. We shared our napkins with them when the woman accidentally put her leg into a deviled egg, laughing with her as she wiped the yolk from her calf. When the movie started—*The Princess Bride*—the kids settled down and Jake stretched out on his back between our blanket and theirs, staring up at the sky with a look of sleepy contentment on his face as the oldest girl absently stroked his belly.

Adelaide leaned back in her chair with her leg propped on the cooler, the ice pack Ben had remembered to bring her resting on her bad knee. We sat beside her in stadium chairs, and as Princess Buttercup began her grand adventure, I leaned into Ben's side and relaxed into his solid hold.

Chapter Sixteen

Chip was waiting in a corner sitting area when I walked into the Hot Pot Monday afternoon; now that Jake was at least somewhat settled at my house, I'd decided it was best to keep an extra layer of distance between me and Chip. Especially after his disturbing message Friday night. An array of pastries and a still-steaming cup of coffee waited for me on the low wooden cocktail table between two orange sofas, and a broad smile stretched Chip's face as though our texts had never happened.

"I couldn't remember how you take your coffee, so I brought over all the sugars and creamers and stuff, and I didn't know what you liked here, so I got one of everything," he announced as I sat on the love seat facing his.

We needed to talk about his inappropriate comment and the texting in general before we discussed anything else. "Chip—" I began.

"So now that Katie's done," he cut in, "I spent all weekend working on my next amends I have to make. I really need your help for this, Doc. I already started the letter." He leaned forward to pull his phone from his pocket.

"Chip, before we do that—"

"Hang on, Doc—I don't want to lose my train of thought. 'Dear Amanda—I know you think I hate you after the things I called you the day we broke up—'"

"Chip, we need to talk about the other night."

"'But I don't hate you. You probably hate me. I don't really think those things about you—but I stand behind what I said about your mom, LOL—'" He looked up, those oceanic eyes sparkling with amusement, as if waiting for me to laugh with him.

"Chip, please stop avoiding this." I kept my voice quiet but firm.

Lowering the phone, he let out a sigh and scrubbed a hand down his face, smoothing his goatee. "I was really hoping we could just ignore it and it would go away," he said finally, setting the phone beside him.

A half smile leaked across my lips. "Not really how therapy works. That's kind of the opposite of therapy, actually."

"Are you going to fire me?" he asked, and his nervous-little-boy expression made me want to erase the furrows from his face.

Shaking my head, I said, "This isn't a formal course of therapy, Chip. And that's not my intention." Over the weekend I'd considered ending whatever this unusual association we were attempting was, but I knew Chip responded to guidance and structure, firm boundaries. I just needed to reestablish them. "But there can't be any more late-night texting."

"Yeah, I know. I was just in a bad way and—"

My palm came up to stop him. "Regardless of the situation, there are...limits in our relationship."

"What if it wasn't so late? Can I text then?"

"We talk *here*. I want to help you, Chip—I'm very much on your side. But I can't allow one person special privileges, or I have to offer them to all my clients. And you can see that that would be overwhelming."

One of those slanted brows lifted, along with a corner of his mouth, and he leaned forward. "I didn't think I was a client, Doc. I thought we were more than that."

I pushed as far back as the small sofa would allow, then wished I hadn't given in to the urge to retreat. "That's the kind of thing I'm talking about, Chip. This is inappropriate behavior. You're...you're *flirting*." Heat speared into my face as the accusation fell out, and I dropped my gaze to my hands clutched on the sofa cushion.

"Well, it took you long enough to notice."

My eyes shot back to Chip. The smile on his face had softened, and he wore that disarmingly sincere expression I'd begun seeing more and more often.

And for once I was rendered speechless. What was I supposed to say to that? Patients got crushes on their therapists—it was called transference. But I'd never had one just baldly state it before.

Silence dropped like a sandbag and lingered for long, uncomfortable moments. I was still staring at him, and I shook myself back into focus. "That's...that's not allowed," I said foolishly.

All amusement had vanished from his expression. "I can't help it, Brook."

"That's not true!" My outburst startled us both. I cleared my throat. "That's not true, Chip. That's what we're trying to get at—that you do have control of your actions, if not always your feelings. We all do." The familiar, therapeutic language soothed me.

Chip stood up and came over to sit on the other end of my love seat, and my heart thunked against my ribs as I scooted back toward the arm behind me. What was happening? How had I lost control of this meeting to the point that I couldn't even—

"Look, Doc—Brook," Chip said quietly, "can we drop the BS for a sec? Just person to person, I like you. I'd like to see more of you. What's wrong with that?"

He sounded so reasonable, his blue-green eyes steady on mine, one hand lifted toward me, palm up. This was the side of Chip that always gave me so much hope that there was a gentler man inside him, trapped under all his barbed edges.

I pressed cold fingers to my cheeks, trying to cool them. "That's...Of course it's nice to hear, but it's...it's unethical. Inappropriate."

"You keep using that word. I do not think it means what you think it means." Chip quoted the line in Inigo Montoya's accent with a wink and a return of his crooked grin, and the reminder of my evening with Ben and his mom sent a surge of guilt through me. He must have seen my reaction, because he leaned away slightly, giving me space, and sobered. "It's just...I feel like maybe there was a reason you didn't want to take me back on as a client this time, Brook," he went on. His sandpaper voice was a low rasp that seemed to hypnotize me, holding me frozen as I stared at him. "Maybe you knew that there was something more here—something I think we both felt that night on the beach—and part of you knew you wanted to keep this out of the professional realm?"

At the memory of us twined together on the sand that night several months ago, my face flamed further. "Chip, I...I don't know what..." I couldn't find words to respond to him. His arguments made sense. There *was* something between us that night—and long before. And he wasn't my client anymore— it was true: I was the one who'd made sure of that. Was he right? Did part of me see this coming all along, and want to leave that possibility open?

"But...but what about your exes...making amends...?" I managed finally.

His lips curved up in a smile I could only call *tender*. "This was always about you, Brook," he said gently. "How have you not known that?"

I reared up to sit straight and squared off with him, indignation a welcome replacement for the uncertainty I was swimming in. "Wait a minute, you mean you...This whole thing about making amends was just some kind of...of *ploy*?"

"What? No, of course not!" He let out a great sigh, close enough for me to feel his breath wash over my face, smell the cigarettes and cinnamon that I had come to associate with Chip. He lifted his hands suddenly, and I flinched before I realized he was raising them to his shaved head. He scraped them along it with a rasping sound, as if he were trying to scrub his brain clean.

"This isn't coming out the way I...Look, Doc—Brook. Here's the thing. You make me want to be a better man. For *you*."

Something twanged powerfully in my chest. "Don't, Chip. Please don't," I murmured. "This can't go anywhere—you have to know that." My voice was wobbly and uncertain, but I knew the words were harsh.

He looked plaintive. "Why not? I don't understand. You know me, Brook—you have to know how rarely I feel this way about anyone."

A wild laugh yipped out of me before I could hold it back. Another inappropriate reaction, but at this point, what did it matter? "Let's not overstate things. We've been working on your making amends to what is apparently a long list of people you've felt this way about."

"It's different." He was adamant, but not aggressive. "That's just dating. This is deeper than that. You get me like no one else has. You make me...I don't know...calmer. Better. You make it easy to be better."

"That's my job. It's very common for patients to confuse that feeling with the feeling of—"

"No—don't do that. Don't hide behind all that psycho mumbo jumbo. See? I get you too. I know that you use all this therapy stuff to keep your own feelings under wraps."

He wasn't wrong—I did pull the logical concepts of psychology over me like a force field when I felt myself drowning in emotions I was afraid to feel. It was actually a big part of the reason I *had* gotten in Chip's truck that night—I'd spent so long pushing everything back behind that shield, it was ready to blow past it when I ran into Chip on one of the lowest points of my breakup with Kendall.

"And I know that you feel something for me too," he pressed, as if sensing my vacillation. "I knew it all the way back when we first worked together."

That was a little close to home. I'd been feeling—and fighting—an attraction to him from almost the first time he came to me at my old practice. I couldn't explain it then and I still couldn't—he was everything I knew was a bad bet, relationship-wise, even if he hadn't been a patient. There was something primal and chemical and basic to the way I was drawn to him—if I hadn't believed in the power of pheromones before, I'd have had to after I met Chip. My body went haywire every time he'd stepped into my old office.

"Doc, there's something here," Chip went on in the face of my confused silence. "I'm not saying we're soul mates or something. Just that it's obvious we have a connection—there's something about us that just works with each other. I didn't expect it any more than you did. But it happened, and I think it's worth exploring."

He sounded so reasonable, so persuasive.

There was a time when I wouldn't have even allowed for the possibility of dating someone like Chip. When my every rational impulse told me one thing while my basic instincts were screaming the exact opposite, it never made sense to overrule my head and follow my...well, whatever always responded so strongly to him.

But things had changed since we knew each other before. *He* had changed—this new Chip was gentler, more genuine. Someone who made me laugh, and who was clearly working to become the person he wanted to be. But more important, *I* had changed. I didn't operate exclusively from my left brain anymore; more and more lately my emotional right-brain side was weighing in—and I was letting it.

Maybe this persistent pull between us was a symptom of that. Maybe, now that I was dropping my rigid shield of rationality, I was more willing to open myself up, to be less predictable, less controlled. Less careful.

"Are you two looking for a little more?"

The voice startled me out of the rabbit warren of thoughts I'd been lost in, and I looked up to see a woman in a white shirt and green apron holding a carafe of coffee in one hand, a pitcher of iced tea in the other.

I hadn't touched my coffee, so there was certainly no need for a refill. Chip nodded at the barista and touched her wrist as she poured more tea into his glass. "Would you mind bringing my friend a fresh cup?" he asked softly. "I think hers has gotten cold."

"Sure thing. Right back." She leaned over to take my cup, flashing an uncertain smile to the wide-eyed mute woman I'd become.

It was such a thoughtful gesture...almost sweet the way he'd called me his friend. Could we be that? Friends?

Or, as the barista had unintentionally said, were we looking for a little more?

I used to always know the right answer in any situation—or thought I did. The maddening downside of the awakening emotions I was discovering was that I couldn't always sort through the chaos jumbling inside me.

Chip wasn't rushing me, wasn't pushing. He sat back with one arm draped behind the love seat, his left leg triangled over his right, giving me space. By the time the woman returned with a new cup of coffee, setting it down in front of me, my croaked "thank you" were the first words we'd spoken in minutes.

I busied myself leaning forward to pour creamer into my coffee and tear open two sugar packets. White crystals spewed all over the cocktail table and the floor.

I took a deep breath to steady myself. "Chip," I said, and then cleared the falter from my voice. "This is a lot to take in. I can't just—"

"I'm not asking you to make some big commitment or anything, Brook," he cut me off. "I'm just saying can't we maybe get to know each other—as people, not like doctor and patient—and just...see?"

If it hadn't been for Ben, I realized with a queasy feeling of guilt, I was ready to say yes.

"I don't know," I said finally. "I have to think."

He nodded. "Okay, I get that. Take your time. I can wait. I *will* wait....How about now?" That little-boy grin was back.

I almost felt an answering smile creep onto my lips, but my thoughts—and my stomach—were still churning.

Chapter Seventeen

Of course I took my dilemma immediately to Sasha.

"What do you think about seeing two guys at one time?"

She mulled my question over. "Honestly, that's the only kind of three-way I'll consider anymore. With two girls I'm just not as into it."

I just stared, pulling my feet back from where they commingled with Sasha's as we each slouched back against an arm of her red velvet sofa.

She kicked my ankle. "Not with you, idiot. That would be like incest."

Dropping my legs back down where they'd been, I reached over to the cocktail table for my wineglass. "I meant dating, actually, though of *course* I can understand your assumption. Don't we *all* have three-ways at some point?"

"I know, right?"

I just shook my head. Did my brother have any idea what he was getting into?

"What if I wanted to date someone besides Ben?" I asked.

Sasha sat up, crossing her legs. "You met someone else? Where?"

"I already knew him, actually."

She grinned. "And he asked you out? You playa!"

"He hasn't actually asked me on a date yet. And I don't even know for sure if I want to go out with him. I just wondered...if I did, would that be bad? I mean, considering Ben?"

"Well, have you and Ben talked about it?"

"About whether I'm going to go out with another guy? No, Sasha, geez!"

"No, duh—about what your relationship is. I mean, you're like some weird sexless Victorian couple, so you can both be forgiven for having no idea where you stand."

"Shut up."

"So who is it? Do I know him?"

Ugh. I was afraid she'd ask. But I couldn't lie to her. "It's Chip Santana."

"What! Oh, my god!" She shot off the couch, turning to face me with hands on hips. "For god's sake, Brook, what's the deal with this guy? You know he's trouble!"

"Oh, come on, Sash. You of all people can't see taking a chance on a guy who's not perfect?"

She raised her eyebrows. "'Not perfect' is one thing. Abusive is another."

I sat up and clinked my glass down on the table. "He's not abusive."

"You told me he strangled some chick!"

"She shot him! He has a temper problem, I admit. But he's working on it, Sasha—and honestly, he's a really sweet guy underneath it."

She rolled her eyes. "That's what all the battered wives say."

I stood up too, pacing across her living area to get out from under her accusing stare. "You don't even know him. And frankly I feel like you're implying I'm an idiot. Don't you think I of all people would know if Chip's a wife-beater?"

"I don't think you're an idiot, Brook. But you've got some kind of weird blind spot with this guy. Like you can't see past the attraction."

Resentment flared up in me. Sasha was a few months into the first healthy relationship of her life, and she suddenly thought she was some kind of expert?

But it died almost as quickly when I met her concerned gaze. All Sasha wanted—all she ever wanted—was what was best for me. If the tables were turned I'd probably be giving her the same warnings. And hadn't she hit on some of my own concerns? I did feel a powerful physical pull to Chip that more than once I'd worried overcame my better judgment. As our night in jail so eloquently demonstrated.

"You're right," I finally admitted into the ringing silence. "It's not a good idea."

Sasha came over to where I still stood near her television and pulled me into a hug. I stood stiff in her embrace for a few moments, and then finally raised my arms around her waist.

"Ben's a really good guy, Brook. It's not worth risking something great that might develop between you two for someone who doesn't deserve you." She pulled back and winked. "And by something great developing, I mean finally getting it on, of course."

"Of course."

I returned her smile, but it took more effort than it should have.

...

I didn't know what to say to Chip, so I took the coward's way out and didn't say anything at all. Work kept me busy enough not to justify avoiding calling him.

Cameron Mitchell had broken up with Wayne Bukowski, and was in the acute stages of mourning. I worried she'd go right back to him if she didn't have someone to talk it over with, so we scheduled several additional sessions over the week. Frank Farqu—a client I'd been seeing for many months, since he first came to me to help him win back his ex and instead I'd realized he needed help to stop stalking her—had met someone new, but couldn't stop thinking about Carole and wanted my blessing to contact her and let her know that (I met with him asap to decline to give it). Lisa Albrecht, my editor at the paper—and my first client—had been working with me on her resentment and rage at her ex-husband. When her sons told her that her ex moved his much younger girlfriend—whom he'd left Lisa for—into his apartment over the weekend, she was desperate for a session to keep her from going over there to slash their tires. Naturally I had to prevent her from getting arrested for vandalism. Between clients, my radio shows, and writing my column, I had my hands too full to worry about Chip.

Whenever I had a few free minutes, I worked with Jake on obedience. Results continued to be uncertain: some days he seemed like the greatest, smartest dog on earth, responding almost immediately to my commands of "sit" and "stay" and "down," grinning eagerly up at me for one of the treats I kept in a fanny pack at my waist. Then other times he refused to engage, leaning up against me for affection, licking my legs to get my attention, and finally throwing himself on the floor at my feet, belly-up, like a dead dog. I didn't know if it was something I was doing wrong as a trainer, or if Jake was simply messing with me.

On Thursday I took Jake over to visit with Adelaide. She was easy to talk to, full of compliments about my column and my radio appearance Monday, and we made dinner together while we chatted. She told me stories about Ben as a curious, busy child always rigging up something: building a working safe out of LEGOs, creating complex Rube Goldberg devices that were set off by his parents opening a door or walking into a room, starting "businesses" for lawn care or car detailing from the time he was twelve.

I couldn't help smiling through her descriptions of a kid who was so similar to the adult he became—industrious, creative, entrepreneurial. Sasha was so right—regardless of whether Chip was a reformed man or not, it wasn't worth jeopardizing things with a man like Ben.

Not that it mattered. I hadn't heard from Chip since his declaration anyway.

I guessed he wasn't that into me after all.

Adelaide told me about Ben's dad, her husband, Jim. Even now her love for him was palpable, as if he'd merely left the room, rather than been dead for years. "We did almost everything we talked about doing," she said as she plated the broiled salmon. "Lived in every city that piqued our interest, traveled, tried surfing and spelunking and whitewater rafting, had Ben. And we told each other everything we wanted to say, before the end," she said. "So I have no regrets."

"But you miss him," I said.

"Every day."

Ben had told me the night I first met him, sitting in the emergency room with his broken arm and my perforated foot, that his mom was having a hard time letting go of his dad. It wasn't my business, but Adelaide was still vibrant and active and pretty, and too outgoing to be alone for the rest of her life.

"It would be nice to be able to do some of those things still, if you could find someone who enjoyed them," I said casually as I took our plates to the table.

"It wasn't the activities as much as it was the company," she answered with a fond smile.

I tried again over dessert. "You know, they say the concept of a soul mate is a construct. There are a lot of people we can be happy with."

"Lightning doesn't strike twice," she said.

"It can, actually," I replied with a grin. "Just not in the exact same way."

Friday nights used to be my "date night" with Sasha, but now her Fridays always seemed full: "Stu and I are going night rowing in Bonita—crazy, right?" "I'm VIP'd in for a new nightclub opening in Naples and Stu's driving my drunk ass home afterward." And the one that always gave me a twinge: "We're just staying home curled up on the couch and watching movies. Come on over!"

Sometimes I did. And sometimes it was like old times—all three of us camped out on the floor, eating takeout food right from containers we passed around like a buffet, heckling whatever stupid movie had tickled us to pick out—*Sharknado* or *Battlefield Earth* or *Freaks*.

But other times I felt like an appendage, the obligatory maiden aunt that my two clearly happy best friends had invited over out of charity. Not because they did anything overt to make me feel like a third wheel—to their credit, Sasha and Stu refrained from cuddling or holding hands or kissing when I was over. But I could see in the occasional naked glance between them, or a brushing of their shoulders on the sofa, or a secret smile, that the two of them now shared something that I didn't with either one of them. So I stayed home with Jake that Friday night, curled up on the sofa as he tried very hard to make me feel less lonely by crawling all the way across my lap—where he promptly fell into a loud snoring sleep.

Even the dog wasn't that interested in my company.

By the time my Saturday-morning group session rolled around, I was more than ready to focus on someone else's problems, as Sherman Schmidt held the claw.

"I can't help the way I feel," he was telling the group. "Feet smell so good, I just want to touch them and tickle them and hold them in my mouth."

Well, that certainly commanded my full attention.

A couple of people tittered, and I glanced over to make sure no one was slinging judgment—especially Dina—but Sherman didn't seem to mind. He dipped his head and gave a bashful smile.

"Yeah, I know—I hear it too; it sounds weird, right? I just got to the point a few years ago where I could say it out loud like that and not feel like there's something wrong with me. Everyone's sexuality is unique—you just have to find someone who gets yours." His face clouded as he slumped back in the red plastic chair. "That's why I'm never going to get over Ruby. She's the one who helped me accept myself. And she...God." He bent in half, elbows on knees and head in hands. He'd moved so fast I worried he'd put an eye out on the claw prongs-up in his lap, but he just sat curled over himself.

Elisa Rodriguez, beside him, reached over and patted his shoulder, and after a moment Sherman angled a look over to her and nodded gratefully, straightening. His silvering hair poked up at the sides of his head where he'd driven his fingers through it.

Sherman looked around at everyone in the group, and I was proud to note that most met his eyes, offered a smile, or gave an encouraging nod. But despite their silent support, Sherman's brown eyes were red at the edges, his face drawn with pain.

"Where'm I ever going to find someone else who doesn't think I'm a freak?" he asked in a voice quiet with despair. "Who else is ever going to accept me?"

No one answered him. After a moment Sherman shook his head, reached into his lap, and pushed to his feet, walking the claw back to the center of the circle and then dropping heavily back into his chair.

"Sherman," I said into the shifting of bodies and whisper of the HVAC system that were the only other sounds in the otherwise silent room. "Did you mean it when you said a moment ago that you had learned to accept yourself? And all of your...preferences?"

One shoulder rose in a half shrug. "Yeah, I guess. No, I did. I do accept it. I know it's a little strange, but...Ruby used to say it's like, everyone likes chocolate cake. Not a lot of people like lima beans. But some people love lima beans. And no one thinks that's deviant."

"Dude, liking lima beans is a little deviant," Antonio Moretti said. "Nasty little fuckers."

Rebecca Forster cackled, and Elisa elbowed her, but she was grinning too. Everybody liked Antonio, and he frequently played to his audience.

Angling a warning glance to the rowdy side of the circle, I went on: "As Antonio has pointed out, liking lima beans might seem odd to some. But you just said some people love them. Do you think feet are worse than lima beans?"

Sherman gave the one-shouldered shrug again. "No. Feet are nothing like lima beans."

"This is a weird conversation," Dina said, but her tone lacked its usual combative edge.

"How do you mean?" I asked Sherman.

His forehead wrinkled with concentration. "Well, I mean, a lot of people like feet. You can look online—there's groups and stuff. There's no lima bean fetish sites online. That I know of."

"Amen to that," Antonio piped up.

"So it's not that unusual to like feet—to be turned on by them?" I asked, making sure the question didn't sound rhetorical.

Sherman said, "Not if you judge by that stuff, no. But online stuff is one thing, Brook. You can find just about anything online. I mean, really, anything—as dirty as you want."

"And amen to *that.*" Antonio was grinning.

"But those are outliers," Sherman went on as if he hadn't heard. "You walk into a party in real life and say you like furries or something, most people are going to back away from you. You guys all know how hard dating is already, finding someone you like, you can trust, you click with." Nods and grunts of agreement rippled around the circle. "If your sexuality is...you know, atypical, it's a million times harder. Your dating pool is so much smaller. Ruby was perfect for me. And I don't think I'm ever going to find someone else like that."

This time I let the silence fill the room. I wanted Sherman to hear his own words and dispute them. I could tell him all day long that that kind of global, absolute thinking was flawed, but if he was ever going to believe it, it had to come from him.

But it wasn't Sherman who spoke up.

"I hate chocolate cake," Sheila said.

Every head swiveled to her.

"Did you just *talk?*" Antonio asked disbelievingly.

Sheila's face had gone so deeply red it was almost purple, but she went on. "I hate it. My mom always made it for my birthday, and she never asked me, never once—" She stopped, swallowing. "She just made it over and over, and I hated it. And I don't know about lima beans. I've never had one. But I'd try them. Why not?"

Antonio was still gaping at her as she finished. Everyone was, I realized—including me—and Sheila dipped her head so the fall of dishwater hair covered her eyes again.

Beside her, Dina Jones was staring intently at Sheila, eyes narrowed, and I prepared to jump in if she went on the attack. Sheila wouldn't hold up to a full-on Dina strike.

Sherman was looking at Sheila too, but his expression was inquisitive. "Seriously? You don't think there's something wrong with lima beans?"

Sheila colored further—who could have thought that was possible?—but shook her head, her long bangs dancing across her eyes. "I'm not saying I'm *into* them . . ."

"No, I know—I just...Thanks, Sheila. Thanks for saying that."

She gave a single nod—and the tiniest of smiles.

"I would try them too," Carolyn Hendry said, and Betty bobbed her head, adding, "Yeah, me too."

"I hate the fuckers," Antonio boomed. He looked directly at Sherman. "But I wouldn't judge someone if they liked lima beans."

"I know a girl at work who *loves* lima beans," Rebecca put in. "And by lima beans right now I'm talking about feet. I could introduce you two." She shot a grin over at Sherman, who was full-on grinning back now, and I felt an answering smile creep over my own face.

...

That night Ben and I had dinner on the patio at Doc's, the restaurant's light and music spilling out toward the gulf behind it. We ate fish sticks and French fries and drank cold Anchor Steam beers, and Jake had a plain kids' hamburger that Ben stripped the bun from. A hot breeze danced through my hair and ruffled the hem of my sundress, but at least the movement offered some relief from the warm, humid summer air. Afterward we sat at the wooden picnic table to finish our beers, still talking, Jake contentedly stretched out underneath it between us.

"... And when I walk into what's going to be the master bedroom, one of the drywall guys is crouched between two joists, and I'm pretty sure his pants are down."

"No," I said. "Please tell me he wasn't—"

"Taking a dump before the plywood goes up so he can wall it into the house? I wish I could."

"Oh, my god. Oh, my *god*! What's wrong with people?" I said, covering my mouth. It felt wrong to be laughing—Ben had had to fire the guy—but I couldn't help it. "Why was he doing that in their *house*?"

"He said Mr. Tannenbaum—the owner—came by earlier that day and really laid into him about plaster drips outside the garage. We fix stuff like that before the owner even has a final walk-through, so I get why Turk might have been pissed off. But honest to God. Was it worth losing his job over?"

"That has to be some serious kind of health code violation, doesn't it?"

"It would certainly not endear me to the building inspector. Or the client," he said, and our soft laughter floated up and out to sea, where the full moon made a path of silvery white across the gentle waves.

The music had turned off as we talked, the night growing abruptly darker as Doc's turned off some of the outside lights.

"Looks like they're getting ready to close," Ben said. "You up for a walk on the beach?"

"Only always."

We walked hand in hand along the shore, Jake loping along beside us on his leash, stopping periodically to sniff the water, a sandcastle, seaweed, shells, the air. I couldn't blame him—the earthy, salty, *alive* scents of the sea always wrapped around me like a second skin, settling into my soul and making me feel like my lungs had opened up. The gentle sounds of water lapping at the shore mixed with Jake's occasional barking to alert us to dangerous sand crabs and the incoming minuscule waves of the gentle gulf.

After a while we stopped and watched him stalk coquina: Jake stared down intently at the water when a wave came in, and then as soon as it retreated plunged his nose into the sand as the little creatures burrowed back in from where the water had revealed them. When he finally looked up at us, sand caked his nose and a puzzled expression rode his face, turning wounded as our laughter sailed down the shore.

"Jakie, come here, buddy. We're laughing with you, not at you," Ben said, rubbing the dog's shaggy side as he leaned his sandy body against Ben's leg.

I bent to look Jake in the eye. "I've got to be honest with you, Jake," I said seriously. "I was laughing *at* you. I'm sorry I hurt your feelings." I took his giant damp head between my hands and rubbed his ears, and Jake lifted his head to give me better access. "Between the two of us I think he's finally getting enough love for once," I said to Ben, watching Jake's eyes close in contentment.

Our heads were almost touching, and Ben's face was inches from mine. His teeth glinted in the moonlight as he scratched the dog's side. "There's never enough love for you, pal, is there?" he said. "He's a high-maintenance dog. Lucky he makes up for it by being so sweet."

I straightened, watching him with Jake—so easy and relaxed, so comfortable showing affection, even when the dog was dirty and wet and a rubbery string of saliva hung out of his mouth. It was so much who Ben was—straightforward and genuine and real.

"Ben...let's go back to my place," I heard myself say. My voice sounded unintentionally husky, and between that and the cheesy way my words had come out, I felt a blush crawl up my cheeks.

He stopped petting abruptly, straightening to look at me. "What?"

"I...I want you to come home with me." *Agh.* Why was this coming out like a bad seventies porn film? What was next? Pointing out where Jake had dampened his jeans and suggesting we get him out of those wet things?

Ben was staring intently at me now, his eyes reflecting the moon. "Brook, do you...Are you sure?"

I nodded, holding his gaze. "This isn't the beer talking. Or even the beach or the gulf or the moonlight. I mean...just so you know..." We'd waited too long. Now it was awkward.

But Ben, as he always seemed to, made it okay. A smile started in his eyes and moved down to curve his lips, and he reached for my hand, pulling me into a soft kiss with Jake squirming delightedly between us.

We walked back to the car hand in hand, Jake bouncing excitedly along, and kept them clasped the whole way back to my house, only the low music from an Amos Lee CD filling the silence of the car. My heart was pounding the whole way.

My hands shook as I opened the front door. Why was I so nervous? Like a virgin bride on her wedding night.

I set my purse on the table in the entryway, and heard Ben follow me inside and shut the door behind him. I'd forgotten to leave a light on, and the only illumination was the glow from a streetlight spilling its light through the slats of the living room blinds. Jake shot by me, beelining for my bedroom, where I kept his dog bed.

Ben showed restraint his dog lacked, staying near the door a few feet away—giving me space, I thought. Room to change my mind.

I was tongue-tied. The only words crawling idiotically through my head were the lyrics of a Barry White song—"Take off your brassiere, my dear"—and I was afraid that it was what would spill out of my mouth if I opened it.

Cowgirl up.

This wasn't the moment I wanted my mother in my head, but her tough-love advice resonated. I didn't have to do this perfectly. I just wanted to do it.

My heart still thudding, I moved closer to Ben—a step...two. He just waited, gaze transfixed on me, and that was the sexiest thing I could imagine.

When I got close enough to touch, he did, putting his hands on my waist and then pulling me to him, and I pressed myself along the length of his body, feeling that he wanted me too.

We'd made out before. We'd even gotten hotter-and-heavier than this. But when his mouth came over mine, his hands pressing against the small of my back, pulling me into him, something let loose in me— maybe just knowing that this time I wasn't going to stop. I clutched his shoulders, pushed myself even closer into him, and let desire wash through me, take me over.

We never made it past the sofa.

...

The first time was quick.

In our defense, the tension had been building for an awfully long time, and I'm sure neither Ben nor I wanted the other one to judge based on the long-deferred release of all that pent-up desire.

But the second time...Holy mama. Not to mention the third, when John Mayer had nothing on our long, leisurely exploration of each other's wonderlands.

Now we lay on my bed in the dark, spent, Jake infiltrating the two inches of space between us to lie with his giant body pressed tight against us both.

"I think he was taken from his mother too young," I said, digging my fingers into the thick fur ringing his neck.

"He's a little needy," Ben agreed, stroking Jake's back. "But if I'd wanted aloof I guess I'd have gotten a cat."

Jake thrust his head into the crook of my neck as if to illustrate, then let out a long, groaning sigh. I wrapped an arm around him, laughing. "He's a hard creature not to love," I said.

I heard the bed shift as Ben rolled onto his side facing me, and then almost inaudibly, "So are you."

My heart slammed into my ribs.

Had I heard him right? I lay straining to hear something more over the pounding of my heartbeat in my ears. My mind raced. Had Ben just said he loved me? And if he had...was I ready to hear that?

Did I love him?

How did you know? I thought I'd loved Kendall, and yet now that I'd broken free of the crazy state of mind his abrupt departure had put me in, and since I'd been seeing Ben, I rarely even thought of him (except once every six weeks, of course, when I went in for tattoo removal). But at the time...at the time it had felt real. Hadn't it?

This felt real too. I knew that I loved Ben's company. I missed him when he was gone. Now I knew making love to him was wonderful. I felt happy when we were together—never with that constricted-chest feeling I'd had with Michael—as if my entire being would implode if he were to disappear from my life (exactly as he ended up doing)—or the comfortable contentment I'd felt with Kendall, but just happy and easy and *safe.*

Was that love?

Jake made a piggy-sounding noise on my chest as he settled more weight onto me—which I wouldn't have thought possible—and blinked up adoringly at my face as if to say, *Yes, Brook. That is exactly what love is.*

But a boyfriend wasn't a dog.

And I was thinking myself in circles.

By then, of course, I'd let a long, awkward pause follow what might have been a very important declaration.

Or might have been a trick of the night.

My heartbeat still drumming in my ears, I stroked Jake's fur, my hand occasionally brushing Ben's as he did the same. I waited, barely breathing, for him to say something else, or repeat himself, or do something to let me know for sure whether I'd heard what I thought I'd heard. Because the only thing worse than not responding to what Ben might have just said would be responding...only to find out he'd never said it.

But after a few silent minutes he simply wrapped his warm hand over mine and we lay there, looking up at the lazy wobbling circles my ancient fan made. And I realized that if we *had* had a moment, I'd missed it.

Gradually my heart settled back into its normal pace, the soothing sounds of Jake's heavy breathing like a lullaby.

"I haven't done this in so long," I said into the darkness after a long while.

"What, lie naked with a dog?"

"No. Just...relaxed. It feels good."

When I heard Ben call my name, I realized I'd drifted off.

"You're exhausted, Brook. You need to sleep."

"God, sorry—was I snoring?" I said groggily.

"I'm pretty sure it was Jake." I felt his hand stroke my arm. "Mom told me you came to see her again this past week. That's really nice of you."

"Mmmm."

"And watching Jake—all of it, Brook." His rumbling baritone was like a lullaby too, I thought as my hectic schedule caught up with me. "I just wanted to tell you..."

My heart leaped like the single blip of a patient just before coding, and I moved my suddenly weighted head to look at him, forcing my eyes open. "Yes?" I could hear the breathiness of my voice.

"Thank you."

Chapter Eighteen

I woke with a start, disoriented, a light in my eyes. I squinted over at it, registering that it came from my phone on the nightstand just as the bed moved and I remembered—Ben. I reached for the phone before it woke him up too.

Chip. I hadn't heard from him since last week. Part of me had hoped his declaration of intent had been a spur-of-the-moment thing, and that as the week went on without our speaking, he'd forgotten all about wanting us to date.

Part of me hoped he hadn't.

Guiltily I hit "answer" and eased out from under the covers. "Hey…hang on," I whispered.

As soon as my toe hit the floor Jake stirred, lumbering to his feet and charging over to my side of the bed. I stroked him as I eased out from under his giant head in my lap, continuing to pet him into submission as he tailed me all the way to the master bedroom door, where I slipped out and quietly shut him inside.

I glanced at the screen before raising the phone to my ear as I crossed the house toward my office so as not to wake Ben. "Chip, it's three a.m."

"Oh, crap, I forgot—you're not a night owl like me." He laughed in soft exhalations that told me he was smoking. "Sorry, Doc. I couldn't sleep. I keep thinking about you."

Heat suffused my body—my naked body—and I wrapped my arms around myself. Talking to Chip like this in the middle of the night had me feeling exposed and vulnerable. And turned-on. And guilty. "Chip—"

"I don't want to rush you. But it's been killing me all week not to hear from you, and I wondered if you'd been thinking over what we talked about."

He'd been waiting for *me* to make the first move? Pride in Chip—he'd come so far in handling his poor impulse control—warred with dismay. I couldn't keep hoping the decision would take care of itself. I had to choose.

Ben was lying not a hundred feet away—in my bed. After telling me—maybe—that he loved me. I'd told Sasha that nothing was worth risking losing him, and I'd meant it.

But making the choice was harder than it should have been.

I took a deep breath. "Chip, I wish I didn't have to—"

"No, wait, Brook—"

"No—I have to say this." The words grated out past my throat. "I'm seeing someone right now, and I...I just can't. I'm sorry."

The silence that fell between us was so absolute I could hear the faint crackle of burning cigarette paper as he took in a deep draw.

Finally his voice came—raspy and hard: "Okay. I get it."

I pressed my eyes closed. "I want you to know that you weren't wrong. There is something between us. In another situation, another time in our lives, maybe, but right now—"

"I'm a big boy, Brook. I don't need a consolation prize." His tone was barbed, but I could hear the hurt underneath it. Chip always covered his vulnerability with anger.

And knowing that—knowing him so well, knowing *I'd* been the one to hurt him—sent another arrow into my chest.

Whenever Stu and I visited friends' houses as kids, my mom would pack us off with the same dictate: "Make sure you leave things a little better than you found them." So my brother and I were the dorky kids who made our own beds at sleepovers, or picked up all the toys, or even once—in a gesture that endeared me forever to Bonnie Krupp's mom—detangled all the mats from their Sheltie dog, Socrates, while Bonnie and I sat on the floor, glued to the TV all night in a *Beverly Hills 90210* marathon.

Twice now I'd failed Chip, first as a therapist and now as a friend—three times, if you counted making out with him and playing my part in landing us in jail. I hadn't done right by him in the end. Chip was no better off than he'd been from the day I met him—at least, not because of anything I did.

I rubbed my aching temple. "Chip, I'm so sorry that we—"

"It's cool, really—don't worry about it. You take care."

He hung up.

...

I don't know how long I sat in the living room, wrapped in a throw blanket from my couch, trying to sort out my thoughts and assuage my conscience, before I crept back into the bedroom, placating Jake into silence with my fingers. I slid into bed next to a mercifully still sleeping Ben.

It was a long time before I got back to sleep.

...

Sunlight illuminating my eyelids woke me, and I opened my eyes and reached for Ben.

But the other side of the bed was empty.

I sat up and looked around the room—no Ben, no Jake.

I got up and retrieved my robe from the back of the bathroom door, pulling it on over my nakedness and walking out into the house, my stomach fluttering with anxiety.

Ben and Jake were in the kitchen, Jake streaking over to me as soon as my bedroom door opened and sticking his nose in impolite places like a hummingbird at a feeder. I pushed him away, but stroked his head as I watched Ben open a cabinet over the percolating coffeepot and take out a mug.

I smiled my relief. "I'll have a cup too."

"This is for you, actually. I have to get going."

"But it's Sunday. I thought..." Was he just going to leave if I hadn't come out?

"I've got some stuff to take care of today. I wanted to get an early start. Sorry if I woke you up."

I frowned. Something was off. Ben was acting like a guy who'd hit it and couldn't quit it fast enough, but I knew him better than that.

Was this about last night? Had he said what I thought I'd heard, and then taken offense when I hadn't replied? It was too awkward to come out and ask, so I tried hinting.

"Is everything okay?" I asked. "I mean, last night was...pretty great." A smile pulled at my lips as I remembered just how great.

He smiled back, but it wasn't his usual easy grin. "It was."

Nothing. I dangled another line. "I hope my phone didn't wake you up in the night," I said carefully.

His attention was focused on pouring coffee into the mug. "Actually it did."

Aha. An unexplained late-night phone call—*that* I could understand. I didn't know how much to tell him, and I worried that no matter how I put it, it would sound bad, so I opted for the tip of the truth iceberg: "Sorry about that. It was a client."

I thought I saw him close his eyes for a moment as he placed the coffeepot back on its burner. He reached for the sugar canister and dropped a spoonful into my coffee, concentrating on stirring it in thoroughly before he straightened and turned in my direction, his expression as blank and unreadable as pudding. "We'll talk later on, okay?" He handed me the mug and I cradled it between my palms, wishing it were his face for the good-morning kiss he hadn't offered. But the man had made me coffee—and remembered how I took it. What was I complaining about?

I nodded, staring intently into his eyes as if I could read there what he was thinking. "Okay. Just call me when you're ready to bring Jake back by."

"I will. Come on, Jake. Bye, Brook."

As I watched him and Jake head to the front door, I shivered despite the heat of the coffee mug I clutched in my hands.

...

The second I heard the door close I called Sasha.

She ignored my first two calls, but finally picked up the third one.

"Geez, Brook, it's freaking seven a.m. on a Sunday. Who's dead?"

"Jerry Garcia, Janis Joplin, Jimi Hendrix. But that's not important. I want to go out on my parents' boat." I needed to talk to her—and I needed to uncoil the knot of tension in my stomach. Nothing would do that like a day out on the water with my best friend.

"Uh, okay. Have fun," she said.

"No, fool—I want you to come too."

"I can't. I'm sleeping."

"No, you're not."

"I *should* be."

I heard my brother's voice in the background.

"It's your insane sister," Sasha said away from the phone. "She wants us to go out on the boat today."

I opened my mouth—I needed to talk to Sash, but I couldn't with Stu there, not the way I wanted to.

But this was their weekend too, I realized—I couldn't just expect Sasha to drop everything immediately for me anymore.

"It's okay," I said, trying to clear my throat of its sudden thickness. "You guys go back to sleep."

"No, we're coming." I heard Sasha yawn. "But don't expect me to sparkle."

"No, really, Sash, it's okay—I know you and Stu—"

"You woke me the hell up; you have to entertain me now. We'll be at your parents' dock at eight. Bring doughnuts." She hung up.

...

Two and a half hours later the three of us eased into the cove on the lee side of Picnic Island, a small comma of land at the mouth of where the Caloosahatchee opened up into the Gulf of Mexico, and I dropped the anchor while Stu backed us up till it caught. Sasha lay stretched along the bow, watching me.

I eyeballed her roughly ten acres of perfect tan skin in the world's smallest bikini. "You make it very hard to be friends with you."

"You can be the smart one," she said, smirking.

"You're an asshole."

She reached out one long thin leg and kicked me.

"Ow! See?"

Sasha sat up, wrapping her arms around her bent legs. "What's wrong?" she demanded.

"Nothing, except the contusion you just gave me."

"Don't play games, Brookie. What's the matter?"

Before I left my house to grab the doughnuts Sasha had demanded, I'd texted Ben: *Headed out to Picnic Island today with my brother and Sasha. Any chance you can join us?*

He hadn't responded.

I'd tried to laugh and engage in our usual banter, Sasha methodically licking the powdered sugar off the doughnuts and Stu eating the rest of each one as we motored down the river and into the bay, but the lump in my belly lay like lead. And Sasha could always read me.

I shot a glance back to the cockpit now, where Stu was fine-tuning the set of the anchor. "We'll talk later," I said. "It's girl stuff."

She shot to her feet. "Hey, Stuvie," she called out, picking her way like a daddy longlegs over the bow and back into the boat. "Brook and I are going to go sunbathe on the beach for a little while. Do you want to stay here and fish?"

Stu gave her a skeptical look, then made a show of peering over the gunwale and into the three crystal-clear feet of water that bore no evidence of sea life. "Fish for...?"

"Compliments, you hottie," she said, and leaned over to plant a kiss on his mouth. "We won't be long." Stu slapped her ass as she turned around.

I was almost getting used to it.

We waded to shore, and within ten minutes Sasha and I were lying on the beach, the way we used to do as kids: no towel, just stomachs flat on the sand, heads pointed toward land and feet in the water. Gentle waves surged up our bodies every few seconds.

The last time I'd been here was with Kendall—the last day we'd been a couple, actually. It had been a perfect day, I'd thought—right up until the end of it, when I'd finally accepted his offer to move in, and instead he'd bugged out.

I hadn't come back since partly out of sheer busy-ness, but I think I'd also feared Kendall had ruined my island for me, the place I'd been coming—usually with our family or just Stu and Sasha—as long as I could remember.

But as the warm gulf water lapped at my legs and I felt myself sinking deeper into the cool sand with every wave, I realized he hadn't spoiled anything. Picnic Island was my happy place—anything by the water was. My worries seemed to wash away with the outgoing tide.

"Oh, I needed this so much, Sash," I said with a sigh. "Thanks for coming. Sorry I horned in on the two of you."

Sasha rolled over onto her side so she was facing me, propping her head on one muscular arm. "Let me tell you something, Brookie. I'm pretty crazy about your brother. But I need you as much as I do him. Maybe more—just don't tell him that. You had me at hello. You complete me."

A grin stretched my salt-tight face as I reached out and pushed her over on her back. "You're an idiot." But her words were like ointment on a wound.

"Now tell Auntie Sasha what's the matter."

So I did, starting with the fact that Ben and I finally had sex—which elicited a whoop of glee and a fist bump, followed by a ruminative frown as I continued a play-by-play of what I thought he might have said afterward, and the evening's odd, unsettling finish. I recapped the phone call from Chip—which met with a stern look of displeasure that flipped into an approving smile when I told her I'd ended things. Then I related the stilted exchange with Ben this morning before he left and took his dog, and my unanswered text. When I finished she commanded, "Okay, tell it to me again, and give me inflections—I need nuance."

This was one of the many reasons Sasha was always the greatest person to parse out dating problems with. With the endless patience of Job, she would listen to every tiny detail, paying close attention, asking for clarification and elaboration, having you go back over the troubling parts over and over and over as she helped try to analyze what it could have meant. Maybe it wasn't the healthiest approach to dissect every little detail so carefully, but there was no such thing as feeling rushed when you were hashing out a problem with Sasha.

"So what does it mean?" I said after the second recitation. "Do I ask him if he said what I thought he said last night and look like an idiot if he didn't? Do I ignore it altogether, and send the message that I didn't want to hear it, if he did say it? Do *I* say it and see what he says in response?"

Sasha frowned. "*Do* you love him?"

I sat up to ponder that, digging my fingers into the sand and watching the holes fill up with water with each wave. "I don't know. I think that's part of the problem. I don't know if I trust myself enough to know what love is anymore."

"Oh, honey." Sash sat up beside me and leaned close enough to touch shoulders. But she didn't feed me false comfort or platitudes—another reason I loved her. "Well," she went on after a moment, "do you *want* him to have said he loved you?"

"I don't know. We were taking it slow, and that was going great. But when I thought he said it, this pang shot through me. A good pang, I think."

"'Taking it slow'?" Sasha shot me a look. "Does *he* know you're taking it slow?"

"Of course he does. I told him—remember?"

Sasha shook her head. "But you changed the rules. You pretty much have custody of his dog—whom you are training. You visit his mom. And he spends almost every second he's in town with you. Look how far you've come into his life, Brook—you're practically his stay-at-home wife, taking care of everything on the home front while he's off at work."

I stared at her, poleaxed. "Do you think he thinks that?"

Sasha threw up her hands. "Who knows? If we knew how the damn creatures think, we wouldn't have conversations like this one."

I laughed with her, and after a few moments I heard her sigh.

"Is it weird if I miss this?" she said.

"Dating?" A little alarm flashed in my head. My biggest fear about Sasha and Stu was what would happen to our lifelong threesome if they ever broke up.

"Yeah. I mean, I don't miss dating—I *am* dating. It's just...as psycho as all my relationship stuff could be before your brother, I always loved talking out all the crazy parts with you. It almost made it all worth it." I peered over at her and saw her smiling wistfully into the clear blue sky. "With Stu, there's no crazy. And I love that. But I miss talking to you."

I scooped up a heavy clump of wet sand and patted it onto her calf, then another one, smoothing it out like a clay mask, the way we'd done when we were kids. "I'm sorry I've been so busy lately," I said quietly.

"You're building your business. I know that." She joined my efforts, adding sand to her other leg until they looked like the long gray stalks of a heron. "It's not forever. Anyway, I know it's my fault too. Now that I have a *boyfriend*." She singsonged the word.

"I know. It's sort of weird that you have this really healthy relationship and I'm the one coming to you for advice."

"And I love it *so much*," she sang out, falling backward onto the sand with her arms thrown wide. "It is the culmination of my life."

I grinned at her antics, adding sand to her belly.

"We need to know if he's called you, or texted," she said after a while. "Where's your phone?"

I tipped my head toward the cove. "Boat."

Sasha shot upright and scrambled to her feet, sand dropping off of her in clumps. "Stu!" she screamed out toward the water, waving my brother down where he sat in the captain's chair with his feet on the dash, reading a magazine. The few other people moored in the cove and walking along the beach snapped their gazes over to my delicate flower of a best friend. "Land ho!"

"I know, babe," he shouted back, not moving. "But don't advertise it to everyone."

Sasha fell onto the sand laughing, and I marveled at how perfect they were for each other.

We finally conveyed that we wanted him to join us, and to bring my phone, and Stu waded in with that, his own towel, and—bless my brother—the cooler full of lunch and drinks that I'd packed.

Sasha rinsed off in the water as we waited, and we scrambled to snatch the phone as soon as he cleared the shoreline.

"Oh, hi, girls. You're welcome. I've missed you too," he said as we scurried back to the towels to check my call log.

Sorry I missed your text! Sounds like fun—maybe next time. Hope you have a great time. You could use a day off.

I stared at it in perplexity.

"What does that mean?" Sasha spoke my thoughts.

"I don't know. It's weird, right?"

She nodded. "Definitely. Stu, come here."

"Yes, mistress. As you command, mistress," he said, trotting over like a dog.

Sasha turned to face him and gave him a long, intent stare. "That's fun. Hang on to that. We can use it later."

"Stop!" I said.

Sasha plucked the phone from my hands. "You have a penis," she said to Stu. "Decode this."

Stu read the message. "This is from a guy?" he asked me, and I nodded. "Ah," he said. "Okay."

"What? What does it mean?" Sasha prodded.

"Well..." He took the phone and peered more closely at it, then fixed me and Sash with a hard glare. "Don't you dare reveal that I let you in on the guy code, okay?"

"We won't," she promised.

"Swear," I added.

"Okay." He held the phone where we could both see it. "See this? What he's actually saying is that he's sorry he missed the call and might like to go next time. But he hopes you went and got to relax. Now forget everything I just told you."

Sasha slapped his arm. "You are such an ass."

My brother was grinning like the Cheshire cat. "When will you girls learn? Quit trying to read guys' subtext. There is none. We have no depth."

While Sasha wrestled Stu to the ground, I read the text one more time, and decided to agree with my brother. There was no sense worrying about it now anyway—I'd know soon enough if something had changed between me and Ben.

Meanwhile, I was starving.

I broke up the cage match at my feet, and we unwrapped the sandwiches I'd thrown together out of whatever was in my kitchen— one roast beef, one cheese and tomato, and one peanut butter and jelly—and we shoved them into our faces between handfuls of Pringles and Fritos. Afterward the three of us lay on the sand, Sasha between me and Stu, the way it had been most of our lives, and let the sunshine lull us into catnaps.

Jerking awake to frigid liquid trickling across my stomach, I yelped and opened my eyes to see my bratty brother pouring icy cooler water from Solo cups onto both me and Sasha, a fiendish grin lighting his features.

And so of course Sasha and I each lunged forward and grabbed a leg, yanking Stu to the ground and proceeding to bury him in sand. Where we left him for a good twenty minutes or so while we wandered off to gather shells, which we then used to create a shell bikini on him, and snapped pics with my phone, which naturally Sasha immediately posted to Facebook.

When he roared and burst through his sand cocoon like the Incredible Hulk, we ran into the water shrieking, and Stu came barreling after us, catching us over and over and throwing us with great cannonball splashes back to the surface.

We laughed so much I got a cramp and had to get out of the water. Sasha and Stu stayed in, taking turns seeing who could float facedown the longest without air.

For this one afternoon we were just like we used to be, our unit of three—carefree and silly and happy. I wished we could stay here—pitch tents like we used to and just not go back to shore—where all my worries waited for me.

I knew we'd go home in a couple of hours. But I pushed the thought away, leaning back in the sand on propped palms, letting myself just enjoy where we were right now. I watched my brother and best friend, sleek as dolphins in the water, as the sun's warmth dried the salt on my skin and seemed to sink all the way into my body.

...

The day had done me more good than I realized. As busy as I'd been lately, it was easy for my tired brain to get caught up in loops of worry and overanalysis. By the time I got home I realized I'd overreacted about Ben. Of course everything was fine.

That feeling lasted up until I scrambled out of the shower to answer my ringing phone, expecting Ben's call, but missed it and listened to his message.

"Hey, Brook—hope you had a great day today. It sounded like fun. I'm headed back to Cedar Key in just a few—just wanted to let you know Mom's knee's a lot better and she's able to keep Jake, so you can finally have a break from the Kraken. Give me a call when you get this, if you get a chance."

And just like that, I felt sick again.

I hadn't imagined it—somehow I'd blown it. Ben *had* said what I thought I'd heard, and when I didn't even acknowledge his feelings...Well, I knew how I'd have reacted if it had happened the other way around.

I'd cut my losses and get out.

I was still dripping on my tile floor where I'd hustled out of the shower. Laying the phone carefully back down on the counter, I used my towel to dab it dry, then wrapped the terry cloth slowly around my body.

Then I sank to the floor, knees drawn up, leaning against the cabinet and staring at nothing as I wondered how everything had gone so wrong, so fast.

...

I didn't call Ben back. If he'd wanted to see me or to talk, he'd have come over, or at least called again. He'd left the call ball in my court, but I'd dated enough to know when I heard a polite copout, and Ben was nothing if not polite and kind.

I just wasn't up for a half-hearted conversation with him, or a distant, awkward call where both of us cordially pretended everything was the same, but the sick feeling in my stomach told me nothing was.

I put on layers of lipstick—the armor my mother always advocated—and headed over to Mom and Dad's for dinner. I thought I did a spectacular job of keeping up my end of the conversation, a smile on my face, but Sasha's furrowed brows every time she caught my eye told me she was seeing through the facade.

In the driveway afterward, as we were leaving, I gave her the quick recap of Ben's call and his not bringing Jake over, and she leaned out the open passenger door of Stu's Jeep for a quick hug. "Remember what the Monty Python boys say," she said encouragingly.

It was an old joke between us from *Sliding Doors*, one of my favorite movies.

"'Nobody expects the Spanish Inquisition,'" I recited.

She pinched my cheek as if I were five and she was eighty. "No. 'It's just a flesh wound.' Chin up, honey. Don't panic."

I went to bed early—tomorrow was my radio show, and Mondays were always hard when the alarm rang at four a.m. I didn't sleep for a long time, though—my mind was too busy churning, and I missed the sound of Jake's snuffles and snores and existential groans beside me. For the first time in a long time, my house felt empty and lonely.

When my phone beeped I lurched over, hope flaring in my chest, only to sputter out when I saw it was Chip instead of Ben.

I just want U to know Im not mad at U. Im still writing letters to my exes, b/c. I want to be better & that has a lot to do w/ U. I know why U can't answer me. But if it's OK with U, I'm just going to text now and then anyway. G'night, Brook.

Stupidly, I felt tears heat my eyes. I held the phone, my thumb hovering over the keypad, but I didn't make a move to respond. It beeped again.

I know U won't text back. Miss U, Doc.

I put the phone down and lay on my back, staring at the ceiling, waiting out the night until it was time to get up.

Chapter Nineteen

I arrived for my radio appearance on Jim Veneer's show at five forty-five the next morning, groggy, irritable, and heartsick. But when I walked into the studio to Jim's big goofy smile and slipped the headphones over my ears, I let it all spiral into the compartment where I kept my personal matters when I was working with clients.

As soon as Jim had done the intros, traffic, and other housekeeping, he pressed the first lit-up button.

"Hey, there, caller—you're on the air with Jim Veneer and the Breakup Doctor," he said in his smooth patter.

"Hey, Breakup Doctor, I'm Gina. I'm not the kind of person who usually calls you."

No one ever was.

"Hi, Gina," I said.

"So I haven't been dumped or anything. Actually just the opposite. I want to break up with someone. I *have*, actually. But then he gets all upset and I feel bad, so we get back together for a while, but the same stuff drives me crazy, and then I try to do it again. He's a really nice guy—just not what I'm looking for. I don't want to hurt him. What's the gentlest way to break up with someone?"

Thoughts of Ben eked into my conscience, and the sick feeling in my stomach was back at her words. Was he wondering the same thing—how to break things off with me gently?

"Well, you may have just saved yourself the trouble if he's listening in," I muttered.

And then ice shot through my body. Ben always listened in on my show at work. Or he used to.

I heard a nervous chuckle on the other end of the call. "Uh, I didn't really think about—"

"You know, maybe this is a miscommunication," I blurted. "Maybe, for some silly reason, he didn't understand something you said, and he's acting in a way that seems odd to you. But really he's just confused about your feelings, and wasn't sure how to answer you."

There was a silence, and I glanced up to see Jim looking at me with a perplexed expression.

"Um..." The caller sounded uncertain. "I don't think that's...I'm sorry, I think I missed something—a misunderstanding about what, exactly?"

"I don't know. Maybe you don't either. Maybe you should just ask him. Or give him a chance to explain, you know?"

"Explain what?" Gina said. She gave a nervous chuckle. "Honestly I just don't want to date the guy anymore."

From the corner of my eye I saw Jim make a wrap-it-up motion with his finger.

"You want to dump the guy?" I said brusquely into my mike. "Fine. Then would you rather have your leg chopped off or sawed off?"

"What? Neither!"

"You've got gangrene. The leg's coming off. Chopped or sawed?"

"Uh...chopped, I guess?"

"Right. They're both going to be awful, but if you feel you have to do it, quick and clean is better. A breakup hurts, but once it's finished the person can start to heal. Sawing is messy, and the pain goes on and on." I dropped my gaze so Jim wouldn't see the moisture I felt in them.

Silence on the line always felt three times as long on-air. Finally the caller said, "Yeah. I guess the leg's coming off either way. So what, I just say it? Just tell him straight-out, 'Dude, I'm done'?"

"You could try to be a little gentler." She laughed again, but I hadn't meant it as a joke. "It's a conversation, like any other—just about a more difficult topic. The hard part about breakups is that they feel like such a personal rejection. Because, of course, they are."

"But he's a great guy—"

I cut Gina off. "Yes, I have no doubt. But clearly not for you."

"Yeah."

"Here's the deal: In situations like this, just man up and tell the truth."

"What?"

I caught myself. "Sorry. Figure of speech. Just have the courage to be honest, knowing the other person is an adult and can take it. 'I've enjoyed what we had. But it's just not working out, and it's not fair to stay in a relationship with you when I know that.' That's it—no need to delineate every single reason you have for not wanting to be with her anymore. Sorry...with *him*." I stopped and took a breath to collect myself. "Be direct, but tactful."

"That's a tall order," Gina said. She sounded uncertain.

"Just try to remember to treat him with respect as a person, whether or not he's the person for you."

"Um, okay. Thanks?"

"Good luck. And remember—" But Jim had already cut the call, and I was talking to dead air.

...

"So that was weird."

I'd taken another handful of callers before the show ended, and my cell phone started ringing almost the second I went off the air. I'd eagerly answered, my heart sinking when it was only Sasha.

"What was weird?"

"That first caller?" she said. "Gina?"

"You listened to the show?"

"Heck, yeah, we always listen to it. Stu needs to know about breakup behaviors, and that if he breaks up with me I'll kneecap him."

It worried me that I was only pretty sure she was kidding.

"What was weird?" I repeated. "I gave her the chopped off/sawed off analogy. You always love that one."

"Uh, yeah. Buried inside a whole bunch of off-topic crazy."

The building's front door was hard to open, as if it had to push through the thick humidity of a Florida morning in July. Blinking against the bright sunshine, I said, "What do you mean?"

"You were all over the map with her, Brook—talking about misunderstandings and second chances. You weren't even listening to her."

"I wasn't?"

"No. She wasn't calling about whether to break up with the guy. She knew she wanted to. She keeps doing it. In fact, I was kind of surprised you didn't tell the woman to examine her own behavior: why she keeps getting back with a man she says she's finished with. She's the one who's kind of stringing the guy along."

I stopped halfway to my car. "Holy crap. You're right. I didn't even see that."

"Eh, you can't bat a thousand all the time. But it was a little strange that you went off on a tangent about letting the guy explain. I'm assuming this is really about Ben?"

My grip on the phone suddenly felt slippery. "Oh, god. Did I really…I *never* bring my own stuff into a client's issues. Never."

"Not sure we can say *that* anymore," she offered cheerfully.

"This isn't funny, Sasha. I just shot all my credibility." I didn't know when I'd started walking again, but I'd somehow reached my car, and I slumped against the driver's door, the metal already warm even this early in the day.

"It wasn't your best advice," Sasha said mildly. "But do *not* freak out about it. I'm serious."

"I have to go."

"Ohhh, no. If you hang up you're going to spiral into beating yourself up. We know where that leads—and based on past events, I'm going to say jail and a whole bunch of crazy. Meet me at Sunrise in twenty."

She hung up before I could argue.

…

In season, the Sunrise Café was so packed for breakfast every day of the week, you could hardly push inside to put your name on the wait list. But in the dead season of July it was a ghost town. Sasha was already waiting for me in an isolated corner, and the server had coffee slapped down in front of me almost before my butt hit the seat.

I held it in my oddly icy fingers and took a grateful sip as I eyed Sasha. She wore a tan pencil skirt that fit her as if it had been stitched onto her body, a cowl-neck coral blouse—and, incongruously, a gaudy yellow plastic choker that was unlike anything my fashionable friend would ever put against her skin. Examining it curiously, I did a double take at the ring of faint blue and purple peeking out just above the awful thing.

"Jesus, Sash—are those bruises around your neck?"

My best friend turned fiery red. "You don't want to know."

"Of course I do. Tell me."

She shook her head, staring down at the wide white mouth of her coffee mug around her black brew.

I reached over and took one of her hands. "Sash, you have to know you can tell me anything. Always. What happened?"

She turned magenta. "I, uh...I tried onomono his face the ocean," she muttered.

Or that's what it sounded like. I leaned in. "What?"

"I tried autoerotic asphyxiation!" she whispered fiercely. "Now shut up!"

My mouth dropped so wide I swore I tasted the steam from my coffee. "You *strangled* yourself for an orgasm?! Why?"

"Really, drop it, Brook," she hissed. "You do *not* want to know more."

Then it was my turn to blush—or so I guessed from the surge of heat flooding my face— as understanding exploded in me. "Oh, dear god. Did *my brother* do this?"

"I made him. He didn't want to," she hastened to assure me. "He's not the type to just strangle me for no reason."

"You *think*?!" I yelped.

"Shhh!"

"Mother of god, Sasha, what were you thinking? It's dangerous! What if he'd accidentally killed you? How on earth would he live with that? How would I?"

"It's supposed to be crazy hot. I just wanted to try it," she whined in a tiny little voice I'd never heard from her. "Would you *please* keep your voice down?"

"You've told me about sexcapades a prostitute would be embarrassed to repeat," I said in disbelief. "Suddenly *this* is over the line?"

"Well..." She shifted in the banquette, looking anywhere but at me. "I threw up. A little bit. On Stu."

"Oh, god."

"And I might have peed on him slightly."

"Oh, my *god*!"

"I couldn't help it! I thought I was going to die—everything just let loose. Except the one thing I was shooting for. Turns out it's *not* hot and sexy, and I do not recommend it."

"Oh, okay, gosh, thanks for saying."

"You did ask," she said primly. "Even after I suggested you not."

"You know what?" I said. "Never answer another question I ask you. Ever. Not as long as you're dating my brother."

"Quit deflecting. Tell me what's going on."

I sighed and took a long sip of my coffee, hoping it would burn out the memory of what she'd told me. Which it did not. The server came and we placed our orders.

"So I guess it's pretty much over," I told her when the woman left. "Because of my stupid reaction—or nonreaction—to his declaration."

"Hold on—we still don't know if he even made a declaration."

"Why else would he leave town without seeing me, Sash? Why keep Jake from me? When a person's normal behavior changes, you have to look at what's different. In this case, everything was different after he maybe said he loved me and I didn't say a thing. Ergo."

Her eyebrows went skyward. "'Ergo'? Really?"

"Or maybe it was about Chip's call. I told him about it, but maybe I need to explain. Do you think I should call him and explain? But now it's only going to draw more attention to it. And what would I say anyway?"

"Hold up, there, crazy."

"Ben's a nice guy. Too nice to actually break up with me. So I'm guessing this is a breakup by attrition—he'll just slowly disappear."

Sasha shook her head. "I really think you're overthinking this. You're making way too much out of what might be an innocuous event."

"You know I'm right," I countered. "If this were you in this situation, you'd already be boiling the bunny."

"True," she said reflectively. "I wonder if I'm maturing, or it's just easier to be rational and objective when it's not me directly involved."

Our food came—gingerbread pancakes and sausage for me, and a fruit-and-yogurt plate for Sasha (why did she even bother eating?)—and as she dug into her dull breakfast with all the fervor of a starving person, which she probably was, I spread butter and syrup on my pancakes and mulled over what she'd said.

"You're right, you know," I said finally, then shoved a bite of pancake into my mouth.

"Usually. About what?"

"I'm catastrophizing," I said around the mouthful. "That's weird. I usually don't do that. Why do you think I am now?"

Sasha bit into a blueberry. "Because you really like this guy."

"I really liked Kendall. I really liked Michael."

"Yes, but since then I think you're turning into a real live boy, Pinocchio."

I threw a packet of sugar at her.

"I'm serious, Brook," she said, dodging it. "You've changed a lot in the last few months—you probably don't even realize it. Ever since last spring you're...I don't know. Softer. More open. Not so intimidating."

I drew my eyebrows into a furrow. "So before I was hard and closed and scary?"

"No. Just...guarded. Like nothing ever really affected you any more than skin-deep. Now things do. I can see it."

I gnawed on a sausage link I'd speared on my fork while I thought about that. "Well, if this is what it feels like all the time, I'm not sure it's an improvement."

Sasha shook her head. "It won't be all the time. You're just getting used to it. It's like when a deaf person gets a cochlear implant and hears for the first time. It's too much at the beginning—overwhelming. Then he learns to filter."

"Sasha, none of your metaphors for me are very flattering."

"Before," she stressed. "That was you *before*."

I swallowed a too-large bite of sausage, washing it down with coffee so I didn't choke. "So basically you're saying that I'll get used to being more...whatever, open. To 'feeling' more. And then this stuff won't hit me so hard."

"Oh, no. It always hits hard. Feels like crap. You just have to accept that, deal with it, and let it go."

"Wow, such an improvement," I said sarcastically.

Sasha put down her fork—she'd made a small dent in the yogurt and taken a few bites of berries—and leaned back in the banquette. "Would you stop? It *is* an improvement. What would you have done at this point as the old Brook?"

"Hard, cold, scary Brook?" I shot back.

"Yes, that sad creature. What would you do?"

"I'd walk away. When you see the ax descending you don't hang around for the decapitation."

"Right!" She leaned forward excitedly. "But how does it feel to think about not having Ben around anymore?"

My throat closed around a bite of pancake and it was an effort to swallow. "Awful."

"Yes! That's great!"

I eyeballed her.

She waved away my skepticism. "Not the awful part. The other part. Now you can admit that it would hurt to lose him, instead of shutting down. Brook, once you shut down it's all over. There's no chance. But I think it's pretty likely this is just a normal relationship stumble—a speed bump. So cowgirl up." I cracked a smile at her use of my mom's phrase. "Take a chance and hang on, stay open. Maybe he does have one foot out the door. But maybe not. Don't take the risk of slamming it right on his leg."

I pushed my plate away and leaned back, letting out a long breath. What Sasha suggested was the total opposite of what I wanted to do: My instincts said cut and run—protect. But I thought about what I would advise a client to do in this situation, and I saw that she was right—I was being precipitous, jumping to a conclusion I didn't yet have enough data to reach with any certainty.

"So I just...what," I asked finally. "Go on as if nothing happened?"

She shrugged. "Why not? Nothing really has."

I stared down at the carnage of my breakfast, thinking. It was hard not to act, but Sasha had a point—right now there was nothing to act on. I just had to chill out, lie low, and be open to whatever happened.

Damn. Sasha's way was so much harder.

"Okay," I said. "I'll just wait and see."

She beamed as if I were a prize pupil. "That's my brave Breakup Doctor! Breakfast is on me," she said, reaching for her purse. "Think of it as the positive reinforcement you mental health people are so fond of."

"Very funny."

She looked up from plucking bills from her wallet and met my eyes, all trace of teasing gone. "Just don't shut down, Brookie. Be open to *anything*. It's like with me and Stu—sometimes the things you expect the least are the very best surprises of all."

Chapter Twenty

Sasha's advice was so good, the next night I wrote my column on it:

Doing Less

It's advice that flies in the face of probably most everything you've heard. We're exhorted by experts to do more in every capacity: more work, more leisure time, more productivity, more efficiency—more, more, more.

But I suggest that, where love is concerned, you try doing less.

I don't mean less of the good things—being attentive, listening, honoring your partner and being present in the relationship.

It's the things that tie us in knots that too often we get wrapped up in doing too much of. We worry; we ruminate; we downright obsess: Does our partner love us? Is he faithful? Have her feelings changed? Are we okay?

Are we doing enough?

When we're so busy dwelling on the secret worries and fears and insecurities that we all have—because we are human—it's impossible to see what's actually there. That can be bad as well as good, of course—if you take time to breathe, to stop stressing about every what-if, every disaster scenario, every secret inadequacy, and look at what is actually happening, maybe you really will find out your fears are based in reality.

But maybe they aren't, and you're suffering for nothing.

Either way, you aren't having the relationship that's going on in your present. You're living in the ones you had in your past that fed all the demons that come trooping out when we let ourselves believe that we could be happy: the ones that remind us of when we thought the same thing once before, and were spectacularly wrong. And we got hurt.

It's human nature to avoid pain—we're hard-wired for it: our nervous system uses pain signals as a barometer for our safety. Pain indicates that something endangers our well-being, and so the natural reaction is to avoid the thing that caused it.

But if you're confusing the relationship you're having now with the ones you had before it, you're reacting to phantom pain. You're anticipating an outcome that may or may not occur—and if our fears get too firm a grasp on us, they may actually bring about the very thing we were so terrified of. If you are so afraid that your partner will cheat on you that you constantly harangue her about it, monitor her communications, and make accusations, for instance, you create an atmosphere of mistrust that may in fact encourage her to look elsewhere for the kind of loving, trusting relationship most of us crave.

If you fear he doesn't love you, it may be due to your own fears that you aren't worthy of love. And if we can't find it in us to love ourselves, as the tired-but-true trope says, how can anybody love us?

Do less—less of the kind of unhealthy, fear-driven thinking that brings about exactly the thing we fear most. Don't twist yourself up in overthinking. Don't torment yourself with every worst-case scenario from every unsuccessful relationship before this one that might—if you just let it—turn into the one that's successful beyond your imagination.

In the wise words of Frankie Goes to Hollywood...relax.

It was only a first draft, and it needed polishing, but I liked it. It was everything I would tell a client in a similar situation. Everything I knew to be true in my head and my heart. My paranoia about Ben wasn't about Ben at all. It was about Michael, and Kendall, and every other time I didn't get the love I wanted.

And it was about me. I'd cringed as I wrote the line about not feeling worthy of love. Of all the therapeutic clichés, that was the one that made everyone roll their eyes. But it was the truest statement of all. Was I really afraid Ben might not love me?

Or was I afraid *I* didn't?

...

Ever since I'd spent time with Ben's mom, I'd been doing some thinking about my own. Despite the thorny relationship we'd had for so long, I loved my mother—why else was I always striving to win her approval? I wanted us to have a relationship—one that was more than Mom telling me how I could do things better and me rolling my eyes. But I'd been waiting angrily for her to offer me what I craved before I'd unbend and open up to her.

I could keep standing on my high horse and being resentful, and have the same distantly loving but troubled dynamic I'd always had with my mom. Or I could do what Adelaide had shown me with Jake: Accept a creature's nature just as it was and modify the way I reacted to it to yield the behavior I wanted.

Yes, it was dog-training my mom. But whatever—it had worked on Jake.

The thought of the big galumph send a shard of pain into my chest. I missed him. I missed Ben.

To distract me from obsessing over him again, I called Mom to see if she could meet me for dinner tomorrow, just the two of us.

She greeted the request with a long silence.

"What's wrong?" she asked finally.

"Nothing, Mom—I just thought it would be nice."

"Are you sick? Pregnant?" she plowed on as if I hadn't spoken. "Oh, lord, are you coming out?"

"What!? Mom, geez, I'm not gay. *Or* pregnant. Or sick, for that matter—I just wanted to have dinner with you."

But her reaction pointed up the fact that I couldn't remember the last time I'd called my mom for no reason, just to hang out. Or whether I ever had, for that matter. We didn't have that kind of relationship.

So maybe it was time we did.

She offered to meet me on her dinner break from rehearsal the next night, somewhere halfway between her theater housing in Naples and Fort Myers. We settled on Tradewinds in Bonita and hung up shortly after, our conversational stores exhausted.

And still there was no text or call from Ben. Even by the time I climbed into bed, fighting the suffocating feeling that threatened to smother me.

...

I was almost expecting Chip's text when it dragged me out of a fitful sleep that night.

Hey, Brook. I heard you on the radio this morning. Hear you all the time, actually. I always listen. I like to hear U help them like you helped me.

His words spread over me like honey after the way I'd been beating myself up.

And, if I were honest with myself, it filled up the aching cavity in my chest from the total radio silence from Ben. I cradled the phone to my chest, knowing there would be more. Sure enough, it buzzed a few seconds later.

You take great care of people who need it. Been wondering if the guy you're seeing takes good care of you.

I gripped the phone, blinking against a sudden heat in my eyes.

I wish that didn't make me jealous, but it does.

I noticed distantly as another text came in that he'd started using more full words, fewer of the abbreviations that always made his texts feel like a teenager's to me.

I don't mean weird jealous. Not like a stalker, LOL! Just...I wish it could be me.

My mouth went dry. The phone buzzed immediately.

Even just as friends.

And immediately again: *It sounds weird, but I think you're the best friend I ever had.*

I was full-out crying now, and feeling stupid for it. Chip's words were achingly sweet, and I was flattered and gratified and even pleased all at once, against the loneliness and rejection and fear filling me up about Ben.

I wanted to reply so badly. Just to acknowledge him. Just because I knew firsthand what it felt like to live in the void of nonanswers that gnawed at your insides and broke down your self-confidence and equanimity and contentment.

It might be opening Pandora's box. But I couldn't let someone else feel the way I was so miserable feeling right now. I thumbed just a few words and hit send:

Thank you, Chip. That means a lot.

I powered the phone down before I could second-guess what I'd done.

Chapter Twenty-one

"Oh, Brook, do you really have to eat so much shrimp?"

My mother frowned at me over her menu as the server took our order at Tradewinds, a once-upscale restaurant near Bonita Beach that was working as hard as an aging Botoxed debutante to mask its slow decline.

I manufactured a smile. "I love shrimp, Mom. You know that."

She sighed. "You have since you were a little girl. You know they're linked to high cholesterol."

"Mom, I'm thirty-two. I think I'm good for now."

"For *now*." She looked up at the server. "I'll have the Nicoise salad, please. No egg," she added, looking pointedly at me.

I bit my tongue for about the twelfth time so far—and we'd barely been here ten minutes.

It probably wasn't the best day to face my mom head-on. I woke this morning and turned my phone on with my breath held, wondering how many texts from Chip would have piled up after my ill-advised response—only to find none. Nor had Ben texted, or left a voice mail.

I buzzed like a live wire all day long as I met with clients, working much harder than usual to stay focused on their issues, rather than masticating my own. At three I came out into the waiting room to greet a new client and found two unfamiliar people there. "I'm so sorry," I said, confused. "I don't do couples therapy." Only for them to shoot strange looks at each other and then at me. "Um...I don't know him," the woman said uncertainly. Turned out I'd double-booked two new clients—and I didn't even remember ever speaking to the man. Probably blushing purple with mortification, I shepherded the woman—Minnie McDermot—into my office, while I pushed out a smile and an apology to the man, and rebooked him—still without knowing his name and too ashamed to ask. Hopefully I'd find it in my records somewhere.

By the time six o'clock rolled around and I'd seen my last client for the day, I felt like a wrung-out sponge. I'd driven to meet Mom on my usual favorite route—Estero Boulevard along the gulf shore—but even the sprawling vistas of sand and bay and ocean failed to pull me out of the funk I'd slipped into.

But I'd made plans with my mom. There was no way I could call them off.

We sat on a deck that overlooked a bayou-type inlet of cypress and mangrove, a trickle of tidal stream giving the place minimal waterfront cred. There was something different about my mother. She wore a pair of loose, flowing palazzo-type pants that were elegant on her, a simple short-sleeved gray cotton top hugging curves I had no idea she had. Her hair was different too—not the careful waves I was used to, but loose curls that framed her face, making her look young and...playful. A word I would never associate with my mom.

"You look awesome, Mom," I said after the server left. I didn't mean for my tone to sound so surprised.

She glanced up at me with a hesitant expression, almost cautious. Then her usual closed-lipped smile. "Thank you." She unfolded her frayed cloth napkin, smoothed it over her lap, then leaned back, hands clasped. "Okay, Brook Lyn. What's this all about?"

I let out a sigh. "Ma, seriously. I just wanted to see you. To have dinner. No agenda, okay?"

The skin between Mom's eyebrows wrinkled as her stare on me intensified, as if she were trying to X-ray my head. "Oh," she finally said. "All right. Well. How are you?"

"I'm fine. How about you?"

"Fine."

The only sound after that was the clink of the ice in my glass as I raised it to my lips for something to do.

"And how are rehearsals?" I plopped into the silence.

That yielded another small smile. "Good. I forgot how much I love being backstage. The theater is always magical, but from the other side of the footlights…it's something else."

"Maybe you could give me a tour after I see the show one night?" I asked offhandedly, and Mom's teeth peeked out between her lips.

"Would you like that? I'd love to."

"Sure. It'd be interesting."

Mom nodded, and sipped her own drink. "So…" she said after a moment, "how's everything with your practice?"

"Good." Usually that was where I'd leave things. It was easier to exchange platitudes with my mom than try to go any deeper—at least with civilities we were less likely to grate on each other and start a fight.

But I was trying for more with her, I reminded myself. Time to put a toe in the water.

"I'm really busy with clients, so that's good. And the group sessions are going pretty well. I think I'm helping a lot of people."

"That's wonderful, Brook Lyn. You always wanted to help. Do you remember 'rescuing' the frog in our backyard when you were younger—around seven or so? You were convinced he was sick and wanted to nurse him back to health."

A grin tugged at my lips. "I did? That's funny." She rarely reminisced with me about my childhood, and I reveled in the moment.

"'He has a fever, Mommy,' you told me when I came to check on you. And you'd rubber-banded an ice cube to the poor creature's back. I don't know if he froze to death or was squeezed to death." Her laughter floated out over the mangrove swamp.

I gritted my teeth. "Really, Mom? That's the story you remember about me liking to help? That I killed something?"

The smile vanished from her face as if I'd kicked her. "Oh, please, Brook Lyn. It was cute. You didn't know any better."

This was going nowhere good. I decided to try another tack, but nothing came to mind that wouldn't be a minefield. With Adelaide—a woman I barely knew—conversation flowed like it was spring-fed. How was it that I couldn't think of a single topic of discussion with the woman I had known my entire life?

Movement from the corner of my eye pulled my focus to our server, bearing a large oval tray with our dinner on it, and I was grateful for something to fill the silence. After setting down our meals and making sure we needed nothing else, she vanished, and I looked back at my mom, who was busy slicing her green beans in halves.

Something about that careful, meticulous gesture tugged on my sympathies, and I took a deep breath. I was trying to break down barriers between us.

"So...how's the cast of the show?"

Mom's eyes flicked up to me, shadowing with disapproval as she saw me pick up a shrimp and bite into it, tearing the flesh out of what remained of its tail. She pointedly looked at my silverware. "You're coming to the opening, aren't you? You'll see them for yourself?"

Reluctantly I picked up my fork. Who the hell ate tail-on shrimp with a fork? "Of course I will," I gritted out with a forced smile. "I just meant, you know...personally. Do you like them? Do you guys hang out together when you aren't rehearsing? Are any of them, like...I don't know...friends?" I couldn't picture my mother yukking it up with a bunch of theater types, but clearly there was a lot I had never known about her.

She nodded cautiously, as though guarding her confessions to an interrogator. "Yes, I like them, for the most part. Yes, we do get dinner together most nights, or meet between rehearsals to run lines. Yes, I guess you could say I've become quite friendly with some of them."

It was a factual and complete answer to my questions, but it didn't really tell me much.

"Ma, how come you never talk to me?" I blurted out before I could think better of it.

Her eyebrows arrowed toward each other. "What are you talking about? What are we doing right now?"

I held out my arms, palms up. "Well, I don't know about you, but I'm desperately searching for a way to get an actual conversation going between us, and judging from your closed-ended answers, you're looking for ways to get me to shut up."

Mom let out a long-suffering sigh, laid her fork down, and stared at her plate as if the tuna might advise her how to deal with her vexing daughter. "What is this really about, Brook Lyn? Did I do something? Tell me what it is."

I clattered my own fork back to the table and pushed back with my palms on the edge. "That's not what I— I just meant—"

"Please keep your voice down and don't make a scene."

"That! *That's* what I'm talking about! You're apparently big buds with your theater people, and you'll talk to Sasha all day long, but with me and Stu all you ever do is criticize and worry and give advice we didn't ask for. Why can't we just *talk*?"

"You're my children." She sounded surprised. "It's my job to worry. To help you make the right choices. Not to make the mistakes I made with my life."

"Mistakes?" I knew my eyes must be wide as eggs. "What do you mean, like *us*—your family?"

"Don't be ridiculous."

"Well, then what did you mean, Mom?" Maybe it wasn't such a great idea to try to change our relationship from its usual cordial civility. This was spiraling fast to a place I'd had no inkling of going. But now that she'd said it, I couldn't let it go. "Do you wish you hadn't had us? Hadn't married Dad? Is that what all this theater stuff is about—you're doing what you really wanted to do with your life finally, now that we're out of the way?" The bitterness in my tone startled me, and I realized my accusation was punching out from somewhere deeply buried.

Mom closed her eyes and shook her head, then looked at me again. "Brook Lyn. Do you want me to tell you that everything in my life happened just the way it was meant to? That I wouldn't change a thing?"

Well, *yes*, actually. That would be nice.

"I can't tell you that," she went on, not waiting for my answer. "I didn't expect to meet your father when I did. And I certainly didn't plan to be pregnant immediately after that. It all happened very quickly, and it just simply was the way things *were* before we had a chance to think about whether it was what we would have planned. It was the situation at hand. I don't know if I'd do things the same way, and I don't believe things are meant to happen. I know this is the way they did happen. And this is the path I'm on, so I embrace it."

I tried to keep the pain her words caused me off my face, but judging from the way her face tightened, I didn't succeed.

She reached across the table for my hand, and I let her, but made no effort to grip her fingers back. "But I can tell you that you kids—and your father—are the best part of my life," she said intently. "I couldn't be prouder of my family. You're all good people. Hard workers. You love each other. You're not on drugs."

Eh, I'd take it.

The tightness in my abdomen loosened ever so slightly, and I swallowed back the lump that threatened to choke me. "But is this what you wanted, Mom? Are you happy?" We'd touched on a raw nerve I hadn't even known was there, and my voice was small, blown away in the breeze off the gulf.

"Brook Lyn." Mom squeezed my hand slightly and then let go, pulling hers back and reaching for her fork. "Happiness is a choice."

...

I thought about my mother's words the whole drive home—straight up 41 this time. I would have been blind to the gulf route anyway with my mind churning the way it was.

Every kid wants to hear her parents say she's the best thing in their lives—and to my surprise, my mom had. Sure, it was amid a handful of caveats and disclaimers that were more like what I expected from my not-exactly-warm-and-fuzzy mom, but if I heard her answer as an adult, as a therapist, instead of as her daughter, I had to admire it.

Happiness is a choice.

I knew from the article Sasha wrote about my mom in the spring that my mother been accepted to Juilliard on a partial acting scholarship when she was younger—the first I'd ever heard of it. I'd known she was good after the first time I saw her act in *Lion in Winter*—but I didn't know she was *that* good.

She had to turn it down, though, because her own parents wouldn't pony up the rest of the tuition, and Mom couldn't afford New York and the pricey school without it. She never got to chase her dream. Instead she had us—again not part of her plan, and yet, despite how much Mom often grated on me, she'd been an amazing mother. She was the one who brought us all together—still—every week for a family dinner. She'd created all of our holiday traditions. It was even Mom who'd initially welcomed Sasha into our family, calling Sasha's parents directly the first time my sad, withdrawn seven-year-old best friend asked if she could stay at our house so she didn't have to go home to their fighting, and making it sound as if they would be doing her an enormous favor if they would entrust their little girl with our family for the weekend so that her own daughter had someone to play with.

I don't remember a time Mom wasn't there when I skinned a knee or fell off my bike or came home crying from some slight from my friends at school—not to wrap her arms around me and comfort me, as I might have wished for, but to pick me up, set me back on my feet, and remind me I was stronger than whatever had knocked me down.

When my father cheated on her while she had two small children at home—a fact he'd confessed to me once in the blackest of my despair over Kendall, and then had never spoken of again, and which Mom had no idea I knew—she'd stood strong then too, somehow working through it with my dad, learning to forgive him, and even loving him wholeheartedly again all through our childhood without any trace of the resentment or anger or rage I know she must have once felt.

She wasn't the kind of squishy-soft mommy I'd always wanted. But maybe she was the one I needed. One who faced challenges head-on and didn't let them mow her down. One who took whatever life handed her and made something out of it that she then decided was exactly what she wanted, and chose to be happy.

The one who'd raised me to be just like her.

I wasn't a victim, the way I'd been acting this past week. I was strong like my mom, and whatever was happening between me and Ben, I could face it. And I could handle it.

And I wasn't the same person I'd been even just a few months ago—when I'd confused strength with hardness, with a cold, rational façade that precluded the genuine strength of vulnerability and openness and the courage to show your feelings. Strength wasn't feeling no fear, as the old saw went. It was feeling the fear and doing it anyway—that thing that was making you afraid.

It was choosing to be happy. No matter the outcome.

I picked up my phone at a red light and dialed Ben.

Chapter Twenty-two

I didn't want to talk things out over the phone, so I kept it short and light, as though nothing had changed between us—we talked about our days, I asked about Jake, and before we hung up I made sure to mention Saturday, our customary date night.

"There's a new Indian restaurant that opened up downtown—Saffron," I said casually. "Feel like checking that out this weekend?"

There was a moment's hesitation, but I didn't let myself freak out about it. Luckily, since it was followed by, "Sure, that sounds good. Meet me there at six thirty?"

I also didn't let myself freak out about his wanting to meet there, instead of picking me up as usual. Maybe he had something going on beforehand, or would already be downtown, or...it could be anything. Harmless.

I agreed and we said good night and hung up.

Things were clearly not the way they always were—there was a tension between us we never had. But Saturday night we'd talk things out, and I'd face it head-on instead of running.

…

The next morning I called Sasha before my first client to tell her about the call with Ben.

"So he said he wanted to *meet* you for your date, and you aren't worried? *Really?*"

"Well, I *wasn't*. Geez, Sash!"

"Sorry. I just...Oh, wait, are you doing that thing where you shut down and act like you don't care?"

I sighed. "No. I'm not going to do that anymore. I'm doing that thing where I try to be a grown-up and not get panicky. Something weird happened that night, and I'm just going to ask him about it. I'm going to tell him how I feel."

"Wow. That's kind of...huge."

"You think it's too much? I shouldn't say anything?" I heard the doubt creep into my tone.

"No, no—I think it's really great, Brookie. I just mean it's huge for *you*. I know you must really like him, and you've gotten so brave about letting yourself be open to your feelings, and...I'm so happy that you..."

"Oh, for god's sake, Sasha. Are you crying?"

"No." She sniffled.

"You're an idiot."

"I'm really proud of you, Brook."

"Okay, Tammy Faye, we'll talk when you've collected yourself," I said dryly.

But as we hung up, I felt a little glow of pride in myself.

...

"I'm Sheila. Amherst."

Sheila held the claw dangling down beside her chair between the tips of two fingers, as though it might burn her. She'd been the first to pick it up when we all settled into our chairs that Saturday morning, surprising me as much as it apparently did everyone else in the group. Except Dina Jones, who leaned back in her chair, arms crossed in her usual position, assessing Sheila as if she were a calculus problem she was working to puzzle out.

"So...um, my fella...Tom...he broke up with me a couple of months ago." Sheila wasn't looking at anyone in the group while she shared this; she kept her eyes trained on the ground, and spoke so softly that I had to make sure the sound of my breathing didn't drown out her words. "Right after I signed up for this group he came back, so I was going to cancel...but I didn't, because...well, I'm worried he might not stay."

I frowned at her terminology. Sheila seemed absent in her summation—a passive recipient of whatever Tom decided to offer her. But I tried to reserve judgment until I heard the rest of her story.

"So I'm here. I guess that's all." She made a quick flick of her wrist that swung the claw forward, and she let it drop to the center of the circle.

Antonio leaned forward to pick it up—he shared nearly every meeting—but I held up a hand to stay him. "Hold on, Antonio. Sheila, let's talk this out a little. You say Tom came back—you mean you two are back together?"

She nodded.

"And are you talking about what happened with your breakup—or have you?"

Sheila lifted a shoulder. "Tom doesn't like to talk about stuff like that. He says that's for women and fa— um, gay people, he means."

"What?!" Dina barked across the circle. But when I looked over at her she had already piped down. She caught my eye, holding up her hands to show she was finished, but shooting a dark scowl over to Sheila, who fortunately was still staring at the ground. I was afraid the fierceness of it might have made the skittish girl implode on the spot if she'd caught Dina's eye.

"Okay," I said, keeping my tone neutral. "You said you're worried he might not stay. What makes you think that?"

Another half shrug. "I don't know. Sometimes things are really great." A soft smile came over her features, which she promptly hid by tipping her head forward, sending a cascade of hair over her face. "I keep trying to make sure they stay that way, but I always manage to say or do the wrong thing. I know his last girlfriend really hurt him, and so I try to be nothing like her, but sometimes I think that's the exact wrong thing to do."

"What do you mean?"

"Well, she was pretty close to perfect. She's smart and successful—she owns her own boutique—and she's confident and really outgoing. She loves to travel—I'm afraid to fly—and she's beautiful and has style, of course, with her job. And I, um"—she indicated her own outfit, a bland beige oversize T-shirt and washed-out jeans—"don't."

"Do you know her?" I asked, confused at Sheila's detailed description.

Sheila shook her head. "No, just from stuff Tom tells me. He doesn't mean to—it just pops out when we have a fight."

There were restive rustling sounds from the group, as if they had to channel their unvoiced reactions into movement.

I could relate; pity flooded my heart. This poor girl was apparently treated to a litany of how wonderful the woman before her was—the woman Sheila was *not*—and made to feel inadequate over it. Judging from her self-effacing demeanor, she clearly suffered from a poor self-image anyway. It sounded like this guy was playing right into her vulnerabilities, using them to control her, to make her feel worse about herself, to raise his own self-esteem by plunging hers to rock-bottom.

"Sheila," I said gently, "it seems like Tom might be comparing you to someone else a lot. Maybe he's not really appreciating who *you* are."

"Oh, no!" Sheila looked up at me with pleading eyes. "I think she—Desiree is her name—I think Desiree just really messed him up, made him feel bad about himself, so sometimes he can't help doing that to someone else. To me, I mean. He doesn't mean it. I just...I guess I hoped maybe you could help me figure out how to help him past it."

My frown drew down further. "Does Tom want that too—is he trying just as hard?" I was afraid I could guess the answer.

Sheila's gaze darted up to me, and then shot right back down. "I think he is. If he says something a little...you know, unkind, and hurts my feelings, he's so sorry about it—he's so sweet and sorry and tries so hard to make it up to me. He says I'm just what he needs—the exact opposite of Desiree."

I heard a muffled cry of outrage from Dina again. I couldn't even chastise her—sympathetic pain knifed through me as well at Sheila's words. This guy—Tom—had set up his previous girlfriend as a paragon, an ideal he made sure Sheila could never reach, and then compounded it by telling her she was nothing at all like this perfect (and I suspected greatly embellished) version of a girlfriend. With a woman like Sheila—low self-esteem, eager to please—it made her strive ever harder to be what he wanted. He was manipulating her by preying on her weaknesses, and she was so caught up in thinking she could "fix" him, she couldn't even see it.

It was unbelievably common, especially with women, but it didn't make me any less sad—or angry—every time I saw it.

"Sheila..." I had to tread carefully. She was clearly still in defensive mode where Tom was concerned, and heaping blame for their difficulties on no shoulders but her own. "Sometimes people try to make others feel worse about themselves because it makes them feel better—more powerful. It's especially egregious when they press on those areas where someone might already be insecure or vulnerable. It can make that person a little bit blind to the fact that maybe their relationship isn't as healthy as it could be."

To my surprise, Sheila seemed to agree wholeheartedly, her head bobbing up and down like a Pez dispenser. "Yes! That's it exactly—that's what Desiree did to Tom, always cutting him down and making him feel like he wasn't good enough. That's what I want to help him with!"

She looked so uncustomarily hopeful, her expression so relieved and validated, I knew I had to leave it alone for now. Sheila wasn't ready to see what was really going on in her relationship, and pushing her to was only going to make her defensive and close her off to further exploration of it. Good therapy didn't always mean forcing someone to examine their life—sometimes you had to back off and let them live it for themselves, even if you could see they were making a huge mistake.

Some people had to scrape bottom before they were ready to admit they were drowning and reach up a hand.

Chapter Twenty-three

I got ready for my date with Ben that night with Sasha-like levels of personal grooming. Which entailed:

- ✓ Shaving my legs—obviously. And as long as I was down there with a razor...I thought I might do something a little creative.

- ✓ Waiting for bleeding in un-Band-Aidable area to taper off.

- ✓ Trying to cover strange bald patch with creative womanscaping, resulting in what looked to be the letter B. Which, while I was committed to making my feelings known tonight, might be a level or three past what I wanted to convey to Ben about them.

- ✓ Stepping away from Lady Town before further damage could be done. I'd make sure the lights were dim this evening, and (sadly) that Ben didn't get too much face time down there.

- ✓ Curling hair, something I was not accustomed to or adept at doing, resulting less in my usual frizzy waves but more...I wasn't sure what. A little bit 1940s pinup girl, a little bit Lenny Kravitz.

- ✓ I opted for a dress between sexy and classy—a formfitting sheath that hugged every curve—until I realized that some of those curves weren't the good ones and would require Spanx. And having Ben remove me from a sausage casing seemed like the least sexy choice for later on. So I discarded that option and, after trying on every single dress in my closet, went with simple: yellow-and-white cotton sundress à la Donna Reed, but with a fitted bust and a slightly shorter length that hopefully suggested a somewhat dirty Donna Reed.

- ✓ Heels. Duh. Strappy and purple and high.

✓ I even tried a smoky eye, which I thought was pretty hot, and then added a bold pink lipstick (because Sasha told me once that bright lipstick mimics the way nature makes lips flush in sexual arousal, and subliminally turns guys on), but the effect was a bit early Eddie Izzard, so I scrubbed it all and started over, going with a simple subtle gold wash on my eyes and a medium-toned coral gloss. It may not have sent primal evolutionary mating signals, but I thought I looked pretty.

And then I waited. Because in my ignorance of how long this type of primping took, I had allotted myself two and a half hours before I had to leave to meet Ben, and it turned out it took about half that.

As I sat on the bed, contemplating breathing into a paper bag to calm my too-fast heartbeat, I tried to figure out what had me so nervous. I needed to therapize myself.

Why was I so scared?

I'd tried rehearsing what I wanted to talk to Ben about—to be honest, I sat down to make a list, intending to commit it to memory so I didn't get tongue-tied and bungle it.

But the truth was, I had no idea what I was going to say.

Last weekend everything had been fine—easy and comfortable and straightforward. Now Ben and I hadn't talked all week. Last week I'd practically had custody of his dog, and felt like his mom and I were creating a unique sort of friendship. This week I hadn't seen or spoken to either one.

Last Saturday Ben had told me he loved me, or something like it—maybe—and I'd said...nothing.

That was just about the worst response I could have given, if he really did say it. "I love you too" is the holy grail of responses. On the other end of the spectrum, "I'm so sorry, but I don't feel the same way" is agony, but at least it's closure. No response was just...indifference. And that was not how I felt.

But did he say it?

And did I love him?

Those were the two unknowns.

...

When I walked into Saffron, where Ben was standing at the front waiting for me, I saw him visibly suck in a breath at my appearance.

Score.

The snaking tension in my belly started to uncoil. It was so good to see him—it felt like weeks instead of the usual five or six days, and my heart thumped into my ribs as I took him in. Brown hair that seemed longer, with a slight curl, carelessly falling over his forehead. Dark hazel eyes that smiled when he smiled—which he was, and that lit me up too. I didn't realize until then my fear that I might never see him smile at me like this again. He reached out one hand and I stepped into the circle of his arm as he pulled me toward him and gave me a light—but stomach-tumbling—kiss on the mouth.

"You look beautiful," he murmured.

"So do you," I whispered idiotically, pressing my palm to his cheek and trying to stop grinning like a fool.

The hostess whisked us off to our seats, and while we talked in the same easy way we always had, we had wine and ordered plates of food that we shared bites of, and I think it must have been delicious, but I didn't taste any of it because I was too happy simply to be here, with everything—blessedly—okay.

After dinner I suggested a walk down to the water, and we strolled along the lighted sidewalks alongside the marina, watching the boats bob in the moon-bleached river, hearing the creaks and *zzzzppp* of their lines pulling and the sibilant splashes of water on their hulls and the dock pilings and the seawall, smelling the earthy, musky, alive scent of the Caloosahatchee—and even then the thing that registered strongest of all was Ben's warm hand clasped around mine.

There were others with the same idea we'd had, strolling in both directions, and we greeted passersby with nods and smiles, pieces of their conversations trailing behind them as they walked past. But we kept walking to where fewer people had wandered, only the occasional figure lit up in the regular puddles of yellow light from the lamps dotting the walkway.

In the darkness I felt the rest of my tension leave me and float out over the river with the slight breeze that stirred my hair and Ben's. Our conversation quieted comfortably, and after a while of the only sound the waves' gentle teasing and our steps on the concrete, I pulled him over to a bench and we sat side by side, looking out over the trail of moonlight dancing over the water's surface.

I took a breath, and then another, but I was much less nervous than I thought I'd be, now that the moment for talking was here.

"Can we talk about last weekend?" I asked into the night noises.

I saw his surprise in the lift of his eyebrows as his head turned to me. He nodded. "Okay."

One more breath, and then I faced the lions head-on: "That night in bed...when I said that Jake was easy to love, I thought I heard you say, 'So are you.'" I was sure he could hear my heartbeat through the fabric of my dress. I'd either finally know where things stood, or I'd made a complete fool of myself.

"I did say that," he said.

His quiet words shot straight through to my belly. "Okay." I nodded. "So...I didn't know that. I was so tired that night anyway, and then I wasn't expecting you to...I wasn't sure. So I sat there trying to figure out if I'd really heard it, and then pondering what it meant if I had, and figuring out how I felt about it, and then I realized a lot of time had passed and it was too late to say anything. So I didn't." My last words came out in a tone of remorse.

Ben was looking intently at me, but a slight smile lifted one side of his mouth. "Wow. Is all that analysis from being a mental health professional, or just a woman?" he teased.

"Both. It's exhausting."

He chuckled, but didn't offer anything else, so I went on.

"Since then I can't stop thinking about it. And things got a little weird with us. And...I thought maybe it was because you said something...important, and I ignored it. But I don't want things to be weird, Ben. I didn't want some stupid misunderstanding from my being tired and neurotic and overanalyzing to change things between us." I reached over and took his hand, and he clasped mine. "Dating you is the best relationship I've had in a long time. I'm happy. I'm calm—meaning I don't have to sit and analyze every little thing about us to decide whether you really like me—this week aside, of course." I gave a half laugh. "You make it clear every second. I always know where I stand with you. I have fun with you. I love your company. I can't wait to see you every weekend. I even like your mom and your dog so much."

Ben let go of our clasped hands. And then he put both his palms alongside my face, and he leaned in for a soft, long kiss.

He pulled away just far enough so he could look into my eyes, but his breath still brushed my face. "What I was trying to say that night, Brook, was that I think I'm falling in love with you."

I felt something explode inside me—like a supernova, filling me up with a burst of warmth and joy so strong I thought it had to shoot out of my chest.

"Me too," I whispered.

Sometimes you can analyze your feelings and the meaning of love until your brain cramps with the effort, but if you shut up all the logical, rational voices trying to carefully decide what it all means, the heart tells you in the simplest, clearest way imaginable.

Ben slid his warm hands across my shoulders, down my arms, and took my hands again. "I actually thought you might have not been ready for that," he admitted into the purple night. "I figured saying nothing was your kind way of not having to say you didn't feel that way about me."

"Is that why this week has been so weird?" I asked. "Why you didn't leave Jake with me? Why we met here?"

Ben squeezed my fingers and looked out over the dark Caloosahatchee. "You told me once about your romantic history, Brook. But I never really told you about mine."

My eyebrows drew together. "Yes, you did." He'd been married when he was young—just twenty-three, to his college girlfriend—and divorced two years later. In the decade since, he'd had girlfriends, but nothing serious. When I met him he'd lived alone for ten years.

He shook his head. "Not all of it. I just...It's in the past, and I didn't think it mattered. But I guess nothing's ever really in the past; you carry a lot of it with you, especially in relationships." He smiled at me. "I read that in a really smart therapist's column this week." The corners of my lips turned up. "Anyway, Michelle and I didn't just get a divorce—we imploded. She started talking about how weird marriage was, committing to spend your whole life with one person when it went against human nature—and this was *after* we'd been married for a year. She said love was meant to be open and inclusive, not cut off and closed down. And still, I thought we were just working through a tough patch, because we were young." He looked down at our joined hands, and my heart ached for him. If I'd been his therapist at the time, I'd have told him he was in dangerous waters.

"She was cheating—of course," he said after a long silence. "And I was blind to it—of course. Or willfully blind, I guess—how could I not have seen what was going on? She was busy all the time with work and social activities that apparently didn't include me. She stopped saying she loved me, stopped answering when I said it to her." He moved his gaze away from mine to look out over the water. "She got late-night calls she never explained," he added quietly.

A sick feeling crept into my belly as I flashed back to my middle-of-the-night conversation with Chip. "I'm sorry, Ben," I said softly. "I'm so sorry. The other night must have felt..."

He nodded. "Just like that. I freaked out, I guess. I know you aren't Michelle. But at the time it was knee-jerk, almost primal—something just kept telling me to hunker down, protect. So I got out of there and I kind of...retreated. I'm sorry."

It was so much like me, I almost wanted to laugh. I was the queen of cut-and-run the second I saw the first rustlings of unrest. I couldn't believe that Ben—steady, confident, openhearted Ben—was the same way. But old scars couldn't always cover up the deepest wounds. I knew that as well as Ben obviously did.

"You can't imagine how much I understand that."

He gave a rueful smile. "I guess I just wanted to get out before you had to figure out how to let me down easily."

"I don't want to let you down easily," I said, grinning happily. "I don't want to let you down at all. In fact, that night I was letting *him* down."

I'd meant the words to underline my commitment to Ben, to us, but I could tell from the way his expression changed that I had said too much.

"I thought you said it was a client?" His tone was still relaxed, but sudden tension stiffened his shoulders.

"Oh, it *was* a client. Or a former client. I didn't want to take him back on in formal therapy because we'd had a history with each other. I mean not like dating!" I rushed to explain. "It was just this one stupid night that we..." Ben's face closed up tight as hurricane shutters. *Dear god, Brook, stop digging and put the shovel down.* But my tongue apparently wasn't connected to my brain tonight. "Anyway, I'd wanted to help him work through some things, but in the course of that it turned out he had these...feelings for me. And yes, he'd told me a few days before that he...he wanted more. But that night I told him no. Because of you. Because of *us*."

He'd turned away from me, staring at the boats bobbing on the river in gentle fluid motions completely at odds with the furious churning in my stomach. He nodded, lines bracketing his mouth. "Why did you have to think about it?"

I released a long breath. "After we hung up I felt bad because he's...well, he's a nice guy, it turns out. And I hurt his feelings, and so I...I sat out in the living room for a while just sort of working that out in my head. I should have explained when I came back to bed—I know it must have looked—"

"No, he said tightly. "I mean before. You said he'd told you a few days earlier about his...his feelings for you. Why did you have to think about it before you told him no?"

My mouth hung open like a hinge had snapped.

A slow chill crept over Ben's expression. I recognized the decent of an icy shield like an old familiar childhood blanket.

"Because...Because I..." Why *hadn't* I told him no right away, that day in the coffee shop? *Why* did I have to think it over?

I had no good answer.

"I've been single a long time, Brook," Ben said in the face of my mute confusion. "I'm not a kid anymore. I know what love is and isn't now. I know what's healthy and what's not. I know what I want."

"I...yes," I said past a dry throat. "Me too."

"Do you?" he asked, and there was no accusation in his quiet tone, only the question. "If you knew about us—if you were sure—would you have had to think about it? Would you have taken that phone call in the middle of the night, and been upset enough about what happened that you couldn't come get back into bed next to me because you were still thinking about someone else?"

I shook my head, willing away the tears that threatened to spill out of my eyes. "I...I wasn't thinking about him like *that*."

Finally he turned to face me, but without the anger or pain I expected—only a shadow of sadness. "Are you sure that you really want something more between us?"

The words lurked just inside my mouth, waiting only for me to give them voice so that the rest of the evening could go as I'd scripted it as I'd gotten ready for our date, what felt like days ago now: Ben in my bed, in my life, our relationship back to the way it was. *Yes, I want more with you. Yes, I'm sure. Yes. Yes. Yes.*

Such an easy word—all soft consonants and a single vowel sound. If I just moved my tongue the slightest bit and pushed out air, it would almost come out without much effort at all.

But *yes* felt like facing the foot of a mountain I wasn't equipped to climb.

And tears shot to my eyes in a surge of heat and wetness, because I was pretty sure that I loved Ben.

And I knew that it wasn't enough.

"This"—I squeezed his loose fingers hard, then let go to grasp his face in my hands—"is exactly what I want. *You* are exactly what I want." I let my hands fall and come to rest in my lap. "But that's all I know right now."

He was looking at the concrete sidewalk, and when he finally lifted his gaze it wasn't to meet mine. Instead he stared out over the water. The trail of white moonlight stabbing across it now looked cold where it had seemed romantic only moments before.

I tried to explain—to both of us. "I think I might want other things—*more* type of things—with you one day. But right now I'm building my business. And that takes so much of my time and energy. And I'm not long out of my last relationship—which as you know turned out to be a complete train wreck—and I don't even know if I've managed to deal with the one before *that* yet. And I need to." Ben still sat close beside me, but I felt as if he were drawing farther and farther away. "I like what we have," I rushed on. "Just the way it is. I mean, not *just* the way. I want to move forward, but slowly." I was losing Ben—I knew it—and I had to say something, anything, to stop it.

I knew even before he spoke that they hadn't been the right things.

"You aren't ready for a serious relationship." It wasn't a question.

A welter of mitigations leaped to my mind, clamoring for a bargain against losing this man. *It depends on your definition of serious. Not just at this moment, but not too long. I don't want to lose you.*

I love you.

But the one I let come out was the only one that mattered. "No."

The syllable physically hurt as it tore out of my mouth.

But not as badly as when Ben stood up, hands in his pockets, turned to me without meeting my eyes, and said quietly, "I guess that's it, then. Come on. I'll walk you back to your car."

Chapter Twenty-four

My drive home felt slightly unreal. McGregor was quiet, my open windows letting in only the sounds of crickets and my own tires on the road, moonlight strobing my car in between the passing royal palms lining the street, broken by an occasional headlight coming the opposite direction.

I held my hands at ten and two on the wheel, strangely calm. It wasn't until I pulled into my own garage that the thought struck me.

We just broke up.

I sat in my car, engine off, for a long time after the garage door shut and the overhead light timed off, still gripping the wheel hard.

How did a night that included that tender kiss by the river, the certainty—finally—about my feelings for Ben, the giddy high of knowing he returned them, end up like this?

Because of my own stupid actions. The clinging residue of my past relationships contaminating this one. The mental health professional who couldn't even manage her own personal baggage.

I dragged myself out of the car finally, feeling as if my body weighed three hundred pounds. Plodded inside and dropped my purse on the back hall table, not even slowing as I headed straight into my bedroom and sank onto the side of my bed.

Which was when the tears finally came. And for a change, I let them.

I don't know how much time passed that way—long enough for me to wind up lying on my side on the bed, still fully clothed, my face tight with dried salt and my stomach cramped from sobs. But when it finally tapered off I pushed myself back up and stood, walking back out to retrieve my phone.

This time I wasn't going to put up a brave front, hold it all in, pretend I was fine. I wasn't fine, and I wanted to talk to Sasha. It was past midnight on a Saturday night, my phone reminded me as I stared at the screen to pull up her number, but that had never mattered to the two of us.

Hey, I texted. *You awake?*

There was a long pause, and I thought she might have been asleep. And then finally: *Yes. What's up?*

Ben and I broke up.

My phone rang so fast, I didn't even know if she'd had time to read the whole message.

"*What?*" she screeched when I answered. I could hear pounding music in the background, a cacophony of voices.

"Geez. Where are you?"

"Not important. Are you okay?"

"I don't know. No. I think I screwed up, Sash."

"What?"

"I screwed up!" I shouted over the noise.

"Hang on," she said. I heard her make a comment to someone near her, and then thought I heard my brother's voice say something back. Then there was a lot of rustling, and after a few moments a loud bang and the noise finally receded somewhat, now just a thudding bass line.

"Where are you?" I asked again.

"What happened?"

"I have no idea. One second we were having the best time, and we talked, and he said he thought he was falling in love with me. And I said me too, Sash."

"Holy shit."

"Everything was fine, and then...and then I started telling him about Chip—"

"You *what*!?"

"I mean not like out of the blue—he asked about Chip's call that night, and I started talking, and it came out really badly, and he just...he left."

There was a pause, and I knew she was considering what I'd said. "Tell me the details. What did you guys say, exactly? I need word-for-word."

The music blared again, and then I heard the bang and it quieted.

"Everything okay, babe?" It was Stu.

"Fine," Sasha said away from the phone. "It's Brook."

"Hey, sis!" he called. "You coming back in, Sash? It's weird being in there without you."

"Can you give me just a few minutes?"

"No—Sash, it's okay," I said, but Stu was talking over me.

"Okay, but I'm not going farther than the door. I've had more fingers all over me than a piano." The music blared again, then the metallic slam.

A memory tickled at my mind at the distinctive sound, and I replayed Stu's words.

"Sash," I said in disbelief, "are you at Sticks and Stones?"

"Okay, replay the whole conversation for me," she said, ignoring my question.

"Sasha...answer me."

A long silence, and then, "You said you didn't want to know this kind of stuff about me and your brother."

"Oh, my god. Is this all you two ever think about?"

Sasha sighed. "Brook, we have a lot of years of unexpressed sexual tension between us to work out. But trust me, we're not just about sex—there's lots of talking and emotional shit too."

"I'm going to hang up," I said. "We can talk about it tomorrow."

"No, no—Stu's fine. Tell me what happened. Are you okay? Do you want me to come over?"

"You're on a...date." A rather loose use of the word.

"Chicks before dicks," Sasha said unhesitatingly.

"Ew—please don't talk about my brother's genitals." But I didn't want to ruin their night out. And I couldn't open up this particular Pandora's box while Stu waited, alone and defenseless, in an S and M bar I knew firsthand was a maul session. "I'm okay, really," I assured her. "I'm probably better off just getting some sleep so I can think more clearly tomorrow. I'll call you in the morning and we can talk it out, okay?"

It took about five more reassurances, but after Sasha made me promise to call as soon as I woke up, I finally convinced her to go rescue Stu because I was going to sleep anyway.

But sleep didn't come.

The middle of the night is the worst time after a breakup. It's when most of the bad stuff happens—in the dark, lonely stillness, rationality recedes. It's when the ache of your solitude is most acute, because the world is sleeping, and you are left alone with the pain of what you've lost, the grief, and the darkness that seems it will never retreat.

Except...I knew one person who was always awake at this hour.

I didn't even try to talk myself out of dialing Chip Santana's number.

The line rang four times before I finally heard his voice.

"Doc?" He sounded disbelieving, and that was when I finally questioned what I was doing. Wasn't Chip the whole reason I was in this situation?

In the background I heard noise—loud voices, the thudding of bass under tinny music. He was out—maybe on a date himself—and I'd been a fool to make this call. An overpowering impulse to simply hang up swept over me, but this wasn't the old days of landlines that hid your stupid decisions from a caller if only you didn't speak to identify yourself. Whether I said anything or not, Chip would know I'd called.

"Brook?" he asked again, and I realized how long a silence I'd let fall.

"Chip," I said, and cleared my throat of its roughness. "I'm sorry— I think I butt-dialed you. My mistake—good night."

"Brook, wait!" he blurted. "Don't hang up, okay?"

"Okay," I answered meekly.

The phone went dead silent for a moment, and I thought we'd lost the connection after all. But a moment later the background noises returned, distant now, and I realized he must have muted himself and gone somewhere quieter.

"Hey, sorry about that," he said, the familiar gravel of his voice filling me with an odd comfort. "I'm really glad you called."

"It was a mistake."

He laughed. "That's okay. A happy accident. How are you doing? It's so great to hear your voice."

"I'm..." *Fine.* My old mantra sprang so readily to my lips, but for once didn't tumble out. "I'm a little low, actually." I gave a weak chuckle. "But I'll be okay. Just one of those things. How are you?"

"Well, that doesn't sound like the Doc Ogden I know." I could hear the frown in his voice. "You all right, Brook? You sound upset. Can I help?"

It was a moment before I could speak past the tears aching in my throat at his kindness, the concern I heard so clearly in his voice. "That's nice of you, Chip. I've clearly interrupted your evening, though, and I...I shouldn't have called."

"Brook." I heard the scrape of his lighter and an inhalation. I imagined the way I'd seen him smoke: standing against a building somewhere in the darkness, one leg propped on the wall behind him, drawing on the cigarette he'd smoke to the filter, then stamp out and put in his pocket to throw away. There was an odd intimacy in the clarity of the image. "You ever hear that old proverb about owing someone who saves your life? You pulled me through some of the lowest parts of mine. Let me at least try to return the favor."

"Actually, I think it's, 'When you save a life, you are then responsible for that life.' So according to that, I owe you, not the other way around."

"Then do me the kindness of telling me what's wrong," he rejoined immediately, "because that's what I want."

I let out a long sigh just as he exhaled what I pictured as a mouthful of smoke, and for a moment we just breathed together.

Finally I gave in to the lonely night.

"I think I just broke up with my...with the guy I've been dating," I said, low.

There was another silence, and then: "I'm sorry."

It was so simple and perfect a thing to say, warmth rushed into my chest and filled at least a little of the aching emptiness. "Thank you."

"He's an idiot, for what it's worth."

"Thanks, but actually I'm the idiot. I did it." Pain stabbed me again.

"Oh. Well, then how come you're so upset?"

I stood up and walked over to my bare bedroom window, where I'd never gotten around to replacing the curtains Jake ate. I never even got to say goodbye to Jake. He was just gone. I looked out at my empty backyard, and my eyes grew hot. "Because I think I love him." I knew the words might hurt Chip, but I couldn't hold them back. "But I couldn't give him what he wanted."

"Why not, Brook?" Chip's voice was low and raspy.

The tears spilled over. "I don't know."

I pressed my palm to the glass, cool even in the warm, humid night, and then let my forehead fall to rest beside it. Tears dropped to the windowsill, and I tried to keep from sniffling audibly.

"Brook...I hate hearing you sad."

Apparently I hadn't succeeded in hiding the sound of my crying. "It's okay. It's normal. It passes," I managed.

He gave a low chuckle. "It must be hard being the doc. You know all the right answers, but it doesn't make it any easier to deal with everything."

That was exactly how I felt. I gripped the phone tighter, knowing I needed to hang up, but still reluctant to let go of this thin thread of connection when I felt so adrift.

But Chip made the decision for me. "Look, Doc, I gotta go right now. But I can call back in a little bit, okay?"

Of course. He was out with friends—or a girl. He couldn't sit here and hold my hand all night while I clung to the most fragile of connections. I pushed away from the window and wiped a hand under my eyes, flushed with the knowledge that I'd crossed a line I shouldn't have.

"That's okay, actually," I said. "You've been really nice, but please don't worry about calling back. I shouldn't have called in the first place."

"No—I'm glad you did. Really, Brook."

"Okay. Well, hope you have a good rest of the night. And...thanks, Chip."

"Talk to you soon, Brook."

He was wrong, I thought as I broke the connection. Chip and I wouldn't be talking again like this anytime soon.

Or ever.

...

There was no way I'd sleep tonight, I realized once I'd finally changed into shorts and a T-shirt and slid beneath my cold covers. My mind hadn't stopped swirling since I left Ben.

Or since Ben left me, I supposed.

But something startled me out of a sound slumber, sending me lurching to sit up. I stilled, palms against the mattress, with my heart racing, disoriented and trying to figure out what had scared me awake.

Then loud noise came again—banging. Pounding.

On my front door.

This time when my heart surged it was from relief. Ben! I pushed out of bed and practically flew into the living room, throwing back the bolt and yanking the door open.

To see Chip Santana standing there, hand still raised into a fist.

Disappointment crashed over me as he jumped at the suddenness of my answering, and then his face relaxed into a grin. "Geez, Doc. You scared the crap out of me."

Every proper answer filtered through my head in a flash—*You're the one who scared me!* Or, *What are you thinking, showing up uninvited in the middle of the night?* Or, given my half-dressed, disheveled state, *This is completely inappropriate.*

But what popped out of my tight throat was, "Why are you here?"

The grin disappeared and his face softened into concern. "You were upset, Doc. I thought maybe you needed a friend."

I shook my head. "Chip..." I didn't know what should come after that. Some version of "thanks anyway, but no." But instead I took a step back and opened the door wider. "Come on in."

Wordlessly he did, and as he passed me I smelled the faint scent of tobacco and his cinnamon scent, and something different—spice and tomatoes. For the first time I noticed the Taco Bell bag in his other hand. I nodded to it. "What's...?"

Chip lifted the bag slightly. "Thought you might be hungry. I was. Kitchen?" he asked, pointing to the doorway at the other corner of the living room, and when I nodded Chip disappeared through it.

When I numbly followed I found him retrieving plates from the cabinet over the microwave as though he'd been in my kitchen dozens of times.

Rather than this being the first time he'd been inside my house.

He plated the food as we stood in silence, opened two drawers as I watched before he found the silverware and placed a fork on each plate, then picked up the restaurant's napkins and both plates, and tipped his head to the left. "Living room or dining room?" he asked.

"Dining," I pushed out in a rough voice. It seemed safer to sit in the late-night darkness with a table between us.

And in fact, it would probably be safer if I weren't standing here with him wearing a thin concert T-shirt from the nineties and no bra.

The last time we'd had a middle-of-the-night encounter with me dressed this way, we'd wound up lying pressed together on a deserted beach, the only thing keeping me from doing something I would have wildly regretted the cop who'd hauled us off to jail. Chip had a way of overriding my better instincts.

"Can you excuse me for a second?" I asked.

He raised an eyebrow. "Yeah."

In my bedroom I changed my shorts for an old faded gray pair of Stu's sweatpants with blown-out knees, a drawstring tie, and gathered ankles that made me look like MC Hammer. I pulled on a bra under the T-shirt and a college hoodie over it, and slid my feet into beat-up shower shoes. I didn't need to check my mirror to know that it was the unsexiest ensemble I could have put together. Although I was unexpectedly glad to see Chip, to have the company to save me from my solitude, I didn't need to send the wrong message. For either of us.

When I came back out to the dining room he was seated at one end of the table, my plate across from his, the cheap recycled-paper napkins folded like cloth beside them, a fork lined up in the middle and two glasses of water carefully set above and to the right of the plates, as though we were fine-dining. Chip shot to his feet when he saw me, gesturing awkwardly to my chair like a maître d' in training.

I was touched by his sweet gesture. "This is nice of you, Chip. I'm glad you came. I could actually use a friend."

"Sounded like it," he said, taking his seat after I did. The grin came back. "Hope you like Gorditas."

Actually, greasy ground beef and oily cheese and a thick, chewy taco shell sounded perfect at the moment. I unwrapped one of the three on my plate—I'd never eat all that—and took a bite, suddenly starving. Chip followed suit, both of us eschewing our forks.

"Oh, god," I moaned through a mouthful. "Why are these so good at three a.m.?"

"Same reason Waffle House is. I think our standards relax after midnight."

"Millions of bar hookups attest to that."

Chip laughed, and so did I, and it felt good for a moment.

"Did I interrupt something tonight?" I asked. "A date? Sounded like you were out."

He gave a one-shouldered shrug. "Nah, just some friends. I'd rather be here with you anyway." He unwrapped his second Gordita and tore into it as ravenously as I was.

His comment was so simple, but it filled me with warmth. This new Chip said what he meant, and I liked it. He asked for nothing from me. There were no demands, no expectations. This moment was what it was, and that was all.

Ben had offered me more than that—offered me what I used to think I wanted: a man who thought of a future with me, rather than just living in the moment.

But I didn't have the emotional depth to accept it.

"So," Chip said after we ate in companionable silence for a few moments. "You want to talk about it?"

"Not really," I said, my voice flat. "It just...I thought I knew what I wanted. But it turns out it's nothing at all like I thought," I went on when he made no reply, just kept looking at me. "I guess I'm not quite who I thought I was."

Chip chewed for a few moments. Then he said, "I don't know if any of us are, Brook. I think we're all capable of doing things that...totally surprise ourselves."

I nodded, considering that as I unwrapped another taco. Chip was talking about himself, I guessed—the way he'd taken the reins of his life and changed everything to be someone he decided he wanted to be, instead of who he had been before. At our core, we're who we are. We can change our actions, our choices, but not the essence of our *selves*. But Chip had changed all the choices he made—nearly every one of them—and in the process he had, if not changed, then at least accessed parts of himself that had remained deeply buried for most of his life.

Was that what I'd just done with Ben? Made a choice that revealed the core of me that I didn't know was there—that all I wanted was a short-term good time with someone, rather than anything meaningful or committed?

It sure felt like that.

"I guess so," I said finally. "I guess we change all the time anyway, so trying to figure out who we are at any given moment is an exercise in futility. You have to just live in the now, right?" I gave what I hoped was a blasé smile.

I reached for another taco, stunned to discover I'd already eaten all three. "Wow. I didn't know I was that hungry."

He held up half of his last Gordita. "You want the rest of mine?" he asked.

"That's nice of you to offer. But that's okay. I don't really want it."

He looked as crestfallen as though I'd slapped away his hand. I would have laughed at the incongruity of his expression, but it reminded me too much of Ben's when I'd rejected what he'd been offering too.

"Wait, okay," I said, wanting to erase the memory. "I'll take it."

"Nah, it's cool."

"No, bring it here—I want the taco."

Chip's smile had always transformed his entire appearance, chasing away the fierceness of what used to be his usual scowl. Now it gave him a boyish, youthful air, and lit up the room.

"Oh, you'll get the taco," he said, pushing back his chair and lifting one of those slanting satyr's eyebrows as he slowly stood. He held the Gordita up in one cocked-back arm, like a paper airplane about to be launched.

"Chip...don't you dare," I said warningly.

"Don't I dare what?" His tone was all innocence. "I'm just bringing you this taco you said you wanted so much. Open the gate—here comes the choo-choo."

"Cut it out. I'm serious."

"Chugga-chugga-chugga...whoo-whoo!" he said, making ridiculous train noises as he rounded the end of the table.

"Chip! I mean it!" I scrambled out of my chair on the opposite side from him and bolted into the kitchen, a tightness in my stomach letting loose at the silly game. This was what I needed—mindless, meaningless interaction.

He was right behind me, so I jagged left to cut into the living room, only to nearly run into his chest as he doubled back and cut me off. I shrieked and broke for the sofa, putting the cocktail table between us.

"No! No taco."

"Taco," he droned inexorably, feinting left.

I squealed and broke right. "No taco!"

He stopped dead still, lowering the hand with the food to his side and staring intently at me. "Brook...you said you wanted the taco." He sounded so earnest and sincere it should have made me laugh.

But instead the bottom dropped out of my stomach. Something in his low, gravelly, dead-serious tone stripped away any sense of playfulness between us, and the air grew thick and charged.

"Stop," I whispered breathlessly, my heart suddenly shaking my rib cage. "Stop it now."

"What?"

"You know what."

Chip stood for a moment that felt frozen, and then folded the taco carefully in its foil and placed it on my cocktail table. *No, Jake will get that*, I almost said before I remembered, with a fresh pang.

"I know this scene from a hundred movies," I said. "And it's not going to happen."

"That's not why I'm here."

"Isn't it?" I was angry now—at Chip, at Ben...I didn't know.

"No. Look, if you want me to go now, I will." His eyes were fixed on me across the cocktail table in our odd stand-off, but I couldn't make out what was in them in the half-light from the moon and the streetlight spilling through a gap in the curtains. "But I came to be a friend. To listen. To cheer you up the way you've done for me. Because whatever else I feel or felt toward you, whatever else you want to believe about us, I care about you, Brook. And I want to help. If you'll let me."

I folded my arms over my chest. "You came here just for that. With no agenda. Just to talk to me about my broken relationship with another guy?"

"If that's what you want. Yes."

"Even though you told me you had feelings for me, you want to sit here and listen to me talk about my feelings for *him*—feelings in general, for that matter—like a girlfriend? Really?" There was no way he could miss the skepticism in my tone.

"Try me."

I gave a sardonic laugh. "Okay. I will. Have a seat."

He sat on the armchair beside him and I took the sofa across from it, the cocktail table a barrier between us.

"I think I love him," I said, hearing the challenge in my tone. Might as well call Chip's bluff now and he could leave.

"I know. You said that." His voice was mild.

"He's a great guy. Kind and open and funny. Smart. Generous. So much fun." I was trying to hurt Chip, but the recitation of Ben's wonderful qualities was only wounding myself. This paragon was the man I had just ended things with.

"That's what you deserve, Brook."

"Then why aren't I with him?" I threw it in his face, but I wasn't asking him the question.

He didn't react, just looked calmly at me, waiting for me to go on. Finally, when I just stared back at him with what must have been a bulldog expression, he said, "I don't know. Why do you think that is?"

Oh, for god's sake. He was therapizing me.

"I don't know! Dammit! I have no idea."

"Maybe you don't love him after all?"

That set every nerve I had on edge with a jangle, a visceral gut reaction that told me the truth. "I do love him. That much I know."

He nodded. "Okay. Maybe he's just not the right person for you then."

I leaned back against the sofa arm, moving my gaze out the crack in the curtains and away from Chip's steady stare. "I don't know," I said softly. "How does anyone know that?"

The question was idle, rhetorical, but Chip's voice filtered over to me, quiet, hesitant. "I think it's when you feel happier around that person, maybe? When they bring out what's best in you. Make you want to...what...I guess live up to all the things you ever hoped for, for yourself? When you're better with them than without them."

I thought about that, still looking out my window where the streetlight dropped an arc of illumination onto the empty street in front of my house. It was a pretty good definition, actually. Did it apply to me and Ben? I did feel happier around him, in the easiest, most basic way—as if everything was simply *right* at that moment, just *enough*. Did he bring out the best in me? I never thought I was much of a caretaker, but I'd been a hands-on helicopter dog mother to Jake. I'd loved spending time with Adelaide, helping her—even when I couldn't bring myself do the same with my own mother.

Was I better with Ben than without him?

Was I?

"I don't know yet."

I didn't realize I'd spoken aloud until I heard Chip's voice again.

"Maybe that's the answer, Brook." I turned my head from the window to look at him. "You said 'yet.' Maybe it's just too soon to know. There's nothing wrong with that. Is there?"

I regarded him for a long time, and he simply met my unswerving stare.

Finally I pushed myself up off the sofa and stood. "I'd better go to bed now. It's late." Chip stood immediately, and I met his eyes. "I'm sorry I was unkind before."

"You weren't."

"You are a good friend, Chip," I said quietly. "Thank you."

"I would do anything for you, Brook."

His simple words brought an ache to my throat. I took one hesitant step closer, then another, and then Chip's arms went around me and he held me, offering nothing more than comfort. I let myself relax into it—giving myself just this one moment of human contact, a balm to my aching soul.

And then something shifted, so suddenly and completely it was like an electric current had shot between us. His clasp changed, subtly firmer—one hand stroked softly along my shoulder blades while the other lowered to the small of my back, pulling me closer, close enough to feel how affected Chip was too. His scent even seemed to intensify, cinnamon and soap and something else.

I pressed into him, every nerve ending completely alive and sensitized as if his naked skin were against mine. And when I felt his upper body shift, pull back slightly, I knew why, and I lifted my head to meet his as he lowered his lips to mine.

I lifted my head. I chose.

That was the last coolheaded realization I had before our mouths met and a jolt shot through my entire body straight to the center of me. After that I stopped analyzing what we were doing, or why—I stopped any rational thought at all. I devoured Chip's soft lips, clung to his hard body, and surrendered completely.

Chapter Twenty-five

Here's when you have to wonder if you have crossed a line: When you wake up with a man next to you, and you have to think for a second to remember who it is.

And here's when you realize you've made a horrible mistake: When you do realize who it is...and it's the wrong guy.

I didn't even have the excuse of being drunk to fall back on for why I'd finally ended up sleeping with Chip. The truth was, it had been in the works for a long time—maybe since he'd first walked into my office and some strange immediate animal attraction had *jing*ed all the way through my body, straight to my groin. There was validity to the idea of chemical reactions, pheromones that drew you to someone on a level well below your conscious volition. Chip and I had been circling that draw for a long time, and even a child could have predicted that being alone with him late at night, when I was in a really poor state of mind, was going to wind up with me finally acting on all those sublimated impulses.

But the timing couldn't possibly have been worse. Even if we'd actually gone all the way on the beach months ago—instead of being caught before the act by Deputy Dodd—rebound sex would have been better than what I'd just done.

And as much as I couldn't deny that I'd wanted to go to bed with Chip (and I have to confess that the sex itself was phenomenal—like, porn-film phenomenal), he wasn't the man I wanted to be waking up with.

Awkward.

He was lying on his side, facing me. A light layer of stubble covered his shaved head, the individual hairs gilded in the sunlight seeping through the window—even his unfairly long lashes seemed to shimmer. The sheet was bunched down around his legs, his bare chest and arms seeming enormous in my queen bed. The tattoos that covered his shoulders and upper arms were a colorful contrast to my plain white sheets. He wasn't snoring exactly, but his mouth drooped open, and I could tell from his steady, deep breathing that he was still asleep.

Oh, and he had morning wood. Huge morning wood.

If we were at his house, I could just tippytoe out. Which was exactly what I wanted to do—I could deal with the fallout later. But this was my house, my bed, and if I wanted the mountain of naked erect unconscious man beside me to leave, I had to wake him up and face the music.

"Chip," I said, my voice cracking the stillness of the morning.

He didn't budge.

I cleared my throat and said louder, "Chip," but still, nothing. Hesitantly I tapped his shoulder, as if I were trying to get a stranger's attention on the subway. *Excuse me, sir, could you move? Your penis is making me really uncomfortable.*

Chip gave a loud snore and snuggled deeper into the pillow. Good lord, had he roofied himself?

I took hold of one shoulder and shook. "Hey, Chip. Wake up!"

Finally his eyes flickered open, and as soon as he saw me a lazy grin drifted over his mouth. "Morning, Doc," he drawled, reaching for me.

And damned if that didn't stir something down in Lady Town, even in my present state of mind. Was I seriously some kind of sex fiend?

I put up my hands as a barrier—though I wasn't sure which one of us I was trying to curb. "Hey...listen, last night was really great...." I sounded like a frat boy who woke up with the dogfight winner, but Chip didn't seem to notice.

"Yeah, it was." He had taken one of my hands in his and was doing that thing where he ran his fingers between the webbing of mine, which sent shivers all the way through me.

"Um...Oh. But I have to...I've got things I have to take care of today, so— Oh, *God*." He'd taken one of my fingers into his mouth and was sucking gently.

"It's Sunday, Doc," he whispered against the sensitive skin of my fingertips, before taking the next finger into his soft, warm mouth. He sucked and then released it while I tried to remember how to breathe. "You don't have to jump right up yet, do you?" He was circling my palm with his thumb, the barest of touches, and then he brought it to his mouth and echoed the motion with his tongue.

I wasn't proud of it, but I moaned.

Chip pulled my moist hand down to where he was still ragingly hard—more so, if that were possible—and I wrapped my fingers around his length.

And despite knowing it was a mistake, despite thinking of Ben, despite hating myself for doing in the rational light of day what I'd at least had the veil of night to hide behind last night, I let myself do it again.

...

It sounds super romantic to wake up to a man staring adoringly at you while you sleep.

But the reality is kind of creepy.

When my eyes cracked open sometime later against the sunshine lighting up my room, Chip was lying on his side facing me, propped up on an elbow this time, his blue-green eyes fixed unswervingly on my face. As soon as my eyes slitted open he gave a big toothy smile.

"Morning, Sleeping Beauty."

I jolted awake, jerking back toward the edge of the bed and pulling the covers higher up my naked body. I brought a hand to my face, checking for drool, for sleep crust in my eyes, wondering whether I'd been snoring, and how long he'd been lying there watching me like a lion toying with the prey he'd brought down.

"What time is it?" I murmured. After exhausting ourselves pretty thoroughly on each other's bodies, we'd both fallen back to sleep.

"Still early," he said, reaching out to trace a line down my cheek. I checked myself just before I pulled away. This fawning Chip was a disconcerting new entity. "Eleven."

"Eleven! Geez!" I said, shooting up to a sitting position. The sheet slipped back down and I yanked it over my breasts.

"Calm down, babe," he said. "It's Sunday."

Babe?

Chip's fingers drew light lines down my neck and ventured lower, toward the edge of the sheet. I gripped it like Excalibur, and an awkward finger-battle ensued as I tried blocking his exploration underneath.

"I...I need to get up, actually," I stammered.

Chip just chuckled and dropped down onto his back, lifting his hands to rest behind his head on the pillow as though he had no plans of being moved anytime soon. "Okay—how about this? Let's get dressed and grab some chow and then we can go out on my boat."

Did he think we were dating now?

And then I thought...Were we?

I mean, it wasn't like Ben and I weren't definitively finished, judging by last night. Oh, god—*last night.* It hadn't even been twenty-four hours since we broke up, and here I was in bed with another man. Ben's side of the bed was barely cold.

Had I even changed the *sheets* since he'd been here?

Ew.

Chip was already up and pulling on his cargo shorts, and before I could scramble out of bed he'd rounded the foot and lowered himself onto the mattress to sit beside me—effectively trapping me in my tainted bedclothes. "Hey," he said quietly. "Just so you know, I'm not going anywhere, Brook. This wasn't a one-night stand."

He was being so sweet. Saying all the things a man should say on the morning after an impulsive night, when a woman's fears were at her most acute.

But I hadn't remotely had time to process what had happened between me and Ben. I certainly wasn't ready to start something new.

I let out a long breath and leaned back against the wall behind my headboardless bed as far as the sheet would allow, trying to create some distance without pulling a total Lady Godiva. "Chip...we need to talk."

He shifted and gave an uncomfortable laugh. "Uh-oh. That's never a good conversation starter. Are you dumping me already, Brook?" He tried to make it a joke, but I could hear the thread of worry in his tone.

It was hardly the best situation to have a serious conversation, with only a cheap cotton sheet between me and total exposure, and Chip's bare chest filling my vision as he sat beside me in the bed where I'd slept with two different men inside of a week.

"Let me make some coffee," I blurted.

"Okay," he said instantly, so eager to please me, and guilt rode up my throat. He shot to his feet and held out a hand as if to help me out of bed.

"Um, do you mind if I...?" I trailed off, heat surging into my face as I indicated the general region lower than my head with a spastic gesture of one arm. It wasn't like he hadn't seen every single naked inch of what I had to offer—in extreme close-up, including my jackass tattoo, which seemed to delight him and turn him on even more—but it felt beyond awkward in the full morning light.

"Oh, sure, right. I'll just be in the kitchen," he said.

As soon as my bedroom door shut behind him I sailed into my closet for something to put on. The antisexy outfit from last night seemed like overkill now (and it wasn't as though it had worked the way I'd planned anyway, was it?). I threw on a pair of pajamas my mom had bought me and I'd never worn: cotton drawstring pants in a pink-and-blue check pattern and a matching short-sleeved button-down top. Leaving my feet bare, I headed to the bathroom to brush my teeth—no one felt confident with morning mouth—and smoothed out my bed head as best I could. That was about as girded as I could get at the moment for the hard talk Chip and I were about to have.

And then, because I was a coward, and slightly panicked, I texted Sasha. *Can you come over in 15-20?*

If nothing else, her arrival would keep the discussion from dragging on, and encourage Chip to leave.

Her response was instant: *See you then.*

When I came out to the kitchen I saw Chip holding the coffeepot in one hand as he stood in front of my open pantry, staring inside. I had a flash of Ben standing in almost this same position just a week ago, and felt ill.

"Oh, hey," he said with an instant smile when he saw me. "I couldn't find the coffee. Or the filters, for that matter."

"That's okay." I passed two feet behind him toward the freezer, where I kept the coffee, and took the bag to the coffeemaker in the corner by the sink, reaching to the cabinet above it for the filters. Chip filled the pot from the faucet while I measured the coffee—I usually used filtered, because Florida water tasted like it had come from a public pool, but didn't correct him—and after I poured it in and turned it on, we stood there in awkward silence punctuated by the trickle of brewing coffee.

I'd never been on this side of the morning after—when *I* was the one wishing I'd woken up alone.

I took a deep breath. "Chip—"

"Doc—Brook—wait," he broke in. "Before you say anything, there's something I need to say to you, okay? I've been wanting to tell you for a while, but...I was afraid."

My heart fell to the kitchen floor with an audible thud. (Almost.) A declaration of love was going to make what I had to say infinitely harder on both of us.

"Oh, Chip, no," I said hastily. "I...Thank you—I can't tell you how flattered I am, and it means a lot—really. But you have to understand it's too soon for that. I'm barely out of my last relationship, and I'm not ready to fall in love with someone else right now. Or you know, who knows—maybe ever?" Chip looked stunned, and I gave a rough laugh. "I don't mean I couldn't ever love you back—that didn't come out like I meant it—I just mean that right now I can't even...I just...It's way too soon for that, Chip."

"Um, Doc..." He laughed, but it was more an uncomfortable discharge of sound. "I think you're awesome, and I'm digging whatever this is between us, but I wasn't going to say the L-word. Geez."

Oh. Dear God. When Ben actually said he loved me I assumed he hadn't—which had basically landed me here. Now I'd assumed Chip was going to say it when he wasn't. I really had to learn to shut up.

"I, okay, I'm sorry, I assumed—but I know what happens when you assume—and I didn't mean to..." Agh. Like now. Time to shut up *now*. "What was it you were going to say, Chip?" I finally pushed out.

He rubbed the back of his neck, moving his gaze out the window over my kitchen sink. "Right. Can we go sit down? Maybe out on the porch?"

My stomach clenched. I couldn't imagine what he was so nervous about, but based on his anxiety I didn't suppose it could be good. But Sasha should be here in ten minutes or so, so what harm could there be in hearing whatever his confession was? "Sure," I said, and while we waited for the coffee to finish brewing I ran through possibilities in my head: *I'm married. I'm an ex-con. I killed a man.*

After we poured our mugs full we stepped onto the lanai and I took the sofa, leaving the chair for Chip, but instead he sat at the other end, each of us holding our coffee.

"Okay, so listen," he said, turning so that our knees almost touched. "I told you how much you've changed me, and that's the truth, Brook. That's why I want to come clean with you. I want you and I to start with a fresh slate, everything on the table."

You and I pinballed from one side of my brain to the other. There was no *you and I* between me and Chip, I realized with a sinking heart. Having him here like this clarified that. It was Ben. It had been Ben from the beginning.

But how could I love Ben and sleep with Chip? Enthusiastically? *Twice?*

I was a complete mess. Where was Sasha? I needed to talk this out with her. I reached to my pocket to check the time, but realized I'd left my phone in the bedroom.

"I don't want to be writing a letter to you one day like you had me write to my other exes, so I'm just going to tell you now," Chip went on, oblivious to my inner stew. "I haven't been totally honest with you."

My eyes shot up to his. "What?"

"Nothing huge," he said quickly. "Just logistics, really."

Logistics? What was he talking about?

He gave me that smile that transformed his face from intimidating to inviting, reaching over to tuck hair behind my ear. "I'm still working at the bar. For now."

I frowned, confused. "Wait...you mean a different bar?"

"No, I mean Floppies."

"The same bar you said you *quit*?"

His smile grew even more dazzling. A Crest commercial. "That's the one. But it's temporary, just till I find something better. Trust me—I'm not going to be a middle-aged drink slinger like some of those idiots I work with."

Unease slithered through my belly. The "idiots" were back. "Are you...what, are you planning to stay there till you graduate?"

"Oh, hell, no. God knows when that will be."

"What do you mean?" Were we having two different conversations? "I thought you were in school full-time?"

He nodded. "I will be. As soon as I save up enough to quit the bar and enroll."

It felt as if my brain tightened inside my skull. "I'm not sure I'm...Enroll? Aren't you already...?" I didn't finish, because when Chip's lips quirked at the corner and he reached over for my hair again, I suspected I knew the answer. I set my coffee down on the table—liquid sloshed over the edges—and quickly stood up, stepping away.

"Chip, are you in school right now? At all?"

"I talked to a counselor. I know what I'm going to major in." His voice was soothing, calm. "I just haven't actually signed on the dotted line yet, you know? I didn't want to lock myself in until I had a clear path set for myself. You always tell me to think of my future."

"Not just *think* of it, Chip. You have to *act* on it." My voice rose into a slightly hysterical register.

He reached into one of the pockets of his cargo shorts—still all he wore—and coolly pulled out a pack of cigarettes and a lighter. I would have asked him not to smoke on my porch, but it seemed like the slightest of my concerns at the moment. "You taught me not to be so impulsive," he said, tapping the pack on the table and then putting one of the white sticks into his mouth. He winked as he lit it, and I wondered what on earth I'd ever found sexy about the deadly habit. "So I'm being careful. Weighing my options. But, Brook, don't worry— that's what I'm telling you." He took a deep draw. "All the things I told you—that's what's going to happen. You'll learn that about me—I make shit happen, always. You can count on that."

Oh, yes, I realized with a feeling of nausea blooming in my belly. Chip certainly made things happen.

But I couldn't blame him entirely. I was equally at fault for the situation I'd gotten myself into.

"Actually, Chip, how can you tell someone to count on you when you've been lying to them? For *weeks*?" My voice was thin in my ears.

"I was afraid you'd see it that way," Chip admitted, as though I'd somehow disappointed him. "Brook, I did all of it for you. You see that, right? I want to be the man you want—the man you deserve. And I'm getting there. I promise, babe."

I gaped at him, unable even to *think* of a reply to that. What did it matter? Why bother saying anything at all? I didn't even understand his reality if talking about something was as good as doing it—if creating an image of what he thought someone else wanted was the same in his mind as actually *being* that person.

All along I'd been seeing what I'd wanted to see—what he wanted me to see. And I hadn't had the insight or savvy to look past it. Chip was who he was, and he'd never change.

Some therapist I was.

I heard Jake's little woof and saw that he'd come to the back door, and I went over to let him in. "Good boy," I said absently, digging my fingers into the thick fur on his neck as he shoved his nose happily into my crotch.

I heard Chip's, "Hey!" exactly at the moment I realized—Jake wasn't staying with me anymore.

My stomach fell to the concrete patio as time slowed down and I saw several things as if all at once:

Chip lounging shirtless on my sofa, lazily smoking a cigarette.

Me in pink pajamas and bare feet.

And Ben coming around the corner of my house, calling my name, his face softening when he saw me, and freezing just as fast as he took in the whole tableau.

He came to the most abrupt of stops in the yard, ten feet away from my screen door.

Which was exactly when I heard Sasha's voice behind me saying, "We brought doughnuts!" and saw her and my brother standing in the open sliding glass door to my house.

Time sped back up and suddenly everything happened in fast forward.

"Oh," Sasha said as she caught sight of the half-naked Chip, who'd dunked his cigarette in his cup of coffee as he stood up. And then "Oh!" again as she took in Jake, and Ben still standing frozen on my lawn. The bag dropped from her hands and Jake beelined for the sudden gift from the universe. I lunged after him, inanely thinking, *He can't have chocolate!*, but tripped on the leg of the chair and went sprawling to the concrete. Chip came to take one arm to help me up, Stu at my other—"Are you okay, sis?"—as I heard Ben sharply calling Jake, who saw that I was down on the ground and assumed it was doggy playtime, throwing all hundred pounds of himself on top of me and eagerly licking my neck.

"Jake!" Ben called again.

"Ben," I said.

"*That* one's Ben?" my brother said incredulously, looking from the shirtless Chip on my lanai to Ben out in the yard. "Who's this?"

"Chip," Sasha muttered darkly, crouching to shove spilled doughnuts back into the bag.

"Chip?" I heard Ben say in a wounded tone that broke my heart.

I scrambled to stand, pushing both Chip and my brother away. "Ben, it's not like it looks."

"What?" Chip said, sounding affronted. "Yeah, it is."

"Shut up, Chip," Sasha said.

"My fault," Ben said tightly. "I called to tell you I was on my way. I shouldn't have come when you didn't answer. Jake, come." His harsh command failed to break through to Jake, who was leaning his whole body weight into me, his brushy tail slapping my thigh so fast it blurred.

"Oh, yeah, we tried calling too, Brook," Sash said. "You *really* ought to answer your phone." She made exaggerated bug eyes between Chip and Ben, as though I could possibly miss her meaning.

You think?! I thought sickly.

"Jake, come!" Ben sounded desperate.

But Jake was too happy to see me, and was busy throwing himself onto his back, teeth showing through gravity-slack lips in an incongruous smile, begging for me to rub his belly. And because I was suddenly swamped with blinding love for this crazy dog, and knew he was the only thing keeping Ben here, I obliged.

Sasha, bless her, tried to take control. "Well, I think the rest of us ought to let you two talk," she said.

"Yeah, thanks," Chip answered.

"Not you," Stu barked, and my head shot to my brother in surprise. "Let's go." He stepped past me and Jake on the lanai to shepherd Chip inside.

"I don't have my clothes!" Chip protested, resisting.

I cringed.

"Don't worry about it—I'm going," Ben said. "Jake!"

"Ben, please," I said, furiously scratching Jake to keep him in place. "Just wait a minute. *Please.*"

"Hey!" Chip said. "Why does he get to stay?"

Sasha had somehow found time to dart inside and was back in place in the sliding glass doorway, holding a men's pair of shoes and Chip's crumpled T-shirt. "Got your things," she said to Chip. "From the *guest room.*"

I wanted to both hug her and roll my eyes at the weak attempt at damage control.

"If he's staying, I'm staying," Chip said obstinately.

"You're not staying," I said, exactly as I heard Ben's voice say, "I'm not staying."

I rose from petting Jake and turned to look at Ben, and once again time froze for just a moment. His mouth pulled down at the corners and his whole face seemed to sag, at the same time his body was stiff as a pole.

I'd done this to him.

"Ben, I'm so sorry," I whispered. But I didn't know whether he heard me.

Through blurred vision I saw a white streak bolt past me toward Ben, who caught the dog's huge head in his hands and fast as lightning clipped a leash I hadn't realized he'd been holding to Jake's collar. Then Ben turned his back on me and walked out, pulling a resistant Jake, the only one still looking back at me.

Something crumbled to dust in my chest.

"Geez, that was awkward."

Chip's voice seemed to come from far away and I turned slowly and raised my eyes to him, distantly registering my brother and Sasha side by side again in the doorway.

"Go. Just go," I said dully. I was talking to everyone. I wanted to be left alone with my shame.

Chip flashed that smile, but this time it only made me want to scratch it from his face. "Brook, come on. You can't always be a lone wolf. We have to start working on stuff as a couple. Could you guys leave us alone?" he said to Sasha and Stu.

Fury surged through me like a jet stream.

"There is no *us*," I grated out in a voice cold and sharp as a glacier. "We aren't a couple. We are nothing, Chip. *Nothing*. Every single second I've known you has been based on lies. You don't even exist. Now get out of my house."

I'd never heard my voice like this—dead and flat and cruel. From the corner of my eye I caught Sasha, pale as milk, looking at me as if I might detonate at any second. Stu's eyes were fixed on me too, bewildered, worried, and I saw him reach to Sasha and put an arm around her.

Protecting her from *me*, I thought.

Chip's expression moved from indulgence to shock to a sneer within milliseconds. "Oh, fuck you. Fuck you, Brook," he said, but I was too far gone to even blanch at his shout. "You're just like every other fucking bitch I've ever dated—you don't even appreciate everything I've done for you."

"That's enough out of you." The roar came from my mild-mannered brother, who charged onto the lanai like Rambo, taking Chip hard by the arm and pushing him toward the sliding door. "You heard Brook. Get out."

"Get your fucking hands off me, dude!" Chip pushed Stu's chest, and my brother, taller by a hair but not as solid, stumbled backward, off balance. His heel caught on the concrete threshold and his ankle twisted. I saw him grimace, saw his leg collapse from under him, and still my brother fought to stay on his feet—to protect his women.

But Chip, like an animal sensing weakness, lunged forward and landed a hard punch directly to Stu's chest. A machine-gun barrage of sounds registered: the sickening *thunk* of Chip's fist against Stu's rib cage, the air whooshing out of my brother as the force of the blow propelled him backward again, a terrifying crack as Stu's head bounced off the corner of the open door, Sasha's enraged scream just before she launched herself right at Chip, attaching herself to him like a feral, clawing cat.

"What the hell, you crazy bitch!" he shouted. "Get the fuck off—I don't hit women!"

"Bullshit!" some primal thing in me screamed at yet another lie, remembering his ex Katie. "Don't you touch her!" I charged toward where the two of them had become a freakish animal of connected torsos and flailing arms and legs, and started pushing between them, trying to stop Chip, to protect Sasha. It was like trying to separate conjoined twins, but finally Sasha let go and dropped away from Chip, her jaw jutted and her arms lifted like Rocky Balboa.

I stepped fast into the space that had opened up between them and turned to Sash. "Okay," I said, panting. "Enough. He'll go—you check on Stu."

Sasha seemed to come back to herself and nodded—and then suddenly her eyes went wide. "Brook!" she yelled.

And that was the last thing I heard before what felt like a ham hock clubbed into the side of my head, my vision went dark, and a slab of granite slammed into my body.

Chapter Twenty-six

When I woke up, I was lying on the concrete floor of my lanai, though something cushioned my head—a pillow from my patio sofa, I saw as I sat up.

Which was a dire mistake, as my brain throbbed like a beating heart inside my head, sending agony shooting out through my eyeballs.

Jesus. What happened?

I heard voices and looked through the open sliding glass door into my house to see Sasha and Stu—the latter with dark blood crusted along his left temple—talking to two uniformed police officers.

Oh. Right.

Chip was nowhere to be seen, but for all I knew he was cuffed and lying facedown on the ground just out of my view.

I hauled myself to my feet, unable to stifle a groan as the ice pick in my head stabbed at me again. My left arm stung, and I saw that I'd badly skinned it, along with my left knee and thigh.

I hobbled into the den like a war refugee.

"Hey, there," I said, as though arriving late to a soiree.

Four faces turned to me.

"You're conscious! We're not supposed to move you—the ambulance is on its way. Sit," Sasha said, pushing me toward a chair.

"What! No, no ambulance—I'm fine. Are you okay, Stu?" I asked reaching toward his bloody head.

He ducked. "I'm fine." Of course he was fine; we were always fine—we were Ogdens.

"Where's Chip?" I asked, looking around the kitchen and den.

"The alleged perpetrator had already left the scene when we arrived, ma'am," one of the officers said. His stiff white-blond crew cut seemed to nearly brush my eight-foot ceiling, and his carved jaw was so sharp I wondered if he broke razor blades against it. "I suggest you seek medical attention, ma'am—you're going to want documentation of the contusions."

I craned my neck to look up at him. This guy took his job dead seriously.

The other cop—swarthy and glowering—brandished a clipboard toward me. "We're going to need you to sign this report."

I glanced at it. "No, I don't want to file a complaint."

"You have to," Sasha said.

I shook my head—another terrible mistake, as my tender brain crashed into my skull. "Things just got out of hand. Thank you, Officers," I said to Starsky and Hutch.

"Brook, he *hit* you," Sasha argued. "He hit Stu. He's dangerous—and a repeat offender."

The blond giant flexed his eyebrows in what looked to be a scowl. "We've been called on a domestic violence assault, ma'am. Charges will be filed by the county whether you fill out a report or not."

Their words joggled something free in my brain. *He doesn't mean it*, Sheila had said of her emotionally abusive boyfriend, Tom. She'd justified his behavior eight ways from Sunday. Just like I had with Chip.

Shame rose up to choke me.

Sheila, whom I'd felt so sorry for because she couldn't see past what she desperately wanted with her boyfriend to the way he manipulated her through her deepest vulnerabilities. Sheila, whom I'd pityingly categorized as a mouse, a victim who wouldn't see what was right in front of her face, who justified Tom's awful behavior toward her because she thought she could change him.

How was I any different?

Chip Santana had been playing me for weeks—maybe months. Blinded by my attraction to him, I'd convinced myself that he meant well. That he'd had some tough breaks. I'd justified what I already knew firsthand—his explosive temper, his volatility, his always simmering rage—and even what I knew of his past behavior with other women, and convinced myself that he had changed. That *I* could help him change. That I could "fix" him.

All the same justifications Sheila gave for Tom.

I was supposed to be the expert—and I'd been conned. I'd *let* myself be conned.

Tom attacked Sheila emotionally. Chip had turned it physical with Katie, with me, and who knew who else. And if I let this go right now, he might go on to do it again—maybe even worse.

"You're right," I croaked at Sasha through a constricted throat, then turned to the shorter cop with the clipboard. "Hand me the form."

…

Except for the momentary excitement of an ambulance wheeling into my driveway, sirens blaring and lights spinning until we convinced them we weren't in need of emergency transport after all, after the police left things went just about back to normal.

Such as it was.

"What will happen to him?" I'd asked the cops as I filled out the complaint form.

The tall Aryan-ideal officer dropped his ice-blue eyes in the vicinity of my face without tipping his head a fraction of an inch. "He'll face assault charges and will likely serve up to a year in jail."

"He'll go to jail?" I repeated in dismay.

Guilt prickled my chest. I didn't think Chip was a monster—just a loaded cannon that needed to be defused. I couldn't think landing in jail was going to help effect that. More likely it would do just the opposite, and the therapist in me railed against sending him somewhere that would almost certainly remove any hope he had of doing better.

The little swarthy fireplug shrugged. "Depends. He could get a reduced sentence, if anyone's willing to plead for lenience for him. But given most cases like this, I don't recommend it." The expression accompanying his mild words suggested the subtext that I might be an idiot.

I didn't know the right thing to do—was my judgment about Chip still clouded, or was there some part of his better nature that was salvageable? I wanted to believe the latter.

But I knew that as a therapist, I had to walk my talk. I signed the complaint. Later, when I wasn't reeling from what had happened and a possible concussion, I'd examine whether it was wise to plead for leniency.

Nurse Sasha assisted as Stu and I cleaned ourselves up—his fall against the glass door had split the skin just above his temple, which bled rather out of proportion to the seriousness of the wound, we learned to our relief when we wiped away the dried blood. Sasha spread Bacitracin over it (I had a vat of it, thanks to my ongoing tattoo removal) and put a butterfly Band-Aid over the cut. His ankle where he'd twisted it had swelled up like a tick, so we wrapped it in an ACE bandage. Chip hadn't broken the skin with his roundhouse punch to the back of my head, so once I got the dirt out of my skinned forearm and leg, a little ointment was all I needed.

"I'm not leaving either of you alone, though, after a head injury," Sasha said.

Stu and I both knew when there was no backing her down, so we ordered pizza and parked in my living room once it arrived to eat in front of a *Friends* rerun—"The One Where Ross and Rachel Take a Break."

"*Friends* covered every relationship situation there is," I said, staring numbly at the episode I'd seen a dozen times—where Ross sleeps with the copy store girl too quickly and ruins everything with Rachel—and thinking, inexorably, of Ben.

"Oh, really?" Sasha asked, sitting on the floor and picking the olives off her slice, popping them into her mouth one by one. "There's no 'One Where the Guy You've Been Counseling and Then Slept with Attacks You and Your Brother.'"

"Cool," Stu put in. "There should have been." We'd planted him on my sofa, with pillows elevating his twisted ankle and an ice pack for the swelling.

"Why'd he hit me?" I asked around a mouthful of pepperoni pie.

"I don't think he meant to. He was trying to reach me," Sasha said.

"Nah," Stu said. "I was watching. He just kind of lost it. You ever hear of berserkers?"

"What, you mean like crazy people?" I asked.

"No, they were soldiers or something, right?" Sasha said.

He nodded. "Norse warriors. They were supposed to fall into this trance state, a fury that they couldn't control, like some kind of animal spirit took them over. That's what it looked like. He just went crazy and started hitting at anything."

"Jesus," Sasha breathed.

Stu muttered something we couldn't hear.

"What?" I said.

"I'm sorry," he mumbled. "I shoulda done something."

"You did," Sasha said. "You charged him. It was pretty badass."

"Yeah, and then I went down like a chump." Stu wouldn't meet our eyes.

"Bro," I said incredulously. "You lunged at a tattooed berserker twice as big as you. And he fought dirty. Who punches a guy who's off balance from a sprained ankle? In the freaking *ribs*?"

Stu rubbed at his torso. "Dude can hit."

"Yeah, well, it seems like he's had plenty of practice," Sasha said darkly, reaching up to stroke Stu's good leg. "I thought you were tough as hell," she told him. "When you're feeling better remember what you did. I might want to do a little role-playing."

I was too bone-tired to even react.

"Look, this wasn't your fault, Stuvie," I said. "If you weren't here it could've been a lot worse." I put down my half-eaten slice, my appetite abruptly gone. "This was all on me. I screwed everything up."

"Brookie, come on," Sasha cajoled. "Don't take the blame for what that asshat did."

I shook my head. "No. I lit the match. I'm the one who agreed to meet with him again, even knowing I shouldn't. I encouraged him when I knew better. I responded when I should have ignored him. I opened a box I should have left closed. And then I..." Shame flooded up again. "I freaking *slept* with Chip Santana. After all your warnings why I should stay far away from him."

Stu shifted uncomfortably. It was probably getting a little feely up in here for him. Or maybe he just didn't want to hear about his sibling's sex life. God knows, I could relate to that.

"Honey," Sasha said, "you were in a rotten place. You were upset. Hurt. We all do things when we're vulnerable that we'd never do in our right minds."

She had that right. I'd fairly well lost the plot just a few short months ago when I was reeling from compound heartaches. But I was a therapist. And I'd gone down a road like this before—hadn't I learned from it? Wasn't I supposed to be getting better at this?

"How did you know?" I asked Sasha. "How did you know about Chip when I didn't, from the beginning, when you first met him at Faryn and Jan's party?"

"Oh, please," Sasha said. "I've *dated* Chip."

"What?" I yelped, and Stu's gaze shot to her, eyebrows at his bandaged hairline.

She waved a hand. "Not Chip, per se, but many Chip-like individuals. That type of guy used to be like a beacon to my uterus."

Stu and I exchanged an awkward glance as Sasha went on.

"Believe me, Brookie, I totally get the appeal of that guy—the bad boy, the one you want to reform, the one who sends those primal signals right to the center of your—"

"Yeah, I get it," I cut her off quickly.

"But you don't have to beat yourself up over that. You think you're the first woman to think with the little head?"

"Sash, girls don't have a—"

"Semantics, Stu. Don't interrupt. The point is this," she continued to me. "You were overdue for one of those guys. Every woman has to have at least one. Or at least a dozen, in my case—sorry, babe," she tossed toward Stu.

"No worries—been there myself," he said, unconcerned. "There are female versions of those guys too. And I nailed a ton of them."

"*Yeah*, you did!" Sasha said, and they high-fived.

I would never understand their relationship.

"But how else do we learn what we want unless we get all up in it with what we don't want?" Sasha went on. "You think I'd be as happy as I am with your brother right now if there hadn't been so many train wrecks before him?" Beside her I saw Stu nod, his face lit up. "No, I'd still be that same poor mess of a girl trying to find gold in a quarry. Be grateful for the Chip Santanas. Sometimes they're the only way to the Stu Ogdens."

My brother cupped the back of her head and pulled her in for a brief, sweet kiss.

"Or the Ben Garretts," I said sadly, watching them.

Sasha reached for my hand and gave it a quick squeeze. "Or the Ben Garretts. But if you ask me, I don't think that train's out of the station yet."

"Oh, Sash, thanks," I said wearily. I pulled out of her grasp and set my plate with its half-finished slice on the cocktail table. I wasn't hungry anymore. "But trust me—that train's halfway to Cleveland at this point."

...

My brother and Sasha—my dearest friends—stayed all day long with me, all of us lounging around the living room, watching crap TV, telling stupid stories to make one another laugh, and doing absolutely nothing.

They did not ask for any details about what had happened with Ben, or Chip, or why I'd done what I'd done, for which I loved them completely.

When five o'clock rolled around Sasha suggested I get dressed and we'd all drive over to Mom and Dad's together.

"You two go on. I'm not going to go."

Their eyes bugged out like cartoon characters.

"What?" Sasha said. "Your mom is going to kill you!" You did not miss Sunday dinner in my family unless there was an act of God or you were dead.

"Tell her I'm sick, you guys," I pleaded. "I'm just not up to it."

They didn't want to leave me alone, they said (though I suspected they were more afraid of showing up without me and having to answer to Mom), but, Gandhi-like, I passively refused to be moved, and ultimately they had little choice.

I didn't even bother getting up to walk them out, just waved them out the door and lounged back on the sofa, tuning in to a *Sex and the City* marathon. Because wherever *Friends* left off in relationships, *SaTC* picked up, and it helped to see Carrie, Miranda, Samantha, and Charlotte making mistakes every bit as stupid as my own.

Except, of course, that theirs were fictional.

I can't say I was entirely surprised to hear a car pull into my driveway a little after eight thirty—I'd expected Stu and Sasha to come back and check on me, just not so early.

My phone buzzed in my hand just as the doorbell rang, and I pulled up a text from Sasha: *CODE RED: The eagle swoops in your direction.*

What the...?

"Brook Lyn, it's your mother."

My head shot up at her voice outside my door.

Dammit. Stu and Sasha must have oversold my imaginary illness. My mother had never, since I'd been living on my own, "dropped by." For her to be here she must think I was dying.

Maybe if I stayed quiet she'd assume I was asleep. Or at the hospital.

The doorbell rang again. "Brook Lyn, answer the door. I know you're home."

Sighing, I rose and shuffled over to let her in.

"Hey, Ma," I said, hoping I sounded sick enough to avoid a litany of my transgressions.

She frowned when she saw me, then scanned her eyes down my body. "You like them," she said, sounding surprised.

I glanced down to the pajamas I'd never changed out of this morning—the ones she'd given me last Christmas. "Oh. Yeah. They're comfortable." I'd never worn them before today, but they actually were. "Look, Ma...I'm sorry I missed dinner."

I knew an apology was like showing my throat to a tiger, but for her to come all the way over, she must be piping mad.

But my mother didn't pounce. Instead she examined my face carefully for a moment, then reached into her oversize purse and pulled out a Tupperware container. "I thought you might be hungry."

I stared at it until my mom held the container out toward me and said, "If you'll let me in I'll heat it up for you. I don't want you drying it out in the microwave."

"Oh...sorry. Yes. Come in." I moved back to make room, and Mom took a step inside—I had a fleeting image of a vampire that had to wait for an invitation to cross the threshold before swooping in to attack—but she simply waited for me to lead the way to the kitchen.

In the awkward silence that often ensued when Mom and I were alone together—and the two of us alone here at my house was a first—she twisted on the front burner and reached below the counter for a pan she placed on it. Then she opened the container and poured its contents—some kind of meat stew—into the saucepan. "Lamb tagine," she said as she opened a drawer for a wooden spoon. "Turns to rubber if you microwave it."

"Sounds good." I manufactured a few coughs.

Her back was to me as she stirred. "I know you aren't sick, Brook Lyn."

The denial was on my tongue, but I held it in. I was too tired to lie, and frankly I didn't feel like insulting her with it. "I'm sorry, Mom," I said again instead. It grew easier.

"I saw your brother's bandage. And his limp. Sasha told me."

Out of my mother's sightline I rolled my eyes. Sasha the snitch—apparently she'd keep any secret I told her, unless it involved brownnosing up to my mom.

But I knew how much she craved my mother's approval and love. How could I begrudge her that?

"What did she tell you?" I asked.

My mom's shoulders lifted and fell. "Probably just the highlights. You broke up with that boy you liked so much. There was another boy. It was bad."

I sighed, glad she was facing away from me as tears pricked my eyes. "Yeah. It was pretty bad."

My mother picked that moment to turn around, mouth open to say something. But whatever she saw in my expression softened her face. "Oh, honey," she said quietly instead.

From the time Stu and I were little, those words were the most soothing balm for any wound. I hadn't heard them in years.

My tears spilled over, but before I could reach up to swipe them away, my mother cupped my face in her hands and wiped them with her thumbs. "I'm so sorry."

"Don't be sorry," I said bitterly. "It's my own fault. I deserve this."

"How do you deserve this?"

"I cheated on Ben." It was hard to say the words to her—I couldn't imagine she'd have much sympathy for her daughter who had done to someone the very thing my father had once done to her. "I broke his heart, and then I cheated on him."

My mother frowned and dropped her hands from my face. "No, you didn't."

That shocked my tears dry. "What?"

She turned back to the tagine. "From what Sasha told me, you and Ben broke up before this other boy. Didn't you?"

"Well...I don't know. Technically, I guess. But still, it's not like we'd been apart for months, or even weeks. Don't you think it was a little precipitous on my part to jump right from one guy to another?"

Mom turned back around. "Brook Lyn, you're the smartest woman I know. How can you sometimes be so stupid?"

I gaped at her, not sure whether to be flattered at her unprecedented compliment or angry at the insult that followed immediately on its heels. "What do you...I don't—"

"It's like you don't trust that you're enough."

Wonder where that *came from,* I thought wryly.

Luckily Mom couldn't read my mind and blithely went on. "There was Michael, then Kendall, now this boy—or boys. And even before all that—always someone." She lifted her eyebrows and pursed her lips in such a caricature of distaste, I had to stifle a snort. "When will you realize you don't need anyone else's approval?"

"Including yours?" I said, trying not to let sarcasm drip too heavily from my words.

My mother gave a great sigh and shook her head. "Don't be ridiculous."

The laugh that erupted out of my mouth startled us both. "That was funny, Mom."

"I'm a very funny person, Brook Lyn. You kids just don't realize it."

Was that another joke?

She flipped off the burner. "Get me a bowl for this, please."

I obeyed, and my mother ladled some of the stew into it and nodded toward my breakfast bar. "Sit. I'll bring you a spoon."

I took a seat on one of my cheap wooden bar stools and Mom set the bowl in front of me, whirling away to seek out the silverware drawer, asking where I kept my napkins. As she busied herself, she talked.

"You and this boy—this Ben—you broke up?"

"Yes," I said to the tagine—which was spicy and hot and delicious.

"And why did you do that?"

I regarded the fresh spoonful I'd just shoveled up, thick with carrot and zucchini and a chunk of lamb. "I don't know. It was idiotic."

"You're not an idiot. So why did you do it?" She'd found a glass in my cupboard and had filled it with ice and water, and she plunked it down in front of me.

I sighed, thinking while I chewed and then swallowed. Mom was standing facing me with hands on hips, clearly not budging until she got an answer to her inquisition. "I don't kn—" She fixed me with a hairy eyeball and I sighed again. "Okay, fine. I guess because I wasn't brave enough to...to take a chance with him. To, you know, move things to the next level."

"Well, I had no idea my daughter was such a coward. And so shallow."

My spine shot straight and every hair on my body bristled. I should have known my mother couldn't keep up this weirdly sympathetic version of herself. "I'm not a coward," I fired back angrily. "And I'm *not* shallow—I really cared about him. I still do. I just wasn't ready for something more serious yet. There's no shame in that!"

My mother just looked at me. Then she turned away, crouching to rummage under my kitchen sink. "Well, if you knew that wasn't what you wanted right now, then that's all there is to it," she said mildly. "Nothing anyone can do about their feelings, unless they want to pretend and fake it to someone they really care about. But it seems to me like that's a much unkinder thing to do."

I stared dumbfounded at her as she sifted through the cleaning products in my cabinet.

She stood up, holding a can of oven cleaner that she stared at as if wondering how it came to be in her hands. "There was a time when I wasn't sure what I wanted anymore, Brook Lyn...so I ended up leaving your father." Her gaze rose up to hold mine. "I came back. But I had to have time on my own before I could know that that was what I wanted."

I had no idea whether she was talking about when she moved out to live in theater housing full-time last spring—or when he'd cheated on her when we were babies. But Mom didn't know I knew about that.

And it didn't matter. I heard what she was saying.

"Thanks, Ma," I said quietly. She set the saucepan in the sink, running water into it. "Hey, Mom...I'm not the smartest woman you know."

She glanced up. "What? Who's..."

I just smiled at her, and my mother rolled her eyes and made a *tsk* noise, waving me off. "Finish that up," she said, indicating my tagine. "And don't leave the dishes in the sink—they draw roaches."

"Okay, Ma."

She set the unused oven cleaner on my counter and reached for her purse. "And take a shower tomorrow, and put on real clothes. And for god's sake, put some lipstick on."

"I will."

She stopped on her way out of the kitchen and turned around, not quite looking at me. "Cowgirl up, Brook Lyn."

"I love you, Mom."

She left, but not before I saw her smile.

Chapter Twenty-seven

Early the next morning, as I prepared for my radio appearance, I followed my mother's instructions: Showering, dressing carefully in a plum-colored pencil-skirt and an ivory fitted silk blouse with teal heels, doing my makeup and—yes—swiping on lipstick.

She was right: It helped.

She was right about a lot of things, I realized as I'd lain awake late into the night, thinking. Since high school I'd basically had one boyfriend after the next—sure, there was some downtime in between, but it was only transition periods. I'd never truly been on my own. To find out who I really was. To think about what I wanted for myself.

I think some part of me had known that, and that was why, when a man I'd cared about—still did—had offered me all the things I'd ever thought I wanted, I'd balked.

I needed to be by myself for a while.

I hadn't trusted that feeling, though—which was what had opened the door to an overwhelming physical attraction that had made me overlook every danger sign with Chip. Second-guessing what I'd done with Ben, filled with remorse and shame, it was so easy to bury all that in the arms of someone who demanded nothing of me, because I knew that nothing real could ever build between us.

It was a human mistake. And I had to forgive myself for that.

But I had to also try to accept culpability for hurting Ben, and make amends. The phrase inexorably made me think of Chip and his exes. Who knew if he'd ever actually written the letters I'd suggested. Who knew if any of it was true at all.

Although after seeing Chip in action Sunday, I suspected that some of his breakup horror stories, at least, were dead true.

Ben wouldn't be back home for another five days, and I knew a phone call wasn't enough, so that evening, after a surprisingly good radio show and a day full of clients, I sat down and labored for hours on a letter to him, trying to get the words right.

Dear Ben,

I'm not writing to try to explain my actions. And I don't expect your forgiveness—I fully understand that you may never offer it.

I am sorrier for hurting you than I am for anything else I've ever done. If nothing else, I want you to know that.

I've known three exceptional men in my life: My father. My brother. And you. I told you the other night that I thought I might be falling in love with you, and I know you can't want to hear that from me, but I meant it.

And yet I hurt you. And I am sorry for that to my soul. I won't try to explain all the reasons for why you found me the way you did yesterday morning—I know it doesn't matter to you anymore. But I hope you will believe me despite this painfully clichéd phrase I never thought I would use, especially to you: It's not you—it's me.

It turns out that's not just something people say in a breakup. It's actually true. You are everything I ever want to have in a partner, Ben. It turns out that I'm just not ready right now to start that partnership— and that made me do something stupid.

If I could change one thing in the world, it would be that, because I know I've destroyed any chance for us.

I'd like to try to explain some things, if you'd be generous enough to let me. I will meet you anywhere, at any time. Or we can talk on the phone, or e-mail, or text. If you're willing to talk, please just tell me when and where.

I am profoundly sorry, Ben. I wish I had not hurt you.

With all my heart,

Brook

I e-mailed it, followed up with a text asking him to check his e-mail, and waited.

...

I kept myself busy that week, trying not to put too much hope into Ben's response, but my heart leaping every time my phone rang or my inbox had mail.

On Tuesday I met my mom at the Neapolitan Theater in Naples for the tour I'd asked for. She truly came alive in the theater, her face animated and glowing as she showed me the set for their production, led me to her dressing room, paraded me through the admin offices, and even climbed with me and the lighting director up a metal ladder to the flies where the lights were hung high over the stage. Mom clearly loved every element of the theater, and my face hurt from smiling at her sheer unfettered joy. "This is my daughter, the therapist," she introduced me proudly to her cast and crew and every single person we saw.

Ben did not call.

Sasha and Stu and I took my dad to dinner on Wednesday, all of us making plans to go together to my mother's opening in two weeks, Stu and Dad spinning fish tales of their latest deep-sea excursion, we three kids telling silly family stories and trying hard, as always, to crack one another—and my dad—up.

Still I heard no reply from Ben.

I wrote my column that week about what had happened between us—sort of. I called it "The Reluctant Breakup," and in it I talked about the times when, despite everything good about a relationship, despite no red flags or deal breakers, despite how much you might care about someone, for whatever reason you aren't able to be together, at least for the moment. I talked about finding a way to be at peace with that— "choosing happiness," as my mom had told me, even in the face of sorrow.

I got more reader e-mail than usual on that column—people writing in with heartfelt stories of relationships that had ended for reasons larger than their love for the person. The stories touched me, made me cringe, broke my heart. Pree Chervaar had broken up with a man who made her happier than she'd ever known, because she knew her traditional Indian family would never accept a black, Jewish son-in-law. "Lindy in Lehigh" had ended things with her married "soul mate" because she couldn't bear to break apart his family. Angie Frost had met an Iraqi man while she was deployed who made her want every domestic, maternal thing she never expected to care about. But since his father had been killed in a bombing attack, his mother was alone, and the man couldn't bear to leave her on her own when Angie returned home to the States.

As I always was, despite the many varied faces of heartbreak I was struck by its universality. Even this narrow nuance of grief and loss by choice was shared by so many of us.

There was comfort in that.

...

It wasn't until Thursday morning, as I was just about to greet my first client of the day, that I opened my inbox and finally saw Ben's name. I opened the message with a racing heart.

Brook,
Thank you for your letter.
I don't think there's anything more to be said.
Ben

...

That evening I went unannounced to Adelaide's. Having Jake's things felt like holding on to some thread of connection. But now that it was clear that there wouldn't be even that, it would be easier to return them now than later, and far easier—on myself, and probably on Ben too—to take them to her, rather than having to see him.

When she answered the door my heart thunked into my chest. Her long silence and her flat expression told me she knew everything. "Brook." The usual warmth was stripped from her tone.

I knew that breakups meant not just losing the person you'd been in a relationship with, but those directly connected with them: Friends, family, no matter how close you might have grown to them, were casualties of war. At least in the immediate aftermath.

But it still hurt.

A hundred pounds of streaking white fur distracted me as Jake barreled past Adelaide and greeted me with excited little yips, rising onto his hind legs—taller than I was—and planting his massive paws on my shoulders. I dropped the bag of his things and wrapped my arms around him, letting him lick my face and hoping it would hide the wetness already there. "Jake," I murmured in a rough voice. "Jakie."

Some casualties of war are more unbearable than others.

"Jake!" Adelaide commanded. "Get down!"

"It's okay," I protested, but he'd already obeyed—Adelaide was always so much better at controlling him than I was.

I braced myself and faced her again. "I brought Jake's things. I'm sorry for not calling. I..." I couldn't think what to add.

Adelaide's expression lost a bit of its cardboard edge, and she opened the door a fraction wider. "Why don't you come in for a moment, Brook."

Inside the condo looked exactly as it had every time I'd been here, even though it felt as if so much had changed. I kept my eyes away from the photos lining every wall. I couldn't bear to see Ben's smiling face.

I held up the red cotton shopping bag. "His bowls are in here, and the extra leash. He had some, um, linens at my house that he especially liked, so I put them in there in case you want to...to..." I reached in and pulled out the drapes I'd taken off the rod in my bedroom—the ones Jake had chewed into shreds. In my grip the tattered fabric looked ridiculous, pathetic. "I'm sorry," I said weakly. "Why would you want this awful...How stupid of me. I..." My throat closed up. "I'm sorry," I pushed out in a choked voice.

I turned to go.

A strong hand on my shoulder stopped me, and when I turned, Adelaide pulled me into her firm embrace.

I cried. A lot.

Finally I pulled away, Adelaide's shoulder damp with tears and, I feared, a healthy amount of snot.

She stepped to the entry table to fetch a tissue that she handed wordlessly to me.

"Thank you, Adelaide. I'm so sorry. I know it doesn't make any sense, but I care so much about Ben. I really do. I wasn't just...This was real for me. I want you to know that, at least. I never meant to hurt him like I did."

She sighed, absently stroking Jake, who was sitting angelically by her side, staring up at me with his panting doggy grin as though he were greatly anticipating some marvelous antic from me. "Brook," she said finally, "my son is a very good man."

Remorse and pain and regret shot through me. "I know."

"And he's also a very smart man. He doesn't try to rebuild a house while it's on fire."

I frowned, confused. Who in the world would do that? "No..."

"But flames die down eventually."

My breath flew out of me in a rush. "Do you mean that—"

Adelaide held up a hand. "I'm not saying anything—I have no idea what Ben is thinking, and I certainly don't know what he might want in the future—any more than you apparently do for your own future at the moment." I nodded, acknowledging the truth of that. "But I do know him. My son is not a man of fickle feeling."

The warm flame that sprang up in my chest felt a tiny bit like hope.

But Adelaide's next words sent it sputtering immediately out: "I'm not going to upset him by trying to maintain our friendship."

"No, ma'am," I said, chastened. I squatted down to say goodbye to Jake, tears spearing into my eyes.

"But..." Adelaide cleared her throat above me. "From time to time we need a dog sitter when I'm not available. And I think Ben agrees that we only leave him with people we trust."

I looked up from where I'd been stroking Jake's ears, Adelaide slightly blurred around her edges.

There must have been a question on my face, because she gave a slight nod. "We'll keep you in mind," she said simply.

And I smiled.

Chapter Twenty-eight

"So...I kind of met someone. A woman."

There was no response to Sherman's announcement—no one interrupted whoever was holding the claw in group session anymore. But smiles broke out around the circle, matching the one spreading across Sherman's face; Betty beamed at him like a proud mama, Carolyn and Rebecca were nodding, and Antonio was clearly about to bust wide-open with the effort not to blurt out something congratulatory. I even thought I saw the beginnings of a shy smile behind the curtain of hair falling over Sheila's down-tipped face.

The group had come together.

Sherman continued, drawing my attention back. "And she might be...Well, I don't want to say perfect for me, but I think she kind of understands my...you know..." He nodded toward his sandaled feet, coloring slightly. He trailed off, dipping his head, but I suspected he wasn't through sharing.

"What makes you say that, Sherman?" I prompted.

"Oh...well..." He looked up at me and I nodded for him to go on. "So, uh, I was home alone, working on a wiring project on the front porch. And I had these zip ties sitting on the table, right? And I'm looking at them and thinking, 'They use these all the time on TV to tie people up. But look at them! How effective can they really be?'"

Sherman looked over at me and shrugged, and I bit the inside of my lip, nodding for him to continue. Antonio gave a snorting laugh; like me, I thought he suspected where this story was going.

"So I thought I'd, uh, you know...just sort of test the theory," Sherman went on hesitantly. "I was barefooted—of course—so I put a zip-tie around my two big toes and pulled it tight." He looked around at the group. "And I thought, Geez, I can totally see why these things are used by police and kidnappers. They don't give you any slack at *all*—and they don't break. It actually felt like it tightened the harder I tried to get free. Like one of those Chinese finger-trap thingies?" A couple of people nodded, more than a few trying to hide their grins. "So I, uh, reached for the needle-nose pliers, but they wouldn't cut the tie, no matter how hard I tried. So I figured I'd just crawl inside to find some scissors, and I'm kind of crab-walking across the porch toward the front door when, uh...I hear footsteps coming up the porch stairs."

This was too much for Antonio. "Oh, shit! No, you didn't!" he burst out. A few of the women giggled.

"Well, yeah," Sherman admitted. "And then I hear this pretty, soft voice say behind me, 'I can see you're tied up right now.'"

The room exploded—even I couldn't help laughing.

Sherman was grinning, despite his clear embarrassment. "And I turn around and this beautiful woman says, 'Hi. I'm from the Democratic Party of Florida.'" He sighed out a weak laugh. "There was really no disguising what was going on—I'm scooting on my butt across the porch, half hogtied with this black zip-tie just obvious as anything around my big toes." He was bright red now, but he didn't stop. "I figured she'd go running for the hills. But instead she sits down on my wicker sofa like we're about to share high tea, and she says, 'I always wondered if those things work the way you see in the movies.' And I swear to god, you guys, I just about fell in love. I kind of leaned back against my front door like I was just lounging around on my porch, and said, casual as all get-out, 'You know, turns out they do.'"

Antonio's roar of laughter was the cue for the rest of the group to join in again. "My *man*!" he exclaimed. "Way to play it!"

"So we have a date for next weekend," Sherman finished proudly, and Antonio slapped him on the back so hard the smaller man nearly came out of his chair. Sherman's grin nearly split his head as he leaned over to lay the claw back in the center of the floor while the rest of the group offered up congratulations.

"This is good to hear, Sherman," I said. "It sounds like she may be pretty accepting of...well, the things you like." He bobbed his head, still smiling like a jack-o'-lantern. "But more important," I went on, "it sounds like *you* are. You didn't try to hide anything from her."

"Uh, that would have been a little difficult under the circumstances," Dina quipped, and the group chuckled.

I acknowledged her with a glance and a smile. "True, Dina. But you went with the situation, Sherman. You didn't let shame or fear hold you back. That's pretty huge."

"Yeah." Sherman's eyebrows lifted, as if he hadn't realized it. "I guess it is. Huh." His smile was back, this time self-satisfied. Antonio held up a fist and Sherman bumped it with his own.

Quick as a cat Antonio leaned over and grabbed the claw. "Okay, I got something, you guys. I met this girl."

A few groans sounded. Carolyn rolled her eyes. Rebecca sat back in her seat, arms crossed, fixing Antonio with a hard stare. I don't know why I'd expected different, but my heart sank at his announcement. Lately I'd thought he was growing up a bit.

"No, no, hang on—hang on!" he blurted, holding out a hand as if to keep us at bay. "I met this girl at the auto parts store. She asked if I knew anything about lube jobs."

More groans. I sighed and leaned back, wondering how far to let Antonio go before I stopped what generally turned into a *Penthouse* Forum letter.

"I know!" Antonio said, eyes practically bugging out of his head. "It was like God was just giving me candy! But, you guys..." He sat up straight, claw forgotten in his lap, and held his hands out like Christ on the cross. "I didn't fuck her! That girl remained unfucked by me!" he trumpeted. I sat up straighter as he caught Carolyn's eye and winked. "Sorry, Carolyn—unfornicated."

Carolyn shot him a thumbs-up with a wink. Antonio lifted one hand and held it palm-out toward Sherman. "Come on, pal. Up top," he encouraged, and Sherman, grinning, slapped his palm with his own. The tension around the room seemed to unwind, and I heard a few murmurs of congratulations, encouragement—and surprise, all of which echoed my own feelings.

"I *coulda* fucked—sorry—fornicated with her," Antonio went on, his tone that of a man bragging about a sexual conquest, rather than that he hadn't made one. "That girl was hot to trot, and she was ready for Moretti, if you know what I'm saying." He nudged Sherman with an elbow.

"We all know what you're saying, Antonio," Sherman offered dryly, to a few chuckles.

"But you know what I did?" he went on. "I pictured you guys instead, and it was like a cold shower. No offense—I'm not saying you guys are a wood killer. I just mean I knew all a you were rooting for me. It was kinda like Popeye's spinach—it gave me this burst of strength, and I said, 'No, thanks, honey—not today.'" He tossed the claw into the center of the circle, then spread his arms wide again—*et voilà*—meeting every single person's gaze in turn as they offered up encouragement.

In the hubbub I nearly missed what happened next.

At first I thought she was collapsing out of her chair; it took me a second to realize that Sheila Amherst had dropped forward as if succumbing to gravity and grabbed the claw, which she was now holding up, arm out and eyes wide, like a slightly terrified Statue of Liberty.

"Can I share? I'd like to share."

I didn't know if anyone else had heard her over the din of approval directed at Antonio, but when the room went dead silent I knew they had. Every head turned to Sheila, and she recoiled like a poked turtle.

Next to her, Dina Jones put a hand on Sheila's leg and said gently, "It's okay, honey. Go on."

Compassion...from *Dina*?

But Sheila was staring at her as if Dina were the Oracle at Delphi. Dina gave her an encouraging smile, then reached up and smoothed the other girl's hair back from her face and behind one ear.

Revealing a shocking sight: Sheila looked gorgeous. I heard a few gasps around the room. Her eyes were a stunning light hazel, played up by mascara and plum shadow across her lids. Her cheekbones were high and defined, and her full mouth shone with a swipe of light peach gloss. Now that she wasn't drawn into herself in her chair, hiding behind her hair, I noticed her wardrobe had changed too—instead of her usual browns and beiges, Sheila had on a mint green top that draped softly at her collarbone and skimmed what turned out to be a slim little shape she'd been hiding under formless clothes. Someone had given this girl a makeover, and judging by the way Dina was gazing proudly upon the girl as if she were her own creation, I thought I had a pretty good idea who.

Sheila took a visible breath, blowing it out as if she were taking a Breathalyzer test. Then she gave a tiny nod, as if to herself, and said in her rabbit voice, "Okay." And then stronger: "Okay. Well, hi, everyone. I'm Sheila—I don't know if you remember."

"Of course we remember, sweetie," Carolyn said, offering her a kind smile.

"Right, okay. Well, so...Tom and I broke up." There were some murmurs around the circle, soft sounds of sympathy, and Sheila waved them away. "I did it. I'm the one," she said, and my eyebrows shot into my hairline. Judging from the expressions on everyone else's faces, I wasn't the only one who hadn't expected Sheila to be the engine of their breakup.

"We had a big fight." She was almost whispering now. "And he told me...he said some things...awful things. And I told him I knew he didn't mean them...that I wanted to help...that I loved him—" Her voice gave out and she stopped, tipping her head down.

Dina leaned close, placing a hand on the girl's back. "You're doing great," she said so softly I almost didn't hear her, but her tone was so fond and kind that I wanted to reach over and hug her. Hug *Dina*.

Sheila's head rose ever so slightly toward Dina, and she nodded, plunging a hand under the curtain of her hair to dash away tears. "I told him I loved him," she repeated in a stronger voice. "And he...he *laughed.*"

An audible gasp echoed around the room, and Antonio let out a loud groan. My hand flew to my heart.

"It turns out we weren't really...Well, he didn't think we were a couple. I was just some...this girl he slept with. He said that was all it was. He said he'd never be with someone like me because...um, because..." Tears were still running down her face, but now Sheila seemed not to notice them. Or to care.

She'd stopped talking and it seemed she wasn't able to go on. The rest of the group sat silent, patiently waiting for Sheila to collect herself and continue. But she had curled back into herself, her hair falling over her face as she cast her eyes down to the floor—or to hell, where I hoped her thoughtless ex would end up—and I knew she was shutting down again.

I stood to walk over and take the claw from Sheila—take the spotlight off of her that was clearly making her feel worse—but Dina caught my eye and held up a staying hand. Not as an order, to my surprise, but a plea. I acknowledged it with a dip of my head and sat back down as Dina scooted her chair a little closer to Sheila's. She reached into her purse and pulled out a packet of tissues, taking out one and handing it to the other girl. It disappeared behind her hair.

"He told her she was too plain," Dina said in a strong voice, looking around the circle at each one of us. "That she was ugly. *This* girl—too ugly for that overweight, overblown, overconfident asshole." As she spoke she again brushed Sheila's hair away from her face, and gently tipped up her head with a finger under the girl's chin. "Does this look plain to you?"

Sheila's eyes darted around the room, but never lit on anyone in the circle.

"Sheila, you're beautiful," Betty spoke up.

Beside her Elisa nodded fiercely. "Gorgeous. But you were even without the makeup. And I'm a lesbian, so you can take that to the bank."

There were a few chuckles.

Carolyn, Rebecca, and Sherman voiced their agreement. Sheila was meeting their gazes now, and I saw the beginnings of belief on her face.

"Honey, you are a hot little cookie," Antonio said fervently. "If I met you out somewhere, I promise you I'd take you somewhere we could be alone and I'd—"

"Okay, Antonio, she gets the idea," I broke in quickly. He meant well, but I didn't think Sheila was ready for a full-on Antonio compliment. "Sheila, you are a beautiful woman," I said sincerely. "With or without makeup, as Elisa said. Why do you think it was so easy to believe Tommy when he told you otherwise, when he compared you to his ex-girlfriend and made you feel inadequate?"

She shrugged, shooting another glance to Dina, who nodded at her.

"Um, I guess because...that's what my mom always said?" Sheila ventured, as if hazarding an answer to a test question she was unsure of.

A daughter formed her self-image first in the reflection from her mother's eyes. I thought of my own mom, who may never have made me feel anything I did was "enough"—but it was because she thought I was capable of absolutely anything. "Your mother said you weren't pretty?"

"Well...no. She just said that it was too bad I wasn't smart, because I'd never get by on my looks."

Carolyn recoiled like she'd been stabbed. "What on earth kind of parent says something like that to her child?" she bit out.

"A crappy one," Betty shot back. "One who's too caught up in her own bullshit to see the wonderful qualities in her own kid."

"Amen, my friend," Carolyn replied, gingerly slapping Betty's outstretched palm. I realized that these two opposite women had grown close over the course of the meetings.

As had Dina and Sheila, apparently. Dina had an arm on the other girl's shoulder and was talking softly to her: "I told you, Sheila. It's your mom who has the problem—that has nothing to do with you."

"Do you see what Dina is saying?" I asked Sheila. "That your mom's words—and Tom's—stem from whatever battles they're fighting inside themselves, and aren't a true reflection of you?"

"I guess," she said. "But when it's your own mom...you know...I love her."

I thought again of my mom. "Of course you do," I said. "But you don't have to let her define you. You can love her despite that—focusing on her good qualities instead of whatever her shortcomings might be. That's how we'd like to think a parent should love her child, but we're all only human," I said. "She has her own challenges, and just because she may not deal with them in a healthy way, that doesn't mean you can't. It doesn't mean you have to define yourself by whatever warped view she may not have learned how to readjust yet. And you certainly don't have to stick around and listen to someone who's always cutting you down."

Dina arced a glance over at me, then back at Sheila. "Well, this time she didn't," she said proudly. "She told him to suck it."

"I didn't..." Sheila protested. "That's not how I—"

Dina patted her on the shoulder. "She said it nicer, because she's a nicer person. A good person," she said, looking directly at Sheila now. "She kicked that asswipe to the curb—finally. And this time she's not going to take him back—right?" Dina sounded almost pleading as she took Sheila's hand in her own grip. "Because you know you are kind, and pretty, and smart. You're awesome. And you deserve better than a dick like Tom."

A few of the group tittered, Antonio clapped loudly, and Sheila cracked a smile. "Okay. I'm going to believe you. For now," she said to Dina.

And that was all any of us could ask for, I thought. Sherman's new love interest might tank on the first date. Next time Antonio got offered a woman on a platter, he might not say no. Sheila might never fully believe in her own beauty and power and that she deserved more than she'd gotten from men, and she might wind up back with Tom regardless of Dina's best mama-bear efforts. But for now they were all taking steps forward.

Me included. My heart felt like it had been torn out of me this week as I'd realized that Ben and I were truly through—and that so much of it was my own doing. And yet I was letting myself go through it. Feeling what I felt, even when it felt like crap, and reaching out to the people I loved—Sasha, Stu...my mom. And part of me was tending that little tiny spark of hope that Adelaide had given me, trying to keep it from going out completely.

I didn't know what might happen in my future. But I was learning to be okay with whatever it was. We all were.

They were little triumphs, but they were triumphs nonetheless.

And at least for now, as Sheila said...that was enough.

[Sneak peek at *Heart Conditions*,
book #3 in the Breakup Doctor series]

Chapter One

Every time, I hoped this would be the day it wouldn't happen. But when I caught sight of the tall, lean figure standing near the picnic tables and grills of Lakes Park, a familiar pain shot through me.

I sighed. Clearly not today.

Ben looked great in a button-down oxford in a light green I knew from memory would bring out the deeper tones in his hazel eyes, and dark-wash jeans clung to his legs with an attentiveness I could understand. Next to him, Jake was straining the leash in every direction, sniffing all the scents the park offered him like a junkie in a crack den.

Jake saw me before Ben did, his vaunted Pyrenees hearing catching the sound of my car door as I stepped out, and the dog nearly pulled Ben off his feet trying to get to me. I lifted a hand back to Ben at his wave as we walked toward each other, and conjured up a breezy smile.

"Hi," I said when I got closer.

Ben was better at the smile than I was. "Hi."

I braced myself for the giant dog's greeting, but to my surprise he didn't plunge his nose between my legs, as was his usual delicate way, but sat at my feet, only his furiously swishing tail giving away his excitement.

"Good, Jake," I said, looking into his eyes instead of Ben's.

The dog's tail wagged so hard I worried he'd leave a fan shape indented into the asphalt, and I couldn't contain myself any longer either. "How's Jakie?" I crooned, dropping to a crouch to ruffle his ears. "How's my boy?" I wrapped my arms around him, hiding my face for a moment in his long fur as Jake shoved a nose into my neck and then pulled back to gaze at me with a joyful open-mouthed smile, and for just that second everything felt right.

"Thanks for this, Brook," Ben said above me. "With Mom gone I wasn't sure what to do with him while I was away."

The moment was over, reality bursting back in. I stood and finally met his eyes. "How's Adelaide doing—have you heard from her since she left?"

"I got an e-mail from her yesterday. She met two women at a poker tournament on-board and they've already gotten pretty tight, it sounds like. Last I heard they were headed to go dancing in the ship's club."

"That's awesome. I'm so glad she's having fun."

He looked at me, familiar smile lines crinkling beside his eyes, and I had to look back down at the dog. "You know she credits you for this, right? She says if you hadn't 'stayed all over her back'—her words, not mine—about dating again, she'd never have done a singles' cruise."

"She'd have dated eventually," I said with a shrug.

"Well, she didn't till she started hanging out with the Breakup Doctor. So thanks."

Adelaide and I hadn't "hung out" for quite some time. The last I saw her, her face had been drawn into tight lines of disappointment. "I hope she has fun," I said.

Ben reached to hand me the leash and our fingers brushed. For a heartbeat there was only that warm touch, the shushing of the palms in the February breeze, the whirring coos of mourning doves, the distant sounds of traffic from Gladiolus—and the steady gaze of those familiar hazel eyes.

Jake's ear-piercing bark shattered the moment, and we both followed the dog's alert focus on Ben's truck, where a willowy redhead now stood in the open passenger door, shielding her eyes against the yellow sun, waving when she saw us looking.

"Well...I guess we need to get going," Ben said. "I'll get you Jake's things."

I made another smile happen across my lips. "I'll come get them. I can say hi to Pamela."

Ben's girlfriend was the kind of woman you never, ever want the ex you still have very complicated feelings for—despite the fact that it was you who torpedoed the relationship—to date. The perfect height—an inch or two above average, but not so tall that men were threatened by her. Slim as a prepubescent boy, but with the full, perfect round breasts of a Madonna. Long red hair with a slight curl. Vivid green eyes and teeth so perfect, you would have asked for the name of her orthodontist, except that you already know that she never wore braces a day in her life.

You know this only because you actually *did* ask for the name of her orthodontist the first time you met her, because your blabbering tongue wouldn't stay in your mouth with your nervousness upon meeting the perfect specimen who replaced you, and you vomited out a number of inane comments like this, and she answered with a disarming smile so appealing that you yourself felt a little stirring of attraction to her, despite the fact that you are solidly heterosexual, and she said with charming self-deprecation, "Believe it or not, I never had braces—my parents have these ridiculously straight teeth they passed on to all us kids."

And you liked her. Despite how much you desperately, desperately wanted to hate her.

Oh—and it turns out she's *a brain surgeon*. For real. On kids. A pediatric brain surgeon with a supermodel's body and the soul of Mother Teresa.

"Hi, Pamela!" I called out as we approached her, my tone overly enthusiastic in the quiet morning.

But of course she didn't point that out. "Hi, Brook. Nice to see you. Looks like Jake is thrilled to see you too." She flashed her perfect teeth.

"He's the best," I said over the stupid lump in my throat, tangling my fingers into the ruff at his neck.

"We need to get going," Ben said, clearly uncomfortable. In his defense, with our history he had every reason to expect me to be a loose cannon. He opened the back hatch. "Is this enough food? I can leave you some money if you need to—"

"We're fine." I waved him off, accepting the bag of Jake's current favorite toys—he went through them pretty quickly with those piranha fangs of his—as Ben picked up half a thirty-pound bag of dog food.

"Let me carry this to your car for you," he said, but I reached for the bag with my free hand.

"No, you guys go—you don't want to miss your flight."

Pamela glanced down at her watch and made an adorable little mew of concern in her throat. On me it would have sounded like hawking up a loogie. "You're right." She stepped gracefully back into the car with a wave. "Have fun, Brook!"

"*You* guys have fun, Pamela!" I sang.

She must have thought I was manic, but Pamela never showed it.

Ben gave me a warm smile that for a while I'd feared I'd never see again, and something uncoiled in my stomach. "Thanks again, Brook. It eases my mind to know Jake's in such good hands."

"I'm glad to do it." I meant that. Even though helping Ben out meant sending him off on what I was sure would be an über-romantic getaway to New York City with a goddess.

"Okay . . . well." He patted his pocket for his keys, a gesture so like my dad I wanted to hug him.

But we weren't there yet—if we ever would be—and I was grateful that the food and leash I held literally took the awkward decision out of my hands.

"Get going, you," I said lightly. "I'll see you Thursday night."

Ben gave one last pet to Jakie's smooth head, and a small wave to me, and then I watched their taillights turn left onto Gladiolus toward Six Mile Cypress and the airport, grateful to let my tired face muscles relax from their perma-smile. It would get easier.

It would.

...

For all that Ben and I were finally beginning to knit together a fragile sort of friendship after almost six months of total radio silence, it was hard to see him, knowing that we'd lost the closeness we'd once had. Harder still to see him with Perfect Pamela.

I rolled down the windows so Jake and I could both breathe in the orange blossom–scented air as we pulled onto Gladiolus, letting my anxiety recede. It was typical February weather for Florida, about seventy-three degrees and cloudless, with not a drop of humidity. This was why snowbirds flocked here when the Northeast got socked in by winter.

As soon as we pulled into my neighborhood Jake's tail started swishing madly, and I buried my fingers in his fur with a smile. Having him back, even for a short time, made up for some of what I'd lost with Ben.

Inside I scattered the dog toys, filled Jake's water dish, and let him outside to frolic around in my fenced yard, where he eagerly proceeded to deepen the impressive hole he'd started digging so many months ago—when I used to keep him during the week while Ben worked a job in Cedar Key—as if he'd never been gone.

I wished I could be as adaptable as Jake.

The sound of the doorbell drew me back inside from my screened lanai, where I'd been watching Jake's antics. Sasha and Stu had taken to bringing over breakfast on weekends more often than not, and helping me with the endless renovations my extreme fixer-upper of a house required. Glad to be distracted from my own agitated thoughts, I left the sliding glass doors open as I crossed to the front door and pulled it open with a welcoming smile.

And came face-to-face with the main reason I'd screwed everything up with Ben.

Michael. The man I hadn't seen since he'd dumped me by phone two years ago.

A month before we made it to the altar.

Chapter Two

I couldn't move. I'm pretty sure I forgot to breathe, judging by the way my lungs started to burn and I suddenly took in a huge gasp of air.

He looked so...normal. So familiar standing in front of me with those grass-green eyes peeking out from under the unruly lock of dark hair that fell over his right eye the way it always did. I had to stop myself from reaching out to push it back, out of habit. He was dressed the way I'd always seen him, in slim-fitting faded jeans and a battered black concert T-shirt, this one from a David Bowie show that had to have happened long before he was born. Like Jake and his hole in my backyard, I could almost let myself believe no time had passed since I saw him last—except for the uncertain expression he wore, instead of the slightly cocky grin I'd been used to.

And the fact that he was standing on the doorstep of my house, which he'd never been to before. The one I bought in a furious blind rush with the rest of our wedding money right after he called it off— the part I didn't lose in nonrefundable deposits.

My mouth was so dry, I couldn't have formed words even if my flatlined brain had provided any. Which it did not.

Michael had moved away shortly after we broke up—I didn't want to know where, just that he was gone. The last time I'd seen him was two years ago May. May 4, to be exact—a date I could never forget because of Michael's stupid repeated joke: "May the fourth be with you." At 7:43 a.m. That was when I'd left his apartment—the one I thought I'd be living in weeks later—with a frustrated admonition for him to *please* not forget our cake tasting that afternoon.

He'd been tangled up in the sheets, logy with sleep and lovemaking, after a late-night gig at the Buddha Bar the night before with his band, the Dogs of Society. He'd blinked sleepy green eyes at me. "Okay."

I stopped in the doorway of the bedroom with a huffing sigh, hands on hips like a fishwife. "I'm *serious*, Michael. Don't space this out, okay? I am not asking you to do much for this wedding—just *please* be there. Okay? Michael?"

He started awake from a doze. "Okay, Brook. Bakery. Four o'clock. Cake. I get it."

Those would have been the last words we'd ever spoken, except for the phone call I got from him eight hours later, en route to the Sweet Dreams Bakery.

"Brook, I'm sorry. I can't do this."

An annoyed sigh had torn out of me. "Oh, for God's sake, Michael—it's cake. Surely you can do cake, at least?"

There was a long silence, and then: "No, not the cake. All of it. Any of it. I can't go through with this."

Ice had seemed to crystallize in every cell of my body. "Okay. That's fine," my mouth said. And I hung up.

That was the epilogue on our two-year relationship. The way I dealt with adversity back then was to push it way down deep and carry on, which I did: I went on to the cake tasting, though I don't remember actually tasting any of the expensive pastries I put in my mouth. The next day I called all the vendors to cancel their services, and had blindly put a down payment on a house within two weeks.

This house. Where the man it had taken me two years, two shattered relationships, and a near nervous breakdown to get over stood on the stoop, staring at me.

"Brook," he finally said, the timbre of his voice lower than I remembered.

I swallowed, trying to remember how words were made. "What are you doing here?"

"I'm sorry. I know it's a surprise."

Behind me I heard the oncoming clickety-clack of Jake's nails on my tile as he shot through the house from the back, having figured out that someone new to play with was here. Without thinking I stepped outside and shut the front door behind me before he could investigate.

That brought Michael and me in close proximity. I could smell his familiar scent—sandalwood—and see the slightly darkened indentations beneath his eyes. He hadn't been sleeping.

I pushed backward against the closed door, where I could hear Jake scratching questioningly on the other side.

"What do you want?" I asked flatly.

"I wanted to see you. To talk to you."

Jake started barking.

"You got a dog," Michael said.

"Yes." I didn't owe him any explanations.

Jake's barking grew louder as he heard our voices but couldn't get to us, trailing off into an ear-piercing, mournful howling that went on and on, as if he were being tortured. Michael's face turned stupefied at the racket, and I panicked as a bubble of hysterical laughter swelled up in my chest and threatened to burst out.

A smile spread over Michael's face, and something panged behind my ribs. His smile had always been like the sun coming out from behind a cloud, shining directly on whomever it was focused on. "You know, he might calm down if we went in."

I had to clench my hands into fists and dig my nails hard into my palms to avoid returning that smile. Letting him in.

"I don't think so. My guess is he'd probably tear you limb from limb."

The smile vanished. "You have a vicious dog?"

"Like Cujo."

"Brook...that's not safe."

Nothing was safe at the moment. But Jake was hardly the threat here.

"I think it's best if you go."

He sighed. "I know you have every reason to be angry." He waited, as if for me to agree. I met his eyes with a steady, flat gaze. "Look, I get that...that this is a bad time. And I caught you off guard. I just didn't know how to..." He let out a gust of air, looking off to his right and then focusing on something there.

"Hey, you have a wasp nest in your eaves," he said. "I can—"

"I'll take care of it." I hoped they stung him.

He looked back at me, and the vulnerability I saw in his eyes almost made me gasp. "Brook, I am...God, I'm endlessly sorry for hurting you."

My eyes heated and I had to look away, staring unseeingly out to where two egrets were picking their way through my shaggy lawn. His words were almost exactly the ones I'd used in my letter to Ben after I'd broken his heart. *I am profoundly sorry.*

It had tortured me to have hurt someone I cared about so much. In Michael's agonized expression I'd seen the reflection of my own remorse, and an unwelcome pinch of empathy wheedled into me.

"Fine," I said grudgingly.

The tension in his face eased just a little. "Thank you. Just for hearing that—thanks." He took a breath, running his hands through his hair in a way I'd seen him do a hundred times. "Look, Brook...can we talk? Please? Just for a minute?"

Jake's anguished howls started up again, and I was suddenly seized with an urgent need to comfort him.

"I don't think that's a very good idea."

"Right." A trailing laugh leaked out of him. "Cujo. Maybe somewhere else, then? Or...another time, maybe?"

He was openly pleading, and the traitorous part of me that had once loved him with everything I had pulled at me to hear him out.

But I couldn't. I needed to think—away from the overwhelming *presence* of him. I shook my head. "No. Not now."

His face cleared as if I'd said yes, and he reached into his front pocket. "Okay. That's fair. But when you're ready—soon, Brook, I hope—will you call me? I'll be here . . . for a while. At least until I hear from you." He pulled his hand out with a creased white card between two fingers, and I took it by reflex when he held it out.

Michael Cooper, Promotions.

Below the name and meaningless job title was a phone number with an area code I didn't recognize, and an email address. I looked up when he started talking again.

"Anytime you say, I'll meet you here. Or anywhere. All I ask is that you listen. And I know you don't owe me that, and I don't have any right to ask for it—"

"No, you don't."

He nodded, plunging a hand through his hair again, still mussed from the last time, and I saw him blink fast, several times. He looked down, and when he looked back up at me his eyes were shiny. "You must hate me," he said softly, and in his unsteady voice I heard an echo of the soul-deep pain he'd caused me.

And I liked it. I wanted to cause him more.

"I did for a while," I said neutrally, and then as soon as his face started to brighten with hope, I snuffed it out:

"But to keep hating you I'd have to somehow summon up some feeling for you...and it seems I just can't."

I swung around to grab the doorknob and stepped inside without turning to see whether my bayonet had hit home, shutting the door in his face.

Heart Conditions
The Breakup Doctor Series #3

Breakup Doctor Brook Ogden has spent the last year sifting through the fallout from the disastrous decision that led to her unconscious uncoupling with boyfriend Ben Garrett. Despite advising her clients you can't be friends with an ex, she and Ben have somehow begun to stitch together a friendship—one Brook hopes is slowly turning into more. That is, until Ben introduces his new girlfriend, Perfect Pamela, a paragon of womanly virtues who is everything Brook is not.

While Brook navigates her newly volatile emotional life, an unwelcome surprise shows up on her doorstep: the ex-fiancé who broke her heart two years ago—one month before their wedding. Between her ex's desire to rekindle their attachment, her best friend Sasha's unexpected crisis, and her own unsquelchable feelings for Ben, Brook finds herself questioning the personal progress she's made in the last two years—and threatened with the highest-stakes Breakup Doctor failures she's ever faced.

A Little Bit of Grace
(coming August 2020 from Berkley Publishing)

Family is everything—Grace McAdams's mom must have said it to her a thousand times before she died. Before Grace's dad ran off with an aspiring actress half his age. Before only-child Grace found out she was unable to have children of her own. Before Brian—her childhood best friend, business partner, and finally her husband—dropped a "bombshell" on her in the form of her stunning new replacement.

Which means Grace now has...nothing.

Until a letter from a woman claiming to be a relative Grace never knew she had sends her on a journey—from the childhood home she had to move back into (three doors down from the happy couple) to a tropical paradise island to meet a total stranger who claims to be family. And Grace starts to uncover answers about the eccentric woman her family never mentioned: an octogenarian who writes a viral relationship-advice blog, a compulsive (and highly successful) matchmaker...and the keeper of an unimaginable family secret held for more than fifty years.

A heartfelt, funny story about family and forgiveness, starting over when the happy ending ends, and handling it all with a little bit of grace.

Bedside Manners Reader's Guide

1.   Brook finds herself torn between two very different men in the story. What is it that she is attracted to in each of them? Why, when she seems to think Ben is perfect for her, is she still drawn to Chip?

2.   Is Brook really confused about what she wants, or does she just say that as a reason to keep things casual with Ben? If so, why?

3.   Brook has a complicated relationship with her mother. Why do they seem to push each other's buttons so easily? Despite her frequent acrimony toward her mom, Brook still seems to crave her approval. Why is this?

4.   When Brook tries to reach out to her mom, she often feels that her mother's reactions ruin her good intentions. Do you agree that Vivian is often the root of the problem? If not, how does Brook contribute to their difficult relationship?

5.   Does Vivian love her daughter? Is she a good parent? Discuss her strengths and shortcomings as a mother.

6.   Is Sasha and Stu's relationship healthy? What is it based on?

7.   Although Brook is happy that Sasha has found love with Stu, she's a bit uncomfortable that her friend is now the one in a seemingly healthy relationship, while Brook is the one floundering. Why is that hard for Brook?

8.   Brook feels left out of the relationship between her brother and her best friend. Is that a factor in her actions in this story? In what way?

9.   Was what Brook did with Chip cheating? Why or why not?

10. Do you think Ben is the right guy for Brook? Why or why not?

11. Brook begins a new Breakup Doc practice via support groups, so she can help more people at once. Do you think the idea of people experiencing heartbreak and talking about it together is really a viable one? Why or why not? Is it something you think would appeal to you in that situation?

12. Were there warning signs that Brook missed in Chip Santana for his later behavior? Have you ever had a relationship with the "warning signs"? Did you ignore them, or heed them? Why?

13. Is Chip abusive, or just a guy who lost his temper? Should Brook make sure he faces consequences for his actions, or should she avoid potentially derailing any future progress he might continue to make?

ACKNOWLEDGMENTS

Thanks to my supportive, knowledgeable agent, Courtney Miller-Callihan at Handspun Literary, who championed this series. My deep thanks also go to Laura Wright, PhD, counseling psychologist at Florida Gulf Coast University, for helping me navigate the field of psychology and therapy—and to the therapists who've helped make me a happier, more competent human.

Great gratitude to my early readers: Kathryn Haydn Hays, Stephanie Davis, Marcie and Doug Walter, Jenny Smith, Richard LeMay, Merritt Graham, and Jan Davis. Special thanks to Kelly Harrell, Amber Novak, and John J. Asher, gifted writers in their own right.

To Camilla Monk for her gorgeous cover concept and design; babycakes, you make me look good. And to Erin George and Rachel Jackson, eagle-eyed editors and stalwart cheerleaders for this series.

And my perpetual gratitude and appreciation for the Dogfather, husband Joel, whose love and support are unflagging, essential, and the best thing in my life.